Malthus Revisited

THE CUP OF WRATH

Malthus Revisited

THE CUP OF WRATH

Lin Wilder

Malthus Revisited
The Cup of Wrath

Lin Wilder

ISBN: 978-1-948018-06-7
Library of Congress Control Number: *to come*

Wilder Books
An Imprint of Wyatt-MacKenzie

Back before I met my husband, a former Marine
and psychologist for ex-combat veterans, I knew nothing
about veterans—specifically, Marine combat soldiers.
During the years of our marriage, I learned.

This book is dedicated to those soldiers: Most of whom we
never hear of, who do and see the unspeakable.

"They, too, will drink the wine of God's fury, which has been
poured full strength into the cup of his wrath."
– Revelation 14:10

"You love evil more than good,
lies more than truth.
You love the destructive word,
you tongue of deceit."
– Psalm 52

"No one becomes depraved all at once."
Juvenal, Satires

July 1995, Srebenica, Bosnia-Hercegovina

He lay motionless. Aware that any movement would give him away, he barely breathed, kept his eyes tightly closed. He tried not to think about the soldiers cutting the throats of his father and three brothers: Adin, who had just turned thirteen; Davud, only ten; and Hakem, his twelve-year-old twin. The laughter and their hideous expressions as they committed cold blooded murder. The blood everywhere, the blood…lakes of it. Or the screams of his mother and fifteen-year-old sister, Fatima. She was strong, fearless. The terror on her face when the leader slung her over his shoulder contorted her beautiful features but did nothing to extinguish the look of fear in her eyes.

"RUN, HIDE."

He did. A family of Bosnian refugees had discovered him wandering in the woods outside his family's burned Sarajevo home. A professor, his wife, and two small girls had taken him with them to Srebrenica, where they would all be safe. The United Nations was protecting the city. The professor had explained in precise language what the UN was, and the power that they had. Mile after mile, the small band of refugees walked toward the eastern coast of Bosnia, Srebenica, where they would find refuge. The teacher reassured them all that they would be safe once the exhausting trip was over. The United Nations had proclaimed that the small town they were headed for was safe from attacks or hostility.

In the war-ravaged debris of what was once Yugoslavia, the hope of a peaceful transition from Communism to a new form of multi-party democracy had been smashed into oblivion.

But the soldiers came again, and this time he could not run away. The professor's blood saved him. This time they were in a hurry, using machine guns rather than knives. More efficient. The words of the kind, learned, and God-fearing man lying dead beside him rang in his ears as he lay waiting for a death that did not come. *We have nothing to fear, the United Nations will protect us. There are UN soldiers who are commissioned to keep us safe.*

Allahu Akbar.

To this day, the Srebrenica massacre is considered the worst genocide in post-second-World-War history. Despite the town's protected status, it was attacked and captured by the Serbian Army. More than 8,000 Bosnian people were killed. An additional 20.000 civilians were expelled from the area in a process described by a tidily euphemistic phrase, *ethnic cleansing.*

A battalion of 450 Dutch soldiers charged with protecting the small town was routed by superior forces of better-armed Serbian soldiers. Dutch Commander Karremans pulled out his entire force when Serbian General Mladic assured him that his men were merely transporting the civilians to another city. The killing began as soon as the UN troops retreated.

December, 2016, Pismo Beach, California

"Why, in the vast universe of Cal Poly undergraduate majors, did I pick physics?" LJ's voice was quivering and her intensely green eyes shone in the half-light of their laptops. There was no response from her best friend Morgan, who sat cross-legged, her own laptop open beside the huge physiology textbook she was studying. Her expression was intense, focused.

LJ groaned, loudly.

Still nothing.

"Morgan, are you even *there*?"

Both dogs jumped at LJ's shout.

"Of course I'm here, where else would I be? You can see me, right?" Her brown eyes were lowered at the two dogs, now sitting at alert. "Max, baby, shhh, it's okay," she whispered so quietly that LJ could barely hear her. "Nothing to get upset about. It's just LJ's drama queen act. Gus, be still, boy. Everything is fine, just fine."

They were a most unlikely pair, Max and Gus. Max, an eighty-five-pound pedigreed red Doberman, and Gus, a forty-one-pound mutt, a strange combination of pug and lab that miraculously worked. Max had the beautiful, almost regal look of the purebred Doberman: long legs, a lean and muscular torso, and expressive amber eyes. Gus was, well, the exact opposite. He had been rescued by Dr. Lindsey McCall and her husband Rich only two months before, after being found cowering behind a dumpster at one of the local restaurants. They had taken Max out for a look around upon finishing their dinner. After they had been walking around the Pismo pier for about ten minutes, they were heading back to the car when they heard the faint barking. Max found the little dog first. He sat down right in front of the terrified animal and lifted his paw as if to shake. Gus instantly stopped barking and began to run around in tight circles, around and around.

"Now that we have the room in the new house, you said you wanted another Dobie—maybe a rescue…" Rich watched Lindsey melt right in front of his eyes. She had bent down to say hi, and Gus had stood up on two short stubby back legs to lick her entire face.

"He's a rescue, right? And Max really likes him." Lindsey and Rich had agreed a while back to get no more dogs from breeders. There were too many beautiful dogs already waiting for a forever home.

Rich smiled because Lindsey had been so adamant about another Doberman, "just like Max," but he said nothing. It was evident that this stray dog was going home with them. Max's stubby tail was wagging furiously at the antics of this new little guy, and he was smiling at Rich and Lindsey as if to say, "Look at my new friend."

Both dogs settled back down at the sound of Morgan's voice. Mirroring each other's splayed-out positions, the two now lay back-to-back, Max facing LJ and Gus's gaze fixed on Morgan.

A pair just as unlikely as the dogs, was LJ Grayson and Morgan Gardner. LJ was the biological daughter of Dr. Lindsey

McCall, and had accepted Lindsey's offer to house her and fund her undergraduate education at California Polytechnic State University.

Adopted at birth and raised in Friendswood, Texas, by Lindsey's best friend Julie and her husband, Ted Grayson, LJ had battled alcoholism as a preteen. The path back to sobriety had cost the young girl most of her childhood while she mined the demons of her psyche and ultimately exposed them to the light. Her given name was Lindsey, but had been shortened to LJ when she came to live with her birth mom. The elder Lindsey's ever-practical husband Rich had nixed the idea of calling his wife either *Linds* or *Lindsey Senior.*

For her part, Lindsey-the-younger absolutely loved her new name. LJ felt like a most suitable label to go with her new life as a California college student, and she'd agreed with Rich that two Lindseys in the same house would be way too confusing. Even her parents had adapted, and were growing accustomed to the new moniker.

LJ regarded her best friend—her only friend, truthfully—again immersed in the physiology textbook and once more oblivious to her presence. *But this is why I feel so close to Morgan. She is never girly. Not once have I had to guess what she was thinking. So what if she often acts like I don't exist? Such an improvement over the girls at Friendswood High, who faked everything. Especially during those bad months when it seemed as if the entire school knew...*

Smiling to herself, LJ reflected on their first conversation, while standing in the long line of incoming freshmen who had waited until September 19th to register. Numerous phone calls to Cal Poly during the summer from her home in Texas had not produced the results she had hoped for. In fact, it was as if she had never spoken with any of these people at all. Deciding this was an excellent opportunity to exercise the willpower that her Texan mom Julie had instilled in her, LJ kept her cool and her head down, moving only when the pair of sandaled feet in front of her inched forward.

"Hi. I'm Morgan Gardner from Des Moines, Iowa. What's your name and where are you from?" LJ had jumped several inches, so surprised at the voice coming from somewhere over the top of her head. When she turned back to address the person standing behind her, LJ had to look up to see the face of the skinny, dark-haired girl wearing large black-rimmed glasses. Morgan had to be over five-foot-ten. From LJ's perspective at just five-two, she had to bend her neck back to even see Morgan's face.

"You're quite pretty. I bet you had a bunch of boyfriends in high school, right?"

Before LJ could reply, Morgan continued, "I know, I'm getting personal way too fast, but when I get nervous, I do that. I am now very nervous. I have ASD."

Noting LJ's puzzled expression, Morgan explained, "Autistic Spectrum Disorder…Aspergers…High Functioning Autism…pick one. If you don't like any of those, I have about ten more depending on which DSM the psychologist is using."

Laughing in delight at the complete lack of guile in this girl, LJ extended her hand and said, "I'm Lindsey Grayson, but now LJ for Lindsey Junior because my biological Mom's name is also Lindsey. Her husband Rich decided that two Lindseys in the Pismo Beach house where I live now would be too confusing for everyone, most of all him. I'm from Friendswood Texas, and I'm an alcoholic." *And am babbling like a total idiot.*

The two young women grasped hands for support as they doubled over in hilarity, sides heaving, unaware of the eyerolls all around them. They were inseparable from that moment on.

Morgan and LJ were cramming for December semi-finals in

LJ's bedroom suite at 37 Bluff Drive, the Pismo Beach house that Lindsey and Rich had bought just a few months before. LJ thought of her biological mother as "Dr. Lindsey," because she was the antithesis of the woman who had adopted and raised her. At least that's what she thought when she had first met her birth mother the previous June.

Julie and Ted Grayson, the people who had always been Mom and Dad to LJ, had told her she'd been adopted as soon as they believed her old enough to understand. At age seven, they sat her down and explained that they had *chosen* her. They had promised that one day, when it was time, LJ would meet her biological mother. When she was eighteen, that day came.

But Dr. Lindsey was a bit more than LJ had bargained for, and she was still trying to get her head around the fact that they shared DNA—that this brilliant, world-famous doctor-researcher was her biological mother! LJ was good-looking, and had known it since her preteen years, but she and her mother looked nothing alike. While Dr. Lindsey was tall and blonde, LJ was short with hair so dark it looked black. Apparently, LJ was a virtual facsimile of Dr. Lindsey's sister, Paula, who ironically, had killed herself. Paula had been an alcoholic, just like LJ.

LJ had thought she was prepared to meet her birth mother. After all, she and her parents had been discussing the meeting for a few weeks before they had even left Texas for Pismo Beach.

"Your mother was a Chief Cardiology Fellow, and had no interest in marrying the surgeon she'd been dating when she got pregnant with you. She asked your Dad and me to adopt you, asking only that we name you Lindsey."

LJ guessed there was a whole lot more to the story, but decided this was enough to take in for now. Her parents explained that Dr. Lindsey was wealthy—loaded in fact—because of a drug she had created to treat heart failure. She had established a trust fund for LJ several years earlier.

At this information, LJ's eyes widened. "How much money is in the trust fund?"

"Enough that you can go to any college you like, and more than adequate to pay for a new car when you need one."

So, okay, this person was an incredibly generous stranger. You would expect LJ to greet her biological mother with civility, at the very least. Why on earth was the first thing that fell out of her mouth so divisive?

"Why didn't you have an abortion?"

That question shattered the smiles on the faces of her parents. Julie's eyes filled with tears. But Dr. Lindsey took a deep breath and narrowed the green eyes that were the exact shade of LJ's and said, "I thought about it, Lindsey. God help me, I planned to do just that at first. In fact, I had scheduled an abortion at Planned Parenthood the very same day I spoke with your mother."

Now LJ's Dad had tears in his eyes as well. The air surrounding the four of them bristled with tension. They sat in one of the various furniture groupings arranged throughout the first floor of the humungous house. It was a party, Julie had explained to LJ, a housewarming party for about thirty close friends that Dr. Lindsey and Rich had thrown to celebrate their move from Texas to California. And here she was, ruining everything within seconds of meeting the woman who had decided not to kill her before she got a chance to be...anything. LJ could feel the stinging threat of tears in her eyes, tears that would come any minute.

"It's okay, Lindsey." Her biological mother was suddenly in front of her and holding her hand, tightly. She knew. LJ grabbed that hand as hard as she possibly could, she was experiencing such an overwhelming assault of emotion that she could do nothing but hold on, as if that hand were a life raft in the middle of an immense ocean.

There was a lull in the conversation. The heavy silence seemed to last for hours, although it had probably been less than two minutes and had muted the sounds of the other guests, making it seem as if no one else was there. Once LJ smiled at this woman kneeling quietly in front of her, and they both relaxed their grip, Dr. Lindsey studied the daughter she had not seen since her birth. After a quick glance at Julie and Ted, she asked, "Want to go meet Rich?" The sounds of multiple voices in a party atmosphere once again filled LJ's ears.

"Yo, ladies, is anyone hungry around here?" The sound of Rich's booming voice startled LJ from her musings. Jumping up, she ran to her closed door, opened it and shouted out into the long hallway, "Rich, Morgan and I are down here, in the back with the boys."

By the time Rich arrived at the door of LJ's bedroom suite, both Max and Gus were standing, mouths open, tongues hanging out, wagging their back ends crazily.

"Lindsey's going to stay overnight in her lab, guys. Morgan, why don't you stay here tonight if you like, and you two can keep studying after we eat?" He turned to leave, then stopped. "I hope you like steak!" Rich had only spoken to Morgan a few times, but his broad smile took up half his face at her reply.

"LJ says you grill the best steaks this side of the Yangtze. You bet I like steak, Mr. Rich."

She sure was different, this best friend of LJ's. Morgan had taught herself Mandarin Chinese as a preteen and spoke Spanish fluently. Either a polyglot or a savant, she had casually mentioned her intention to learn Russian next.

Rich knew next to nothing about autism, but because of this fascinating young woman, he'd read a couple of books by Temple Grandin, the well-known autistic animal researcher. That was all it took to realize that much of the superficial knowledge of ASD he had picked up was wholly and utterly wrong.

Whistling to himself, Rich left the girls to their studies. *Dr. Lindsey and Mr. Rich...who'd have thunk it? I hope Morgan takes us up on our offer to move out of the dorm and live here with the three of us. Her presence here is good for LJ...and Lindsey...and me too.*

Smiling as he walked to the kitchen to marinate the steaks, Rich considered Morgan's effect on Max and Gus, the two dogs. Max remained his dog. Like most Dobermans, Max was uniquely bonded to one person, and that was Rich, his favored human. But the big dog had a connection with Morgan from the first, different than the way he was with Lindsey, LJ, or other people close to the family. Rich had never seen Max do that before. It had captivated his attention, and once again, got him thinking. *She has a wealth of knowledge and a really intriguing way of looking at her world and the people in it. Morgan's candor, her almost child-like way of relating, was charming to him. Somehow, Rich never got annoyed at her questions, which could be relentless. No subject seemed out of bounds.*

Of course, LJ was no slouch either. Her physical resemblance to Lindsey's dead sister Paula was initially shocking for Linds, but the better I get to know LJ, the more I see the presence of Lindsey's DNA within.

Rich had met LJ about two-and-a-half years earlier, while still working as Chief Warden over the Huntsville Prisons in Texas. He had risked his job, reputation, and bar license when he agreed to help his former law partner, Todd Kensington, file an appeal to overturn the murder conviction of Dr. Lindsey

McCall. Lindsey had been convicted of intentional murder for using an unapproved cardiac drug of her own invention on her mother. Rich's mind wandered back to that first meeting with LJ's mother, Julie Grayson.

"I want to thank you again for making the trek out here from Huntsville; it's a long drive, and you've still got to get back home, so I'd suggest we get started." Her eyes darted outside as she did what looked like a quick body count of kids, then turned back to Rich, fixing two slightly down-turned almond-shaped brown eyes on his face. Smiling again, Julie suggested in her lilting Texas drawl, "Why don't I tell you about Lindsey and me?"

Thirty minutes later, Julie had covered her close friendship with Lindsey since first grade, a relationship that had continued through college at Rice, but began to fade when Lindsey entered medical school. Julie seemed matter of fact about the way the two had drifted apart as life took them in different directions, but she made it obvious that Lindsey had always been important in her life.

At one point, Julie picked up a thick, leather-bound book and handed it to Rich. "I started this when Lindsey and I graduated from Rice. I followed everything she did in med school and everything else I could find, which, as you can see, was a whole lot." Her grin could not have been more genuine nor more loving had she been talking about one of her children. "Lindsey McCall is a remarkable woman, and I am"—the soft voice choked for a moment and Julie swallowed, then took a sip of her wine to stem the tidal surge of love and sorrow she felt for her best friend—"*proud* to be her friend."

"Julie, thank you very much for lending me this material. I cannot imagine the hours that you must have spent finding and copying all of this." Rich was overwhelmed by the span of time covered in the book; Julie had been maintaining this tribute to her friend for almost twenty-five years. Each page was numbered and protected by a plastic page cover. Looking up again, he met Julie's gaze as she was openly scrutinizing him. Rich had been waiting for the question, but was surprised it had taken Julie over an hour to ask it.

"Why are you doing this, Rich?" Julie's soft brown eyes were darker, and the expression on her face was one of deep concentration, the way she must look when grading calculus finals or determining whether one of her kids was lying. She sat motionless through his ten-minute account of the events of the week, then softly repeated her question, "But why are you doing *this*?"

Rich laughed. Julie Grayson would be one hell of a lawyer, he thought fleetingly, and felt exactly as he had at the age of eight, after taking the dare of his friend Timmy to dive off the high diving board. The water of the sparkling blue swimming pool had looked as if it were twenty miles below.

"Because I can't let Lindsey remain in prison." This was the first time Rich had admitted he believed in Lindsey's innocence—even to himself. His legal training, plus his years as a cop, had shaped a man who believed in the rule of law and he was loath to push those boundaries. Of course, there were countless situations where he had been forced to think outside the box; that was implicit in any life, but particularly that of a soldier, a cop, or a lawyer. The difference was that almost all of those situations were circumstances where lives were in danger, either his own or those for whom he was responsible.

This situation was unique in Rich's experience. There was no time crisis here, no imperative to *act*; the crises were over and the judicial system had been followed. It was an imperfect system, Rich knew, but arguably the best in the world. This was dangerous territory for him—hazardous on many levels. Rich's eyes found Julie's as he calmly and quietly stated, "I am certain that she did nothing to warrant an indictment for murder."

A burst of two and four-footed creatures appearing on the deck jolted him out of his reverie and back to the present. Rich was surprised at the joy these two young girls evoked in him. Their zest for life was infectious and he tended to laugh a lot more with them around.

He was happy to be of some help to Morgan and her mom as well. Anne Gardner had made it clear that the invitation he and Lindsey had extended was a godsend, when they had 'met' online via webcam and discussed the girl's close friendship. Rich and Lindsey had wanted to make sure Anne would approve of the idea before they made the offer to Morgan to live at their home. The college professor had tears in her eyes when she thanked them, touched by both their generosity and their true appreciation of her daughter.

CHAPTER TWO

San Luis Obispo, California

"Do you think they really mean it?"

LJ was driving the new red Toyota Prius that Dr. Lindsey had bought her when she started school. She had grinned as she agreed with LJ that the red one was the prettiest car on the lot, and that red was a cool color, but she couldn't help adding some advice. "Drivers of red cars are stopped more often, LJ. Knowing that may keep you at the speed limit."

LJ had looked it up and found it to be a myth, but she didn't want to test it. She always drove carefully, just under the speed limit.

When Morgan asked her question, LJ had been reciting a mnemonic under her breath for the Bernoulli's equation, which she was sure would be on her physics test. She had to think for a second about what her friend was referring to. Morgan habitually continued conversations that had taken place hours or even days earlier, expecting LJ to automatically revisit the subject effortlessly. At first, LJ had found it annoying, but later decided it was good mental discipline. She thought for a few seconds. "Are you asking if Lindsey and Rich meant it when they said you could move in with us, or are you asking whether my Texas parents really want you to come home with me for Christmas?"

"Both."

Suppressing a smile at her friend's brusque reply, LJ nodded for emphasis. "Yes, Morgan. They mean it. All of them. Rich and Lindsey have already told you several times that they'd love to have you at the Pismo house." About to move on to the topic of her Texas parents, LJ looked in the rearview mirror and saw a California State Trooper on her tail.

"Oh NO!"

"What oh no? They didn't mean it after all?"

"Do NOT turn around Morgan, but there's a cop right behind us." Sighing, LJ grimaced as Morgan not only turned around, but waved at the trooper. Checking her speed again to make sure she was right at fifty-five, LJ frowned when the officer flashed his lights and turned on his siren. Then breathed a sigh of relief as he passed her to chase after someone else. Morgan was oblivious, her brain dominated by her current obsession.

"And Julie and Ted?"

"Right, same same there, Morgan. My mom never says anything she doesn't mean." Aware of how literal Morgan could be, LJ added hastily, "Dad doesn't either. They would love to have you come home with me for Christmas break." Glancing quickly over at her friend, she saw what she expected to see. Morgan was staring straight ahead, her face expressionless, giving no indication of what she was thinking or feeling. But LJ knew that inside Morgan's brain, she was examining her options. Morgan had learned through several bad experiences to be wary of invitations like LJ's. Like many young girls with ASD, she had often misinterpreted the body language of people, especially the gestures of other young girls. Numerous times, what Morgan had perceived to be an offer of friendship was actually ridicule expressed in the typical eye-rolling and sarcasm of preteen girls. She didn't figure out what was really going on until the boisterous laughter and pointing began.

LJ was confident that her friend was calculating the effects of the offers that had been extended by both sets of parents. The speed with which Morgan could solve mathematical formulas reminded LJ of her Texas mom, who was a high school calculus teacher. Morgan's own mom was a professor of economics at Drake University in Des Moines, who made decent money, but the outlay of twenty-five thousand per year for Morgan's tuition dug deep into her savings. Anne was determined that Morgan would not be saddled with crippling debt once she'd completed her undergraduate education. Saving Morgan's mom almost eleven thousand a year seemed like a no-brainer to LJ, but she knew better than to push her friend for a decision. She hated when people did that to her.

"Why don't you act like most girls? Is it because you became addicted to alcohol and got made fun of too?" For LJ, that simple, ingenuous question had cemented both their friendship and her trust in this most unusual young woman. Unlike just about all her high school "friends" back in Texas, Morgan's disarming questions about LJ's alcoholism were only part of the things LJ appreciated about her. Her honesty was just a quality, like her black hair and green eyes. Everyone else treated the subject as if it were taboo—especially Dr. Lindsey and Rich. Until that night at dinner, when LJ decided it was time.

Lindsey, LJ, and Rich were eating dinner one Sunday night out on the deck. The deck encircled the entire second level, affording ocean viewing areas of varying sizes outside each of the five bedrooms as well as the great room and gourmet kitchen. A modular, overstuffed linen couch sat at the eastern corner, surrounding the steel fire pit, while two large, dark brown and white chairs with ottomans sat with their backs to the filigreed ocean with a glass table between them. Large area rugs of the same dark brown and white color scheme, lay underneath the modular couch and at the entry onto the deck, completed the effect of a living room hovering over the sea.

Now that there were three of them, Lindsey had decreed that they should eat dinner together at least once a week. Rich and LJ had laughed when she had suggested it, thinking she was joking, but their smiles disappeared when they saw the look on her face.

"Really. Is that too much to ask of us? Like a real—"

"Family," said Rich and LJ simultaneously, agreeing with her, and understanding why it was important.

Since the best time for the "family dinner" was after Sunday Mass, the appointed day became Sunday. About six weeks earlier, Lindsey had asked LJ if she was certain that she wanted to live at home rather than at college, giving her the opportunity finally, to talk about "it," the subject yet unspoken.

"LJ, we love to have you here, but you know that I'm more than happy to pay room and board at school, right?"

LJ nodded, but didn't look up from her plate. "Yes, I do." *Here's a perfect time. Take it slow and easy. Neither of these two knows anything about kids. She feels guilty for giving me up, but weirdly I get why she did it. Mom told me every detail about that day when she called. And about how, six months later, when I was born, she and Dad had been so excited to go get me from the hospital. They told me all about their agreement that Lindsey would not have anything to do with me, believing that would be best for all of us. That was, until I decided I wanted to go to Cal Poly for undergrad, and Lindsey and Rich just happened to have moved out here because Lindsey had accepted a job as Co-Director of the Animal Science Research Lab at Cal Poly. Coincidence?*

Rich watched the two women thoughtfully. They were still guarded with one another, but overall, they were doing remarkably well, he thought. Neither his wife nor her daughter was comfortable expressing anything but superficial emotion, at least for now. Moving into that terrain was too threatening. Although LJ was barely eighteen, she acted thirty, maybe older. *I'll bet Lindsey was a lot like LJ at her age.*

Rich lingered on the comparison for a few minutes. While Lindsey hadn't had the problem of alcoholism to deal with, she'd had plenty of experience with catastrophe in her young life—including an invalid mother and the loss of her father, who was killed when he crashed his NASA test plane during Lindsey's freshman year at Rice University. In fact, LJ's personality was kind of similar to Lindsey's in more than a few ways. Both were beautiful and seemed to view that fact as something independent of themselves. They applied only minimal makeup in the morning, and dressed to subtly accentuate their good looks, nothing more. They each wore their looks naturally, as if they should confer no extra advantage or gain. They both believed benefits would come from their achievements—and LJ was just beginning to figure out what it was she wanted to achieve.

"Rich, you're staring at me. Why are you staring?" LJ's voice was sharp, sharper than she'd intended. Both dogs jumped up from their snooze to look around. Once satisfied there was no catastrophe requiring a canine solution, they circled a few times and went back to sleep.

LJ's face was hot. The flush had started at her neck and now both cheeks were bright red. She was incredibly nervous. The tremendous energy she needed to tackle this subject was causing her to appear angry. It happened when she was nervous and she knew it was confusing to people, but she couldn't help it. LJ was about to ask for something no normal eighteen-year-old would ever request. Despite many assurances from her Texas mom during phone and Skype conversations, LJ's mouth was suddenly parched, her heart rate accelerating and her breath quickening. *Just get this over with...now!*

Glaring first at Rich, then at Lindsey, LJ pointed to the half-eaten pork loin sitting on the table. "That elephant in the middle of the table," the attempt at a smile failing, "it looks like a pork loin, but it's not." Deliberately and precisely placing her fork and knife on either side of her plate, she declared, "You both know that I'm an alcoholic."

Both Rich and Lindsey glanced guiltily at their half-full glasses of Cabernet.

"Please don't go there!"

Startled, Lindsey and Rich stared at LJ, but all vestiges of her anger had dissipated. She regarded them gravely and earnestly as she worked to be understood.

"That guilty look on your faces? I've seen that look before. After two months of following the first shrink's advice to keep all the wine and alcohol locked up, Mom and Dad decided to have a glass of wine. It was late, after midnight, and they figured I was asleep. But I heard them laughing. They hadn't laughed since it had all started. I came downstairs just as they were opening up a bottle—the first time after they'd discovered me so trashed they had to rush me to the emergency room to have my stomach pumped. They looked *exactly* like you just did."

The penetrating emerald eyes that gazed at them were so like Lindsey's, but made a startling contrast to her dark hair. She waited until their eyes met hers again, then continued. "*Please* don't think you have to stop drinking because of me. Or that you need to lock up your wine cellar. But we need to *talk* about this...I need to be able to say it—that I'm an alcoholic—and know that I'm not ruining your life by saying the dreaded word. I'm not afraid of being around that wine," she narrowed her eyes. "At least not here. With you."

A sudden smile lit up her face. "It's beautiful, by the way. Mom and Dad—Julie and Ted—would love it. The wine cellar, I mean. I hope they saw it when they were here in June." Uncharacteristically, LJ was chattering. Drenched in relief and ten million other unidentifiable feelings, she felt almost euphoric. "Morgan and I checked it out last week. We tried but lost count of all the wines you have stored there. Pretty impressive." LJ could feel the tension draining out of her, along with a tangible surge of gratitude—a dawning awareness that the facts of this family of hers were complicated but not dark. Anything but.

Raising her hand to stop both Lindsey and Rich from speaking, LJ said, "Look, all I'm asking for is the ability to talk to you, to explain myself and to thank you for all you are doing for me. I've been planning this conversation ever since I got here in June."

Getting up from where she sat on the overstuffed sectional couch nearest to the ocean, LJ walked around the fire pit that served as a table. She moved their plates to the side and sat down on the marble edge in front of Rich and Lindsey, who were seated side by side on the long L of the couch facing the water. She grabbed each of their hands, but her eyes remained on Lindsey. "I'll never understand all that it must have cost you to decide to have me. And then to ask Mom and Dad to adopt me. But I know it had to make everything more difficult for you. There aren't any suitable words to thank you for that." The sheen of tears in her eyes was evident, but none were shed. LJ pressed on because she knew she had to. "But I do, you see. *I do thank you.*" Now the tears hovered on the edges of her eyelashes. "See, I knew three girls in high school who had abortions. It was so easy for them, and they even joked about it.

Their mothers took them to do it, and they were back playing soccer the next day, like nothing had happened. Life was back to normal."

Rich resolutely kept himself from looking at Lindsey or touching this stouthearted teenager. *Stouthearted,* he thought, was a most fitting word to describe the girl whose words he was listening to. *Yep, this is Lindsey McCall's kid, all right.*

"Once we all decided to accept your generosity and move me out here for college, Mom and Dad, Julie and Ted—" Stammering now, LJ was still having trouble with names and labels. Who was her mother? Her Texas parents were the very best parents she could ever have, but it, this was confusing.

Wisely, Lindsey and Rich just listened. Lindsey felt drilled to the couch, with no idea of what to say to the child who sat there baring her soul. She wished with all her heart that Julie Grayson were there, sitting beside her. Julie would know what to say. Lindsey could only sit still, silent as a stone. Mind racing, all Lindsey could think of was the hell that Julie and Ted had gone through. She was just beginning to fully understand the wisdom of her decision eighteen years ago. *I could never have dealt with this, not after Paula.* Lindsey's sister Paula had begun drinking at thirteen and never stopped.

"They told me the whole story. Who you were, and what you were doing at the time. They answered all my questions, even when I asked them over and over again! So I thought I was prepared for this." LJ stood and stretched out her arms toward them, then turned slightly away to face the ocean. "How could anyone be prepared for beauty like that?" Then she swung back to them and exclaimed, "And this house? Mom and Dad have a very nice house back home in Texas, but this, this isn't a house, it's a—" Her uncharacteristic agitation threatened to choke her for a second.

"Mansion?" offered Rich, in an attempt to head off a series

of explanations and excuses from Lindsey. Guessing what she was thinking and feeling, he placed his hand on his wife's thigh to keep her quiet. She had been burdened with enough guilt and remorse for several lifetimes.

"Money is a funny thing, LJ," Rich said, smiling. "Back when I was in Houston homicide, I saw plenty of guys who had mega millions, yet killed to get more and more." Taking a sip from the glass of Cabernet he'd not touched since the girl's soliloquy had begun, he lifted it first to LJ and to Lindsey, then drank. "Thanks for telling us that our enjoying a little wine is not a problem for you. Just like Ted and Julie, we do like to drink it with dinner." Rich paused to reach out for LJ's hand and pull her back down to her perch on the edge of the firepit. "Thank you also for the first frank conversation the three of us have had since you got here. I want to hear everything you want to tell us, LJ, but there are a few things I'd like to say to you about your Mom here."

Ignoring the uncomfortable squirms he could sense from Lindsey, he leaned forward just a bit. "Unlike those men who craved money, your mother has little interest in it. When she was a few years younger than you are, your grandmother, her Mom, was diagnosed with heart failure. She became bedridden and was frequently sick from the side effects of the digitalis, the drug that kept her heart going." He paused and turned to Lindsey, suggesting gently, "Drink your wine, Linds, it's really very nice. Let me tell your daughter a little bit about this astounding woman who gave birth to her, please?" Rich watched as Lindsey picked up her glass, began to sip from it, and leaned back into the couch.

Lindsey breathed in deeply and said, "Okay, Rich." The smile she beamed at him was radiant. "I do love you, husband," and then, in a whisper, "and need you."

Watching these two demonstrating their love so openly, LJ

was surprised that she felt no embarrassment. Instead, she was suddenly aware of what she'd been ignoring since she had decided to begin this *talk*. The chilly September ocean breeze that played with her hair, the shadows created by the setting sun, the snores of Max and Gus as they slept in their beds, an aching sense of appreciation, and so much more. Aware of the changes in Lindsey just because Rich had decided to pull back some of the layers that obscured her true nature, LJ felt calm and secure, just as she did at home in Texas, surrounded by the love of her parents.

"Lindsey decided to create a new molecule for digitalis," Rich continued, "one that would not cause the awful side effects she'd witnessed in her mother. She wanted to find a way to augment the beneficial effects of the drug without the toxicity." Each time Rich thought of these years, the long nights and weekends required, his wonder at the tenacity of his wife engulfed him. "She worked on this new molecule during most of her non-working time throughout college, medical school, and twelve years of Residency." Rich picked up his glass in a second silent toast to Lindsey. "And, you know what? She did it. Billions of people all over the world are now being helped by Digipro, the new drug she created with Hank and Liisa Reardon at their pharmaceutical company, Andrews, Sacks, and Levine." He shook his head at the thought. "It took her twenty years, LJ, while she worked her day job. The money in your trust fund, your tuition, the car—all of that comes out of the Digipro money. And does she want to retire? Hell no! She's working with Liisa on a new drug, Longevive, a drug they think can double the human lifespan! I could go on, LJ, but my wife's elbow keeps jabbing into my ribs."

Rich kept talking, but his tone was more earthbound. "Anyway, I want to get back to the subject of the house for a minute. You should know that we had more than a little trouble with the decision to buy this place. I had a real hard time seeing myself living here in a place like this, a gated community with a swimming pool, our own spa, and this view." As he looked out, the sun was in his eyes, causing him to squint as he went on. "But I talked Lindsey into it. She'd found it online before coming out here to interview at Cal Poly and was excited about it. She had never lived in a place like this either. Once I saw it, I realized this beautiful place was *made* for her. This was her house. It *is* her house LJ. She's the one who wrote the check, not me."

Rich considered but discarded the idea of sharing the additional morsel about Lindsey's wrongful murder conviction. Instead, he leaned back against the cushion. He'd said enough.

For a few moments, the three sat in silence with only the occasional cry of seagulls as background music. LJ felt weird. She knew her mother was smart, most likely a genius. But what could she say about what Rich had just revealed? She—anyone actually—would be in awe of someone who had accomplished even half of what Lindsey McCall had. But this was her *mother!* Since she had no idea how to respond, she did what her mom had taught her: Be still and *think*. Open yourself up to your feelings, no matter how ugly or embarrassing they are. When you're with someone who makes you uncomfortable, know that the discomfort comes from you, not from the other person. Ask the questions of yourself that no one wants to ask. Am I jealous? What am I afraid of? Is it rejection? Success? The expectations of others?

LJ smiled at the long list of questions that her wise mother had taught her to ask and answer honestly.

Speak it. Once you speak it, it loses all power over you.

Quite suddenly, LJ was flooded with infinite gratitude for both of these women, her two mothers.

"I'm afraid I will disappoint you," LJ said, looking from

Lindsey to Rich, and back again. "Here you both are, opening up your lives to…a stranger, paying for everything…and you have absolutely no idea of who I am, except that I'm an alcoholic." LJ was standing now and pacing from sheer nervous energy. "Lindsey, I don't think you'll ever know how deeply I appreciate your offer to pay another forty thousand dollars for my room and board, but the thing is, I don't really trust myself to be among a bunch of freshmen college kids, at parties, bars…anywhere." The memories were assaulting her brain…boys she hardly knew who she'd allowed to give her pills, liquor, and even to undress her. She remembered little of what happened after that. Had she had sex with one of them, or ten? She didn't even know if she was still a virgin—how disgusting was that?

LJ's voice was quivering, her knees trembling. "Mom and Dad worked so hard with me for the last two years, it would kill me if I gave in and started drinking again." Ignoring the tears coursing down her cheeks, she sat down and stared at Lindsey. "Do you *mind* if I stay here, at least this year?"

CHAPTER THREE

San Luis Obispo, California

LJ and Morgan pulled up to the parking lot adjacent to the Baker Building on the Cal Poly Campus. Before she'd even turned off the ignition, Morgan had her door open.

"Wait, Morgan, we have time. It's only seven thirty. If we go in there now, I'll be climbing the walls. The exams won't be distributed until eight. They made that perfectly clear. Let's make a plan. Midterms end on Friday but for freshmen, Thursday. Friday is free, a perfect day to move you out of the dorm and into the bedroom next to mine. You'll save your mom five thousand dollars! Lindsey talked with someone over at the administrative office and was told that the money could be returned to your mother if you left by the end of the semester. That's Friday, by five in the afternoon."

"Five thousand two hundred ninety-eight dollars and fifty cents."

"Huh?"

"That's how much my mother will get back."

"Does that mean you want to do it, Morgan?"

"Yes." Morgan knew LJ wanted to talk more about it, but she couldn't. Not now. She'd had that nightmare again the previous night. The same one as last month, then twice this past week. Morgan had never been so terrified in her life. What if it was a warning? How could she even describe what she was seeing and hearing when she didn't even understand it herself?

About a ten-minute walk away from the Baker Building, Lindsey stood with six Dobermans in the exercise area of the newly built Animal Science Research Center. The building had been a condition of Lindsey's appointment, and a win-win for everyone, since the two-million-dollar investment cost the university nothing. The Research Center had been wholly financed by Dr. Lindsey McCall, and sat adjacent to the administrative offices of the Animal Science Center. Although she'd been offered a space in the crowded building, Lindsey had preferred to be in the labs, close to her animals. Since she was a medical doctor and not a veterinarian or animal physiologist, she'd solicited help with the design of the center from two members of the faculty who were experts in animal research. The 1,500 square foot exercise area had been the subject of vigorous debate among Lindsey and her two advisors—not for the cost, but for the amount of space devoted to it. Like any university, Cal Poly was under immense pressures for space, especially for research. Ultimately, Lindsey was granted a total of only 10,000 square feet for her entire building.

Thank you, Jodi and Chuck, for forcing this issue. My idea for an exercise area just a third of this size was stupid. These are relatively average-sized Dobermans, and I have six more coming over the next few weeks.

"Dr. McCall! Take a break from your kids and join Jodi and me for lunch."

The head of the Animal Science Department stood there in all his corpulent splendor, in his usual long black Jesuit robes. Reverend Blaise Roderick held a Ph.D. in organic chemistry from Cal Tech, as well as a doctorate in physics from MIT.

With an intellect, heart, and personality even more massive than his 300 pound body, Father Blaise was a study in contrasts. Hard science and religion, ascetic Jesuit and morbidly obese, hagiographer and devotee of mystery novels, scholar and movie buff. The list was long, but these were the most evident to Lindsey. Closing the gate to the exercise area, she whispered to Ally, a five-year-old red male with the most pronounced cardiac dilation of the five dogs, "I'll be back baby boy, you're just fine with your buddies here." She pointed at his bed and said, "Sit Ally boy, and I'll give you your chewie." The big dog climbed onto the bed, then sat with an expectant look in his eyes. Lindsey walked over to the row of white cabinet doors, reached into the first on the left, and pulled out a white berber dog toy shaped like a gingerbread man. Then she walked back to the sitting dog and handed it to him. Ally took it softly, lay down and began to suckle the toy.

"Lindsey, if I hadn't seen this I'd never have believed it!" Dr. Jodi Tamarack stood beside Fr. Blaise shaking her head and chuckling. "These dogs have been here what—a month? Six weeks? They are already acting like they belong here...the others will arrive this next week, right?

Just as Lindsey was about to reply, a fleshy black-sleeved arm wrapped around her waist and none too gently pulled her toward the hallway. "Ladies, we need sustenance. Man cannot live on Dobermans alone. Surely you don't want to be the cause of the hundred-pound weight loss my doctor keeps advising?"

"Okay, okay, I get it but let's walk, we need the exercise." Lindsey had not run in the last couple of days and was feeling the inactivity.

At the look on both Jodi's and Fr. Roderick's face, Lindsey looked out of the window. It was pouring. The central coast had been in severe drought conditions for close to a decade, and the connecting entrance between the central offices and animal science center had been the butt of numerous jokes as an unnecessary architectural flourish. Until this winter. No one made fun of it now that December's rainfall had reached twelve inches in just seven days, and there was no end in sight. The locals were considering a revision of the water restriction policies that had been in effect for as long as anyone could remember. With flooding the new and constant danger, the old regulations now seemed absurd.

Grabbing her slicker off a hook in the entryway, Lindsey said, "I'll run to get my car. Meet me at the front of the admin building so you won't get soaked."

Ten minutes later, they sat at 19 Metro, one of the few decent options for a meal on campus. It was a favorite of Fr. Blaise since it served breakfast until early afternoon. Digging into a large stack of buckwheat pancakes drenched with syrup, the priest popped the glutinous mess into his mouth, closing his eyes while he chewed. "Heavenly." Smiling at Lindsey's egg-white frittata with squash, he declared, "It's a rule."

"What's a rule?"

"Those who don't need to watch their weight eat as if they do."

Shrugging, Jodi sighed, eyed the garlic parmesan breadstick she was about to devour, then placed it back on her plate. "Father, just once, I'd like to finish my meal without feeling guilty about my unhealthy eating habits. It's bad enough watching Lindsey contentedly surviving on well-seasoned grass."

"'There is nothing either good or bad. It's thinking makes it so,' the good Bard said long ago. Jodi, my dear, the Lord gives us each unique gifts. Fasting has never been one of mine—or yours."

Defiantly picking up the breadstick, she ate the whole thing. "Rather than discussing our inability to fast, let's talk about the dogs, and whether Lindsey can get them to keep eating kale. That's far more interesting!" The veterinarian looked expectantly at Lindsey.

"It's hard to believe, but the short answer is yes, we can. Dobermans love to eat. I've mixed huge batches of spinach, kale, collards, and turnip greens with olive oil and chicken broth. They gobble it down as if it's hamburger. Already the dogs are better. Their Holter monitors show only occasional ventricular ectopy, and their exercise tolerance has improved significantly."

Lindsey had learned to ignore the mostly congenial scrapping between Father Blaise and Jodi. "Jodi, I'm hoping you or one of your grad students can start doing echocardiograms on them later today, so we can confirm what I see clinically."

The expressions of both the priest and Jodi were thoughtful while Lindsey explained. Neither of them had been enthusiastic about Lindsey's decision to bring in a bunch of Dobermans with cardiac disease to kick off the first experiment in the brand new research center. Jodi's interest lay in large animals, primarily cattle, followed distantly by sheep and horses. Dogs were far down her list. But she was a team player, and Lindsey's contributions to the center had to be acknowledged. The vet would cooperate in any way she could. Besides, she was finding that the Dobes were altogether different from her image of them. Far from the aggressive creatures their appearance suggested, they were love hounds. Jodi and Sami, a post-doc veterinarian from U.C. Davis, had performed the admission echos on the six dogs when they'd arrived. Both had been amazed at the cooperation of the large dogs, their friendliness and the complete absence of offensive behavior.

Fr. Blaise was a bench scientist. With doctoral training in both physics and chemistry, he could have his pick of positions in any number of prestigious labs in the world. But his contrarian approach to almost everything would have limited his success in the highly political world of academia. In fact, before hiring Lindsey, Roderick had fired five researchers, each with outstanding pedigrees. The terminations had resulted in such severe blowback for the president that Roderick's job as the director had been in jeopardy. But the emergence of Dr. Lindsey McCall at Cal Poly, along with her insistence on financing the multimillion-dollar research center, had returned the priest to the good graces of the president's office—a fact the Jesuit found most amusing.

"You think there are epigenetic changes already, don't you?" His sharp, dark-blue-eyed gaze never left Lindsey's face while Fr. Blaise sliced off a piece of sausage with surprising delicacy, popped it into his mouth and chewed. "But then again, it could be the Digipro you have them on, how can you distinguish between them? I thought you said there would be no need for control groups?"

Jodi had stopped eating and was listening attentively. She had been wondering the same thing.

"Honestly, I can't distinguish. Ardis has found six more Dobermans in either early or moderate stage of heart failure. We should have all six new dogs by the end of next week. Given that each does have cardiomyopathy, this group will be on Digipro only. I'll not be adding the megadoses of K2 from the leafy dark green veggies to the diet of this group."

Ardis Braun ran one of the largest Doberman rescues in the country, the Dobies and Little Paws Rescue Center in Fillmore, California—about 250 miles south of San Luis Obispo. She had been in Dobie rescue for close to thirty years and had a national reputation for the quality of her shelter.

When Lindsey had explained to her the kind of research she planned to do at Cal Poly, Ardis's reply was as emphatic as it was supportive." Hey, Dr. Lindsey, you tell me how many Dobies with heart failure you can treat, and I will locate and help get them to you!"

"Do they all have a splice site mutation for PDK4?" asked Fr. Roderick.

"Yes, boss, they do indeed." Lindsey's smile widened as she thought back to her first meeting with this man. He'd shown very little interest in the study she wanted to implement as soon as the new lab was ready. Here was a man who had never done clinical research and whose attitude had bordered on rudeness. Now, seven months later, he was well-versed in the most technical components of her research.

At that first meeting, once the details of Lindsey's new job had been agreed upon, the priest had stood as if to hasten her out the door. Lindsey had stayed seated. "There is something else we need to decide before I can agree to come on board."

Tersely, without turning back to face her, the black-robed figure had barked, "And what would that be, Dr. McCall?"

"Father, I need to explain it to you, and I'd prefer to do it to your face rather than your back."

Taking a seat behind his desk, surrounded by piles of papers she knew now had dealt with the furor over the dismissal of five members of the Cal Poly faculty, Roderick growled, "Five minutes. That's it."

More quickly than she would have thought possible, Lindsey explained the subset of young girls among the millions of patients taking Digipro who had stopped needing the drug. The ASL researchers had accidentally discovered about forty of them who had developed cardiomyopathy before the age of ten.

Cardiomyopathy is a puzzling and almost universally fatal

type of heart failure, thought to be caused by a virus in adults and a genetic abnormality in children. Malformations in the DNA have been found in some kids, but the actual mechanism of the disease is poorly understood. However, its course is all too well known: increasing heart failure and incapacitation over time, and eventual death if not treated with heart transplantation.

Liisa Reardon and her team at ASL theorized that the cause of the disease among these youngsters may have been the sudden activation of the inactive X chromosome. After reading about how a physician had beaten her own multiple sclerosis with a strict nutritional regimen, Liisa and two colleagues had wondered if diet could affect cardiac failure in a similar way. With the help of an epidemiologist, they incentivized the parents of the cardiac-impaired girls by offering six months of free medication in exchange for precise control of what their kids ate. They found that after a few months on the dietary regimen they designed—basically, a strict Paleo diet but with more greens—most were off the Digipro or down to a much lower dose. The science emerging about the critical importance of vitamin K, magnesium, zinc, and potassium in healing the mitochondria was incontrovertible.

Lindsey wondered if Dobermans with cardiomyopathy were like those young girls. There was even a genetic marker identifying it in large-breed dogs such as these. There was now a DNA test for it.

Lindsey would have sworn that Roderick had heard little if any of what she had told him all those months ago, but apparently she was mistaken.

Father Roderick plucked a breadstick from Jodi's plate and winked at Lindsey as he asked, rhetorically, "Want to know the three best components of our first non-livestock animal research undertaking?"

Lindsey merely waited while he dispatched the breadstick, wiped his mouth and multiple chins with his napkin, and leaned back with his hands folded over his bulging abdomen.

"I'll be reporting at the President's Council meeting this coming Friday that we are..." with his left hand, Fr. Blaise ticked off three extended fleshy fingers on his right as he spoke, "testing a noninvasive procedure; doing it on rescue Dobermans, twelve dogs who would die without treatment; and have reversed the clinical research order from human to dog rather than dog to human." Blue eyes twinkling, he extended a fourth finger. "And I can report that the dogs are already exhibiting improvement in their cardiac function. We welcome, therefore, a visit from the animal activist groups who have voiced so much concern over dog research at Cal Poly!"

Rich carefully balanced the food and coffee in one hand while pulling open the door of Lindsey's research building with the other. He could hear the dogs the minute he was through the door, the barks, whines, and scrabbling of nails growing louder as he walked past the mostly empty offices and headed into the exercise area. *Sure sounds like a lot more than six Dobies.* Progressing into the cavernous space, he realized why. *It's because there are now twelve!*

Lindsey stood in the middle of the melee, baffled as to what had excited the dogs until she turned to see Rich standing in the doorway bearing gifts.

"You are a life saver, thank you! How did you know I'd be absolutely starving?" Lindsey's eyes danced with anticipation. She was salivating at the fragrance of the takeout omelet breakfast from their favorite spot, Lil' Bits in Grover Beach.

"Maybe because you were too tired to eat dinner last night before falling into bed—and then were back here before six this morning?"

"What would I do without you, husband of mine?" Lindsey grabbed a container, opened it, and popped a crispy chunk of home fries into her mouth. "Yum, oh gosh, this is so good."

Rich followed Lindsey into the conference room, away

from the dogs. Grinning while he watched his wife tear into the food, he said, "You'd be a whole lot thinner without me, that's for sure!" Slowly letting his gaze roam over her form, he added, "And we don't need any weight loss off certain parts, nope not a single ounce!" Pointing to a Starbucks coffee cup that she hadn't noticed, he said, "If you don't want this, I'll drink it."

Lindsey swallowed then shook her head, "No, thanks, go ahead, I've already had three cups. If I drink any more coffee, I'll be on the ceiling." Her hunger beginning to abate, she sat back, looked happily at Rich and asked, "So what are your plans for the day?" Then, before he could answer, she frowned and asked, "I forgot to ask how your case for Alicia was coming along? Do you think we should call Hank Reardon and see if anything else has come out about Dimitri's death?"

"To your first question about my plans, not much, just some paperwork. The second? Surprisingly well. Alicia's nutty ex-boyfriend seems to be respecting the restraining order. She's back in her condo, apparently feeling safe. And the other thing? Yes, I think we should call Hank—maybe tonight if you get home earlier than last night. Like maybe for dinner? LJ leaves for Texas in two days, you know."

Right. Today is Thursday.

"In fact, her last day of exams is tonight. How about we make dinner a priority? A little celebration for her finishing her exams and you rivaling Ardis as the fastest growing Doberman Animal Shelter in California?" Regarding his wife's sudden frown, he decided to press. "When can you leave here so I can plan dinner?" *If she doesn't have a deadline, she'll stay here until eight or nine, minimum.* Calmly, he watched annoyance begin to build in her posture and expression. The tightening of her mouth and jaw. Rich merely waited and watched her toy with the remainder of her food.

Rich was accustomed to this dance. There were times he

understood Dr. Lindsey McCall far better than she knew herself. LJ's candor at dinner the previous Sunday night had left vast residues of emotion that Lindsey didn't want to deal with. Since she had been a small child, intense study and work had been her way of staving off unpleasant or painful emotions. Rich recognized the process in action.

After his first wife, Laura, had been killed in a car accident, he'd worked nonstop as captain of Houston Homicide. That is, until a gunshot flattened him. Literally. Only then did he deal with the awful pain of Laura's death. Many times during that hellaciously hot Houston summer, he had thought he'd never make it...and didn't want to. In fact, if it hadn't been for Max and the immensity of that dog's heart, he was quite sure he wouldn't have. But what Lindsey was dealing with was considerably more complicated than grief. Sometimes he thought he understood, then something would happen to make him realize he had no clue. Like during last Sunday's dinner.

LJ had taken huge risks that night. Rich winced when he thought back to Lindsey's silence after LJ's request to live with them rather than face the temptations of full-time campus life. Only after she had repeated herself had Lindsey answered, "Of course you can stay here—as long as you'd like, LJ." She'd done so in her "clinician persona," a flat, detached voice and expressionless face. That was it. LJ must have felt like a fool to have made herself so vulnerable. Rich had been angry at Lindsey in that moment, knowing that her feelings were nothing like what she'd presented. That robotic affect had been a sign that she was frightened. Lindsey McCall was scared to death of her daughter, though LJ had no way of knowing that.

Lindsey stared at the remains of her breakfast, trying to get control of herself, trying to unlock her jaws and force herself to look at Rich. *God, why is this so hard? Why can't I act like an ordinary loving mother? But of course I am not her mother. Julie is.*

Ever since LJ had arrived, these thoughts and prayers had played inside Lindsey incessantly. Here at work, Lindsey absorbed herself in the ever-needy dogs and her lengthy list of tasks. Several times, Jodi had offered her own help and that of the grad students, but Lindsey had refused. That was selfish she knew, and unfair to the dogs, but it was what she needed to do. Closing her eyes for another few seconds, she took a breath, opened them, and looked up at her husband, who sat there regarding her evenly.

"You're right," she said, finally.

"Yes, I am." There was no humor in Rich's face. In fact, Lindsey noted, he looked sad.

"But I don't want a repeat of a dinner like last Sunday's. I…I just couldn't take it."

Good, a crack in the façade. Rich cocked his head and raised an eyebrow. "What do you mean?"

"I don't want to go back there…to feel all that guilt over giving her away to Julie and Ted. All those years when I never thought about her…never even wondered what she looked like." Her voice dropped to a whisper. "Imagine never wondering about the face of your own child?"

"Then what prompted you to ask her to live with us, Lindsey? You can't have this girl in your house without dealing with what happened eighteen years ago."

Rich's sadness was gone, replaced with frustration. Sometimes, he really didn't understand, and he was sick of trying and failing to do so. He wondered if his wife should see someone, either a spiritual adviser or a psychiatrist. Maybe he needed to call Father John Tobin to come out and visit them. The priest was a trusted friend and counselor to them both.

"Rich, how do I tell my daughter that she got the better mother? How do I tell her what a disaster of a life she would have had if Julie and Ted hadn't adopted her? How do I explain that *I wouldn't have been any good at being her mother?*" A huge single tear sat at the edge of her left eye, then fell, followed by several more. But she made no sound.

You think LJ doesn't know this? Aloud, he merely said, "You tell her exactly that, Lindsey. Just like you just said it to me." Watching her face, beautiful even with the dark circles of fatigue smudged under her eyes, he suddenly knew that this would resolve itself. Finally, she would find peace with the decision she'd made all those years before. Lindsey had never said these words out loud to him before. At no time had she ever suggested that giving up LJ had been the best option—for the baby as well as for her.

Rich guessed that she'd never expressed these feelings to him because it had taken her all these years to reveal them to herself—to let them float up through all the debris left by her inability to prevent the deaths of her mother and her older sister. He'd read somewhere that each family has a sacrificial child, one that carries the pain of all the other family members. Lindsey had been that child in the McCall family.

Rich knew, too, that the insomnia she'd had as long as he'd known her would disappear. As she forgave herself for all her failures, real and imagined, sleep would begin to come more easily. He said a quick prayer of thanksgiving as he watched her pick up her phone to call her daughter.

"LJ, it's me. Rich and I want to have a celebration for you acing your exams. Oh, I'm sure you did! And to thank you for being the gritty girl you are." Her voice lowered. "And LJ, please forgive me for being such a total jerk Sunday night. We love you—I love you—and I hope you know that you can live with us as long as you can stand us!"

She was speaking to LJ's voicemail, but it was a start. LJ would get it.

Pismo Beach

As his vintage 1992 380 SL Mercedes effortlessly crested the slight rise on Route 101, a stunning panorama was revealed. Rich exhaled loudly in pure pleasure at what may have been the premiere coastline and ocean view in the world. The sight never failed to amaze him. The morning sun sliced through the December drizzle and fog to reveal the enormous boulder in Pismo Bay, hundreds of feet below, eternally pounded by the restless Pacific Ocean.

Quickly glancing to his right, Rich smiled as Max lifted his left paw and placed it on Rich's right hand as it lay on the gear shift, curling the pads of his paw around the edge of Rich's hand. *Thank God you're not one of those Dobies with cardiomyopathy Max, my boy. We're family. First, it was just you and me. Then Lindsey came into the picture, now LJ and maybe Morgan. And you welcomed all of us into that huge heart of yours. You know how much I owe you, right?*

Rich had left Max in the Mercedes while he went in to visit Lindsey, suspecting that all those rescue Dobes might be a bit more than even he could handle. He had left their new little rescue guy, Gus, at home. When he came back to the car, he brought Max two grain-free biscuits that were inhaled with gratitude.

Sitting erect in the passenger seat, Max got a lot of double-takes, as always, from other motorists as they flew by along the highway. Occasionally, the big red dog would return the stare of a driver, adopting that quintessential Doberman look. *You think you're looking at just an ordinary dog? No way, look again!*

Cal Poly was just fifteen minutes from the Pismo house, at the northern edge of San Luis Obispo. Rich smiled as he considered the commute he'd had to his office in downtown Houston. The legendary Houston traffic had turned it into a two-hour ordeal unless he left by five in the morning. That he worked out of a home office now, with Lindsey just twenty minutes away, seemed surreal.

Traffic notwithstanding, Rich had been deliriously happy in Texas with his new wife. He'd enjoyed the challenges presented by his return to the practice of criminal defense law after ten years in homicide, and had totally loved working with Zach Cunningham.

The move to California had been Lindsey's idea and he'd agreed to it immediately—but Rich had felt a little uncertain, even a bit wary, about what their life there would be like. Would the transition from conservative Houston to the most assuredly liberal central coast of California work out? When he'd told LJ that purchasing the house had been a hard decision, he meant it. Embroiled in a complicated case in Oklahoma City at the time, Rich had never even seen the place in person until the day they bought it.

Once she'd accepted the new job at Cal Poly, Lindsey had stayed in California to look for a place for them to live. She had sent dozens of pictures of Pismo Beach and the Oceano dunes, each one more spectacular than the last. He'd had to agree with her that the beaches were stunning, equaling Cannes, and the Greek islands. Each time she called, he'd ended up laughing at her over-the-top descriptions.

Then there was the matter of his license. Rich would need to retake the Bar Exam to practice law in California.

The reality was that California boasted the highest failure rate of all US Bar applicants—some 60 percent. Although Rich had made light of his concerns, he had cause to worry.

For practicing lawyers, Calfornia administers a two-day exam consisting of six essay questions and two performance test questions, instead of the four days required by new graduates. But that was good news and bad news. Rich's law partner, Zach Cunningham, had warned him about the performance test questions. Zach had been a grader for several state bar exams and considered the California performance test questions tricky and ambiguous for even an experienced lawyer. Concerned that Rich had just under a month to prepare, he had graciously offered to take the lead in Dr. Simmons' restraining order, with Rich functioning under the limited-practice guidelines of a non-California attorney.

When Rich decided to risk the abbrevated two day exam, Zach spent hours drilling him with examples from past exams. When he finally received his California license that past October, Rich had felt like the boulder he'd seen in that stunning ocean view was finally off his back.

CHAPTER SIX

"Any chance you two could spend another Christmas in Lausanne?"

Rich and Lindsey blinked at the webcam computer image of Hank Reardon waiting for their answer. The two were shocked speechless. They'd been kidding around for the last four hours about all the kinky fun they planned to have, now that they were alone for the first time since June. They'd gotten up at three that morning to get LJ and Morgan to their nine am. flight to Houston for Christmas break. Now, they were drinking celebratory glasses of Cava in anticipation of an early bedtime. In contrast to their light mood, Hank's was uncharacteristically solemn.

"Hank, what's wrong?" Lindsey asked, frowning at the screen. Her upraised hand, holding the champagne glass that had been offered as a toast, floated back down to the table. It was only seven a.m. in his time zone. "You look—"

"Hank, can we call you back in about an hour?" Rich interjected, cutting Lindsey off abruptly and clicking out of the call.

Staring at the now-blank computer screen, Lindsey said, "Would you care to explain what just happened?" But she found herself talking to his back; Rich had jumped up and was pulling on his jeans. Sensing tension in the room, the dogs stirred and sat up, suddenly vigilant.

"Stay Max," Rich said, gently. "You stay here and watch the house. Lindsey, we need to get to a pay phone, so get dressed. It might take some doing to find one. I don't imagine there's a pay phone on every corner out here anymore."

Puzzled but recognizing her husband's sense of urgency, Lindsey grabbed and donned a pair of yoga pants and a loose top, then jogged down the hallway after him. The dogs looked down the hall after them, but obeyed the command to 'stay.'"

Fifteen minutes later, the couple found a pay phone at a 7-Eleven on Dolliver Street. While Rich dialed 0170, Lindsey glanced around at the graffiti etched into the plexiglass walls of the enclosure, still in the dark about what was going on. She listened as Rich recited Hank Reardon's telephone number to an international operator. *Must be too important for cell phones,* she figured, *but how had Rich figured that out?* Her conjecture disappeared with Rich's first exclamation.

"Dimitri is alive?"

Somewhere over the North Atlantic

"Why are you laughing? What's so funny?"

"I can't believe we're doing this. Again. For the third time in less than a year!" Lindsey picked up her champagne flute, drained it, and nodded a, "Yes, please" at the Swiss Airlines steward who stood waiting with a refill. Turning to Rich, she held the now-full glass up in a mock toast. "Here's to our quiet Christmas alone in Pismo Beach." After a big swallow, she continued, a bit coldly, "Humor me, please. Exactly how did you decide that Hank shouldn't say anymore? Who on earth would have tapped his phones or bugged his house? And why would they even consider doing that?"

Lindsey wasn't happy about this unplanned trip to Lausanne, and she wanted to make sure her husband knew it. She'd gritted her teeth throughout the previous two days of lining up Jodi Tamarack and a dozen Cal Poly grad students to care for the Dobermans and the new batch of Agouti research mice that had finally arrived for the Longevive study. Getting them had been far more complicated than either she or Liisa Reardon had thought it would be.

To eliminate genetic variation among the mice they were

studying, the scientists used what are known as agouti mice. These mice had jumpstarted epigenetic research when both the function and switchoff of the agouti gene was understood, ending, once and for all, the myth that DNA is destiny.

The agouti gene causes mice to be voracious eaters, born with abnormally yellow-colored fur instead of the usual brown. Agouti mice are prone to obesity, cancer, diabetes, and early death. Remarkably, the gene can be switched off simply by feeding pregnant mice foods rich in methyl donors, such as strawberries, onions, and leafy green vegetables. The result is lean, brown mice. It was the agouti mice experiments that had made the kind of epigenetic research Lindsey and Liisa were doing with Longevive possible. They had also formed the basis of Lindsey's research with the Dobermans.

Because Lindsey would merely be duplicating Liisa's research, the two scientists had planned to breed at least two generations of control and research mice by mid-December. But Ariana, Liisa's head tech, had promised their entire collection of Agouti mice to other ASL researchers, and the wait for the mice had put them behind.

It wasn't that the Longevive protocol was complicated. Quite the opposite. It merely involved separating the group of sixty-four animals into two groups, one *control*, the second *experimental*, then giving the drug to the experimental group only. They would then conduct seven simple physical measurements of both groups daily. It wasn't that different from any Junior High science experiment, but Lindsey was nervous about it. It had been over two years since she'd conducted any animal research with mice—since before she'd been indicted. Perhaps that was why she found herself resenting the hell out of this interruption due to another crisis at Andrews, Sacks, and Levine.

Glaring across at Rich in the hope of more verbal jousting

to vent her extreme frustration, she saw that he was dead to the world. *Good thing you didn't hear a word I said,* she thought. *It's not as if racing off to Switzerland is your idea of a fun way to spend Christmas, either.* She sat back and collected herself. *I hate you when you act like this, Lindsey McCall.* She shook her head and smiled at her own over-reaction. The hovering Swiss steward misinterpreted the gesture and wordlessly asked if she'd like a third glass.

"No, I've had more than enough, thanks," she whispered, not wanting to awaken her husband. Glancing at him, she wondered—not for the first time—just why this remarkable man had decided to marry her. Lindsey knew she was anything but easy, that there was a side to her nearly impossible to love. Both her mother and sister had detested the intellectual, unemotional aspect of her personality, but Rich seemed to take it in stride.

Lindsey knew that her shortcomings were also her strengths. It was her detachment that made her good at handling the life-threatening emergencies she faced in her job, and her exacting nature helped her understand the most complex science. But the cost of these characteristics had been devastating. This was probably why she liked that Kelly Clarkson song, "Dark Side," and had even memorized most of the lyrics. Humming under her breath, Lindsey thought rather than sang the words:

Will you love me?
Even with my dark side?
But she changed the first line to *Can you love me?*

Until Rich Jansen had come along, she'd pushed every man out of her life in short order. Rich simply wouldn't allow it. Thank God.

"How very good to see you," Dimitri Vlasov said as he enveloped Rich and Lindsey in his arms and planted a kiss on each of their foreheads.

Recovering first, Rich exclaimed, "I'm damn happy to see you, too, buddy! I thought you were dead!" Then, looking over at Hank Reardon, he added, "Maybe that's because Hank called me back in August to tell me so."

Rich had been sitting on their deck sipping coffee and watching the ocean, when Hank had called.

"Hank Reardon, how are you this beautiful morning?"

"One day, Jansen, I swear I am going to call you and Lindsey just to chat. Is she there?"

Rich put his coffee down and stood up, instantly alert. "No, she's at Cal Poly. She's pretty excited about the early effects of Longevive on a test group of dogs with markers of cardiac disease. Dobermans, actually…" Realizing he was chattering to postpone what was most assuredly bad news, he got to the point, "But obviously, you didn't call to chat about Lindsey's work. What's up?"

"Dimitri was found dead at his home this morning. Without him, the case against Diedrich Braun is toast." Reardon exhaled a long slow breath that sounded more like a sob. "Lindsey will not be testifying Monday."

The Swiss special ops detective had persuaded the Switzerland office of the Attorney General to indict Diedrich Braun for two criminal felonies: conspiracy to murder Matthew Adams, CEO of the American Pharmaceutical Company Adams and Adams, and industrial espionage—specifically a robbery at the animal research laboratory of Andrews, Sacks, and Levine. Lindsey had been one of the principal witnesses for the prosecution.

Rich had been surprised when Dimitri had called a few months earlier, exuberant. After months of painstaking work on his part, the Swiss AG's office had agreed to indict. Thanks to pressure by FedPol, the case was fast-tracked. Still, the evidence against Braun was wholly circumstantial, resting entirely on the written claims of Eric, Braun's dead son. A decent criminal defense attorney could find hundreds of holes in the case, and Braun had all the money he needed to hire the very best. Rich had tried to dissuade Dimitri from pursuing it before he and Lindsey had left Switzerland.

"How did he die?"

"Heart attack."

Dimitri Vlasov had been a fit, forty-something man. The Ukrainian cop had worked out almost obsessively and ate like an ascetic.

"Are they buying it?" Rich asked, referring to the people at FedPol.

"It was Commander Evan who called me this morning. No, he and the DA think it was a hit ordered by Braun. It's not terribly difficult to make a murder look like a heart attack if you know what you're doing."

They stood in Hank Reardon's library at his Lausanne, Switzerland, home. Lindsey absently wiped tears away and stared fixedly at the Fedpol cop as wave after wave of memories assaulted her. The kidnapping of Liisa Reardon and the head animal research technician at ASL, Ariana Dumas; the fear that both women were dead; and all the confusion about Joe Cairns. Who was he, anyway?

"Lindsey and Rich, please say hello to Commander Evan Evan, Dimitri's superior at the Tigris Unit of FedPol."

Grateful that Hank had interrupted the frenzied flashbacks chasing themselves around her brain, Lindsey smiled at the head cop. Evan looked like an accountant, or maybe a tax attorney, shorter than she by about two inches and weighing about the same. He resembled old photos of Harry Truman, with gray hair, wireless spectacles, thin lips, and an entirely unassuming air.

Shaking Evan's hand, Rich thought, *I'll bet this guy is lethal.* One of his own best cops had that milquetoast look, too, but he was anything but. These absent-minded Columbo types could be deadly in interrogations.

CHAPTER SEVEN

Lausanne, Switzerland

Incredulously, Lindsey exclaimed, "Your offices have been wiretapped by Diedrich Braun and his people since last June?"

The unassuming cop then told a tale that rivaled the best spy novel. Transfixed, she and Rich listened for the better part of two hours while Dimitri explained. "It was a fluke. There is no good reason that our tech Lara should have gone back to Liisa's office after Eric's body had been removed. Each time we asked, she only said she had a feeling that something had been missed. Once she found the first camera, we brought the entire team back.

"Someone had inserted cameras throughout the animal research labs, Liisa's office, and Mr. Reardon's home office. Incoming phone lines there were tapped as were the cell phones of Liisa, Ariana, and Hank." A broad smile altered his face. "With the permission of the Reardons, we have kept all the devices in place, leading Braun to believe that he is still monitoring everything happening with all of the new drugs ASL is working on." The smile widened even more. "We're showing him all false data, of course. Exactly like the report of my fatal heart attack."

Dimitri Vlasak was not a handsome man. Far from it. His features were too flat, eyes too close together, and nose too broad. In a crowd, he could easily be overlooked. But when engaged in conversation, Dimitri was mesmerizing—even for people who had been awake for close to twenty-four hours, like Rich and Lindsey.

It's those eyes, Lindsey thought. *The same color as the Caribbean...not exactly turquoise, almost aquamarine. Contrasted with that dark skin...*

"Lindsey, is there something you'd like to say?"

Blushing, Lindsey shook her head, "No, Dimitri, just thinking. Sorry." But her thoughts lingered. Her curiosity about the man had an appetite.

Faking a fatal heart attack is not easily done, despite the way it might be portrayed in films. Lindsey figured they had to have used potassium chloride or calcium gluconate administered intravenously. The high dose required would be extremely painful—it would burn. The victim would have to have been immobilized somehow. How did he survive? Clearly, these people were pros. Finally, she decided to just ask him.

"Honestly, Dimitri, I'm trying to figure out how you faked your death. There are not that many ways to simulate a heart attack and live to tell the story."

Dimitri's smile faded. His gaze left hers and wandered around the room. He looked uncomfortable. "I was lucky, I guess."

Right. Luck. Lindsey did not bother to hide her annoyance at Dimitri's cagey reply. Suddenly, the quiet in the room seemed charged, but she kept her mouth shut.

The guy is nervous, thought Rich. *He keeps staring at Evan, who has not opened his mouth since he got here. Reardon is jumpy, too. The other shoe is about to drop. I wonder why Lindsey hasn't picked it up? She's usually far more observant than I am...it must be those twenty-eight hours on the plane. At least I grabbed a few hours of sleep, but she probably didn't sleep a wink. Plus, she's fixated on the faked heart attack, and that's hardly the point. Dimitri's lying and he knows we're all aware of it.*

Out of the corner of his eye, Rich watched the slight sixty-eight-year-old billionaire and CEO of one of the most successful pharmaceutical companies in the world begin to pace slowly around the large room.

Stella burst into the room with a tray of croissants and fresh coffee, which she positioned carefully on the coffee table. The stout Irish woman then refilled everyone's coffee cups and quietly left.

The southwest corner of the library, where the two sharp angles of welded glass met, had been put to practical use by the architect; a built-in upholstered bench overlooked the south side of the mountains and lake below. Hank stood staring out at the beauty.

Rich followed his gaze and thought of a morning the previous June when he had stood in that exact spot, staring out at the magnificent landscaping that had been a project of Hanks's wife, Peg, who had died of ovarian cancer two years before. She had configured islands of vegetation and achieved an effect that was natural while serving to soften and lighten the harsh lines of the hexagonal house. There had been roses of every color interspersed with daisies, veronica, pansies, Russian and perennial sage, and asters, in a brilliant mix that looked accidental, wild. Rich recalled his sense that the wild profusion of color had been mocking him and Reardon. Now, the colors were gone.

At that time, the two men had concluded that both Liisa Reardon and the chief animal tech of the research labs, Ariana Dumas, had been murdered. Thankfully they had been wrong. Looking out the windows now, Rich saw only an unbroken expanse of snow, silent, as if waiting. *I give it twenty seconds before one of these guys gives,* Rich thought. But it was just ten seconds before Hank Reardon turned around and fixed his bright-blue gaze on Rich and Lindsey. "Obviously, we invited you here for a reason, guys. This thing is huge and growing legs by the second."

Puzzled, Lindsey asked, "You mean Longevive? Did Braun and his Diedrich Gruppe Pharmaceuticals finally figure out the formula? But why? It would be a huge time-burner to fight it, but the patent is good, we would eventually win. What is the point of that?"

"If only it were that simple," Reardon sighed. "Back in June, when we discovered the hidden cameras and phone surveillance, we moved our research offices to Paris. Liisa, Ariana, and the two researchers who replaced Eric are working there. The research done here in the corporate offices has been faked, exactly like the heart attack that Dimitri never had." Reardon's smile did not reach his eyes. "In late July, two weeks *after* the DA had dropped the case against Braun, someone tried to kill Dimitri."

He looked over at Dimitri, who took the cue and continued the story, his voice and expression as flat as the Belgian waffle he had just selected from Stella's full breakfast cart. "I heard them come in. It was the middle of the night and I heard the locks click open on the front door of my condo. They were good, but not good enough." Dimitri's eyes darted around the room as if looking again for the intruders sent to kill him. "There were two of them, no ID, seemed ex-military. The fact that the hit happened *after* the AG dropped our case suggested to us that there was something far bigger than pharmaceutical fraud and a conspiracy to commit murder. So, we made up the story and fed it to the press." His smile was more of an apologetic grimace. "And to you, figuring that Braun and his goons might relax and make some mistakes if they believed I was dead." Dimitri looked over at Commander Pierre, nodding his head as he did so.

It felt like a tennis match. All heads turned to watch the unpretentious Evan slowly rise from the corner chair where he had been sitting, silent up until this point. Directing his gaze at Lindsey, he quietly answered the question she'd posed. "Of course, you are correct, Dr. McCall. Pharmaceutical espionage is not a concern of ours." His diction was precise, with just the barest hint of an accent. Standing alone in the large room, the Swiss head of the Tigris Unit looked more like an academic than cop.

That guy weighs maybe a buck forty. Dripping wet. Rich was enjoying this show, which seemed to him a bit like one of the Pink Panther movies. Evan even resembled Peter Sellers, but without the mustache. Absorbed in his reverie, Rich missed the first two times that Evan addressed him. It was not until Lindsey spoke his name that he tuned in to the conversation—which was no movie.

"Am I to understand that you want Rich to talk Joe Cairns into working undercover for you at Diedrich Gruppe?" Lindsey said.

Blinking a few times in a vain hope of waking up from this nightmare, Rich narrowed his eyes at Hank and the two Swiss cops.

"Run that by me again?"

Evan stepped over to Rich, picking his way along the hardwood floor as if to avoid landmines, and sat down in a flowered chair. His gray eyes were grave behind his rimless glasses. His next remarks were not couched or mitigated, merely stated matter of factly, for Rich to accept or reject. Rich was beginning to get a sense of how Evan had gotten where he was.

"Joe Cairns respects you. We know Braun wanted Cairns

to kill you—all of you, not just the kidnapped women, but you and Mr. Reardon as well. He did not carry out those executions."

Rich was catapulted back to a morning in June. After thirty-six hours of increasing stress about the fate of his daughter, Liisa, and chief animal tech Ariana Dumas, Hank Reardon had insisted on doing something. Anything was preferable to inactivity at that point. Believing he could find the farmhouse where they suspected the women were imprisoned, he and Rich had driven west to the small town of Bonvillars, known for the best truffles in Switzerland. Hank had slowed his car when he saw what looked like smoke, then parked and climbed out to get a better look. At the sight of a burning structure, Hank had collapsed at the side of the road, certain that the two women had burned to death. Rich knew he could not pick up an unconscious adult man by himself, and he wasn't getting any cell service, making it impossible to call for help.

Joe Cairns had pulled up, rolled down his window, and said, matter-of-factly, "Looks like you need some help." By that time, Rich had reasoned that Cairns was involved in the kidnapping and was perhaps even a killer.

Cairns had jumped out of the vehicle, helped Rich carry the unconscious man to his car and driven them both to the University of Lausanne Emergency Center, where it turned out all Reardon needed was rest and fluids. Rich recalled the grimace on Cairns' face at the number on his ringing cell phone. "I've got to take this," he had told Rich, and that was the last time Rich had seen Joe Cairns.

"Maybe it's because you were both Marines," Evan paused thoughtfully. "That sense of comradeship is powerful. We believe he will listen to what you have to say." After pausing a moment to let that sink in, he continued. "Several months ago, we planted one of our agents who is also a scientist in Braun's pharmaceutical company. Until four days ago, we were receiving daily updates from him. We've had no communication since last Thursday morning which can mean only one of two things: either Sebastian is dead, or he is being tortured and soon will be." His gaze narrowed but remained trained on Rich. "Just before he went dark, Sebastian sent evidence of a plan to weaponize prion disease." Evan's tone remained cool, as if everyone understood the implications.

Apparently, Rich was the only one in the room who didn't, because all heads nodded at Lindsey's horrified question, "You think they've figured out a way to use Creutzfeldt-Jakob—" glancing quickly at Rich she added, "mad cow disease—as a biological weapon?" Without waiting for confirmation, Lindsey continued, her tone dispassionate. "You have decided not to alert the CDC, the WHO, or any of the hundreds of other international agencies committed to the safety of humanity? You've decided to keep the people who know about this to just a handful." Extending the fingers of her right hand, she stared, then nodded her assent. "You're right, of course. Making this threat public would result in total chaos, anarchy eventually, and..." her voice drifted off, the enormity of her words compressing her voice into a whisper.

To the uninitiated, she seemed composed, calm. But Rich recognized the set of her jaw and tenor of her voice. She was working hard to stay in control, and it was hard to blame her. The population of the entire world was in the scope of an assassin.

Apparently, Rich had been volunteered to persuade a killer to get himself rehired by Diedrich Braun. Exactly how or why Joe Cairns would listen to a single word he had to say was a puzzle. Or why Braun would even consider rehiring Cairns, since he had quit without completing his deadly assignment:

to kill the entire leadership at ASL. On top of everything else, Rich was to persuade Cairns to work as a double agent for the Swiss cops—more precisely, their version of the American CIA, the Tigris Unit. To help save the world. *Lord, if I ever again complain about handling boring domestic abuse cases like Alicia Simmons, strike me dead.*

As one of the three founders of the International Criminal Police Organization—known to the world as Interpol—Switzerland was a leader in active international police cooperation. Its police jurisdictions tended to be far freer of the internal turf wars seen throughout the rest of the world, particularly in America.

But in 2009, the revelation of the fourteen member Tigris unit, dubbed by the Swiss media as "supercops," galvanized huge controversy both in the Swiss legislature and among the public. There had been two previous attempts to create a covert intelligence group like Trigris. Jurisdictional arguments among the canons had doomed the new force in 1978 and again in 2002. The third attempt succeeded solely because Tigris was covertly created by a handful of people. The unit had been operational for some years before Swiss officials or the public were aware of its existence.

Objections to the existence of the unit were based primarily on jusifiable fears that a small, highly trained, and well-financed group of operatives might function outside the established boundaries of police work, perhaps ignoring other national and international agencies and their laws. This is precisely what the Americans had been accused of doing.

Since close to fifty pharmaceutical companies maintained international offices in Switzerland, the policing of fake drugs had become a top priority for the Swiss local and Federal Police forces. In fact, several pharmaceutical companies had hired their own cyber version of supercops: intelligence analysts capable of investigating pharmaceutical crimes and identifying fraudulent sources of drugs. The landscape for Swiss policemen was rapidly developing into a twenty-first-century iteration of the American West: ready, fire, aim.

CHAPTER EIGHT

Delphi, Greece

When Joe Cairns sauntered into Demetrius' small bar adjoining the hotel, the bartender's eyes had darted over to a guy in sunglasses before he nodded to Cairns. For normally glum, bored Demetrius, the quick glance followed by the nod was the equivalent of a shouted warning. Then he poured a tall mug of surprisingly good draft beer and set it in front of Cairns.

Guess I shouldn't be surprised that they found me. Question is, whose goon is this? Braun's or Fedpol's?

In the mirror over the bar, Cairns checked out the man as he stood in front of a beer that had not been touched. He was somewhere in his early forties, hair too short, physically fit, thick neck, broad shoulders, narrow waist: *Gym rat.* There was no gym within miles of this sleepy little resort town, so the logical assumption was cop or military.

Vacation over, time to leave. Wonder how they found me?

Cairns downed his beer, set the empty mug on the bar, and looked at Demetrius in appreciation. "Your draft beer is excellent, thanks," he said.

The bartender's smile was the first one Cairns had seen

in ten days. "Thank you, Joe," he said in heavily accented English.

Cairns walked casually out of the bar. Leisurely. No hurry. He stopped at a few shop windows, then crossed the street as if returning to the little hotel where he'd been staying for the last ten days. The guy was sure to be following.

It was December and chilly, so not many people were out and about. He could hear the inevitable footsteps about fifty, maybe seventy-five yards behind. Popping into a coffee-and-pastry shop, which was empty because they were about to close for the day, Joe smiled at the middle-aged owner and asked in a mixture of English and Greek, "Do you have a back door?"

She looked puzzled and pointed down a small hallway at the toilet he had used just a day earlier.

Shit, I said toualéta.

Sheepishly, Cairns gave up showing off his lousy Greek and asked in English, "Sorry, I meant back door, do you have one?"

Opening a metal door in the shop's back room, Cairns exited and moved silently along a narrow alley. Dark and deserted. Prepared for something like this, he had parked his truck down by the ruins, about half a mile away from town. Trusting that the woman would treat the goon the way she did all tourists—rudely and pretending she understood no English—he began to jog. *I'll grab a few hours sleep in the SUV then take off.*

CHAPTER NINE

Route A-4, thirty miles east of Milan, Italy

Cairns leaned over to increase the bass on the radio as he sang along with Bob Seger at the top of his lungs. He was a little off key, but who cared?

He had been driving for over twelve hours, but was excited to be back in the game. The anticipation of a new op always gave him a high. What was he heading into? What would it cost him?

Taking the E-70 out of Greece had been smart—dull but fast. Stopping only for coffee and bathroom breaks, he was averaging sixty-five miles an hour. Cairns figured he would make his destination with time to spare. Barring accidents or detours unforeseen by the Garmin, he should be back at ASL well before the six p.m. meeting with Rich Jansen.

Cairns had not planned to end his nearly twenty-year stretch in the Marines. With a string of medals no one would see, for operations no one would ever hear about, Cairns was one of the top go-to guys in the Marine Raiders. Never married, by nature a loner, he never complained or made excuses. He preferred working alone, and his superiors quickly learned they could assign him to anything, anywhere, and the job would get done. Or he would die trying.

Cairns had been on an undercover job in Berlin. Force Recon and the Federal Intelligence Service were cooperating in a joint op to find and execute a Muslim terrorist who had masterminded multiple successful bombings in London, Mumbai, and Madrid. After three days of tracking the mass murderer and dealing with a few way-too-close-for-comfort screw-ups, the target had finally been found and terminated, along with two of his associates. Cairns and a German captain he'd been working with ended up in a small bar favored by the man and his colleagues: Bei Schlawinchen, located off Kotbusser Dam.

"If it's such a great job, why don't *you* take it?"

Lighting his fourth cigarette within ten minutes, the guy stared at Joe and replied, "I would if I didn't have a wife, four kids, and a new baby on the way. I'd take it in a heartbeat."

Cairns watched him enviously as he exhaled the smoke slowly, luxuriously, almost elegantly even. It had been ten years, but he still thought about lighting up, especially when he was drinking. He took a deep breath, gladly inhaling the second-hand smoke.

"You said you're not married and don't have a family, right?"

Cairns nodded, impressed, as always, with the command of English so many non-Americans possessed. The captain's diction was precise, in the way of non-native speakers. He surprised himself when he expressed interest in meeting this man, Diedrich Braun. "Tell me more."

He met Braun the following day and signed, as they say, on the dotted line. His first assignment was the murder of the CEO of an American pharmaceutical company so that Braun could acquire the company in a hostile takeover.

Although it felt weird to be in Chicago rather than some

backwater country in the Middle East or Africa, to Cairns, it was business as usual. He'd had every intention of doing his job by eliminating the top research team at ASL, until King David had reappeared in his life after an absence of—what—fifteen years?

Damn good thing I have no friends. They would tell me I have finally lost it; crazy, a complete loon. Nuts. Goneza. Ready to be in a padded room with a straitjacket.

He hadn't always been friendless. It was David who had kept Cairns out of trouble on many occasions. Albeit an aberrant one, David had been the only friend he could trust.

"Warriors don't cheat."

Cairns had been about to lie about the final phase of his close-quarters combat training for the Raiders. A buddy of his had said he could change Cairns' results from failing to passing, when Cairns had heard David's voice in his head. He refused the offer, though he was sure he'd get kicked out. Instead, he got commended. He'd actually passed with flying colors. It had all been a set-up to test his integrity.

Cairns was headed back toward Lausanne at the behest of David—the biblical Israeli King—who was apparently to be his new employer. He considered what lay in store for him. At the very least, several life sentences for murder, if the Swiss Feds or local police were to figure out what he had done in Switzerland alone.

"Return to Switzerland now."

The voice had so startled him that the SUV had swerved close to the side of the narrow road and shuddered as Cairns fought to regain control of the massive vehicle. Once the car had stabilized, he glanced over to the passenger seat. There sat David, clothed in a one-piece single linen shift, regarding him calmly. Joe slowed the vehicle and pulled over to the side of the road, staring in wonder at the ancient figure.

You're back...

"If I go back there, I'll end up in prison." Despite the clarity with which Cairns could see David, he felt like two people. One sat serenely conversing with a long-dead Israeli king, the other was screaming denials, epithets, and dire predictions.

You complete and utter fool! This is not real! It's probably that pizza you ate for dinner last night. You'll be thrown in prison—or worse—if you go back there. The cops, Reardon, and Jansen...they all know you murdered the German couple and would have killed that tech Ariana, too, if—

His inner argument was stopped short by the knowledge that the only reason the chief animal tech at ASL was not dead was the mighty hand of this ghost.

Cairns thought back to moment he'd knelt beside the French woman, Ariana Dumas, and held his gun to her temple. She was already bleeding profusely, and he was seconds away from pulling the trigger to end her life. She'd stared at him, then closed her eyes, reciting the Our Father in French for the third time. Quite clearly, Cairns had heard her beg, in English, "Father, forgive him." Her face had been peaceful, full of light.

Just then, he'd felt the iron vise of a hand surrounding his own so powerfully that the blood flow was cut off. His hand was paralyzed.

Had the girl's prayers summoned help?

His mother, a devout Irish Catholic, had made sure that Joe and his three older brothers had made it to Mass consistently enough to be accepted as altar boys, back in the days when only boys were eligible.

He had been a kid, no more than six or seven, when he had first seen the man chosen as God's anointed.

"Who are you?" he had asked.

"I am the womb of Adonai," was the reply.

He had made the mistake of talking about his friend just

once. A priest had asked the class to explain who King David was. The twelve-year-old Cairns had replied, "The womb of Adonai." The dumbfounded priest had asked the boy to stay after class to explain where he had heard that phrase. Never again did Cairns mention anything about it to anyone.

The David who stood in the mists of that small forest next to Ariana's body was a sight the likes of which Cairns had never seen. He was covered in blood, as if he'd been in a continual battle for centuries and was wearing the blood of all the men he had slain. He was holding a long spear from which fresh blood dripped. The sweetish coppery smell of blood was suffusing the mist.

Although Cairns had never seen David's mouth move until that moment in the forest, he could always hear him.

"Joseph James."

The voice was pitched low, a resonant baritone befitting a king. And he spoke in English. Despite not having heard the voice for so long, Joe had to restrain himself from dropping to one knee on the carpet of pine needles as he wondered at the reappearance in this time and place. And…English? *He would not speak English.* Cairns laughed at himself sardonically as he thought back to that first appearance in so many years… *as if any of the rest of this makes any sense!*

He had been named by his mother after two saints. She'd told him so just before her early death from a heart attack when he was only fourteen. "Saint Joseph and Saint James will always guard you, Joe," she'd repeated several times on the day she died.

The moment the vision spoke his first and middle names, the mists surrounding David evaporated, and Joe could see his face clearly. And those eyes. Good and gracious God, what eyes—brimming with the dark, awful knowledge of killing and death. Looking into them enveloped Cairns with grief and regret. The reek of all the bloodshed, that cloying smell of blood—oceans of it—he could never have imagined such a thing. And the dreadful weight of David's words, "No more. No more killing. Enough. There has been more than enough killing." Those words seemed to sear down into the depths of the soul Cairns had forgotten he had.

Only then had he realized that killing for the US government or for Diedrich Braun had not fixed a thing. He was sick to death of the killing, but had not faced the fact until he was standing there, over the French girl, Ariana. Even now, Cairns could see her face, the repose on her features in spite of the fact that she was critically wounded, most likely dying, and fully expecting him to hasten the process. He had every intention of doing so until David stopped him.

"Perhaps," came the response to his statement that if he went back to Switzerland, he would go to prison.

Great.

Ignoring his chaotic internal chorus, Cairns found himself asking, crazily, "Why do you call yourself 'the womb of Adonai?'"

The clarity of the personage of David sitting calmly next to him in the SUV was startling. Cairns lingered over the shoulder length curly brown hair, the long sharp nose, full lips, and those eyes. They were brown but not exactly brown, more amber with flecks of gold. As he gazed at David, Joe felt himself being drawn in, almost as if those eyes were whirlpools, mesmerizing whirlpools. This was the David who had been at his side during the early years, when he had felt a commitment to something bigger. Someone. As his mentor waited for him to respond, Joe felt the sting of tears, but not of sorrow. They were tears of relief, gratitude, peace—and much more.

The generous mouth in the ever young and handsome face

turned upward in a kind of smile. "Three sets of fourteen generations," he said, and his face began to shimmer. He was leaving.

"Wait! Why do I need to go back? What do you want me to do there?"

"You are to meet with Rich Jansen and listen to what he tells you."

With that he was gone.

CHAPTER TEN

Lausanne, Switzerland

Evan continued speaking into the silence. "We've had a guy watching Cairns for the last few days, but Cairns spotted him last night and took off. We have no idea where he is now."

Taking a gulp of steaming coffee to fortify himself, Rich asked, "In the unlikely event that I can get Joe to meet with me, what incentive can I use to convince him to go back to work for Braun?" Narrowing his eyes as he looked from Evan to Dimitri, he added, "... and in all likelihood, get him killed in the process."

Barely listening, Lindsey's thoughts were racing. *A weaponized version of Cruetzfeld-Jacob disease. Dear God in heaven, what kind of evil mind could have conjured that up and then made it a reality? Whoever it was, they'd need to reduce the incubation period from years to months, or more likely days.*

As the men talked, Lindsey continued trying to wrap her mind around how an abnormality of a cellular protein, a prion, could be altered enough to become infectious. If it could be done—if it had been—it could launch a plague potentially more monstrous than any in history. *The prion would have to be some kind of genetic hybrid, created in some research lab.*

Not all that long ago, before she had decided to accept the job at Cal Poly, Lindsey and Jodi Tamarack shared a dinner together. It was on the flight back to Houston the day after she'd decided to make the move to California. Jodi's passion for her work was contagious and she'd become infected with it; she was so eager to work with this woman, to feel that kind of passion again.

As they'd lingered over their wine, neither wanting the evening to end, Jodi had looked intently at Lindsey. "You know the worst fear of the World Health Organization, right?"

"Sure, a pandemic resistant to every antibiotic we have. It would be the end of antibiotics. Some say it would be the end of medicine, and could lead to the end of the human race."

A broad array of factors was contributing to the possibility Lindsey was referring to. Over-utilization of antibiotics worldwide had been a growing menace for several decades. Combined with the widespread use of low-level antibiotics in animal feed, the evolution of organisms resistant to all antibiotics—"superbugs"—was taking place at an alarming rate. Deaths from infectious microorganisms resistant to antibiotics ranged from about twenty to twenty-five thousand per year, and the number was rising. The Centers for Disease Control estimated that over ten million people could die from antibiotic-resistant diseases by the middle of the century—a mortality rate rivalling that of the 1918 Swine Flu epidemic.

In 1918, one out of three members of the planet's population had been infected with the deadliest strain of influenza ever to be seen. Fifty million people were killed—more than the number of lives lost in the Great War. With superbugs and the globalization of travel, a repeat of that catastrophe was far too possible.

Lindsey recalled the Google search she had done that revealed Jodi had published more than 100 articles in journals such as *Nature, Biology,* and *Epidemiology.* Not only was she trained in Veterinary Medicine, but also in Public Health, with a specialty in Epidemiology.

"You're right Lindsey, but I am talking about a zoonotic disease on the scale of the AIDS virus, only worse."

Transmission of bacteria and viruses from animals to humans was not a new threat to public health, as Lindsey well knew. Rabies, brucellosis, psittacosis, and of course, the plague, were only a few of the diseases that could be contracted from animals. *Fortunately, we've managed to prevent significant outbreaks,* she thought. *At least up until now.* Jodi's characterization of AIDS as a zoonotic disease was frankly terrifying.

In med school, Lindsey had been taught that AIDS was not considered to be of zoonotic origin because direct evidence of monkey-to-human transmission could never be proved. In fact, medical researchers were unanimous in their belief that none had occurred. Watching the casual certainty on Jodi's face now, Lindsey wondered if those researchers had merely followed the safest path because the alternative was too terrifying to contemplate: a cunning, deadly disease smart enough to adapt itself and jump species. That could pave the way to an apocalypse, for real.

If that were true of AIDS, could the same sort of bug be engineered?

"He would have to be a genius, a mad genius," Evan commented.

"He is exactly that." Lindsey didn't realize she had spoken her thought aloud, and the men turned in her direction.

"Who? Diedrich Braun?" Reardon asked the cops.

"No. Viktor Dragovik," said Dimitri and Evan simultaneously.

Rich took a deep breath, his headache worsening by the nanosecond. Ever since that concussion Joe Cairns had given him back in June, he was making up for a lifetime without them. Add stress to fatigue, and the result was a migraine.

This was beginning to feel like a remake of the horrors of the past June. Before he could ask who Dragovik was, Lindsey told him.

"Dragovik is the guy Braun hired to run that pharmaceutical company he acquired by killing the CEO and the others. But if he has figured out how to weaponize a prion disease, he must have switched from organic chemistry to biotechnology—and picked up some genius along the way."

It was as if she were thinking out loud. She had that look on her face that both her husband and Hank knew all too well. The Swiss policemen, on the other hand, seemed dumbfounded at the way she cut right to the chase, and shot incredulous looks at each other.

Rich's voice interrupted Lindsey's thoughts. "So, you're saying that Braun is no longer the threat? That Dragovik is? He's heading up Braun's pharmaceutical company now?" He was having trouble switching his fear from one evil enemy to another, even worse. *Can this evil even be measured? Compared?*

"Correct on all counts, Mr. Jansen. Viktor Dragovik is the…heir apparent, as it were, not only to the American pharmaceutical company, but to the entire Diedrich Gruppe empire."

As Evan slowly circled the area in front of the coffee table that held the residue of breakfast, he seemed visibly uncomfortable for the first time. "You ask if Braun remains a threat," he cleared his throat and glanced quickly at Dimitri.

Rich watched Evan becoming just a little uneasy for the first time. The gaze behind the rimless glasses narrowed. *Reardon must be right. Waiting for the 'other shoe to drop' doesn't cut it. By my count, he's dropped three to date, so just how many legs does this thing have?*

Evan continued, "Before Sebastian disappeared, he sent two videos of Braun. One was from an event where he introduced Sebastian to the key staff of the company, the second was shot just before we lost contact with him. In the second, Braun is close to death: comatose, having constant seizures. There was a nurse with Braun full-time. According to Sebastian, this happened in less than three days."

"Oh, my God," exclaimed Hank, jumping to the same conclusion as everyone else in the room. "Dragovik used Braun as his first human research subject!"

Braun was not a man Hank had admired even before he tried to steal their new anti-aging drug. Uncomfortably, he recalled what he had told the police about Braun back in June. Dimitri had asked if Hank had ever met him and if so, what his impressions had been.

"Sure, I've been around him several times," Hank had said. "There is no delicate way of putting it, when I think of Diedrich Braun, I think of Hitler's SS. There is something so strange about him, so detached…it's like he has no soul. For example, I called his home twice, attempting to speak with him about his son Eric's death. Evidently, one cannot speak with Braun unless they go through this man Claus for an appointment. At the scheduled time, I called and was on hold for at least ten minutes." Hank thought back to that chilling conversation.

"Diedrich, this is Hank Reardon calling. We met—"

"I know who you are, Mr. Reardon. How can I help you?" The voice was icy, imperious.

"Your son Eric has worked for us at ASL for close to three years. This afternoon, he died from complications of a grand mal seizure. My associate, Dr. Lindsey McCall, believes that

Eric had been suffering from a brain tumor for some time. I am so very sorry..."

"Thank you for calling, Mr. Reardon."

Hank heard the sound of a dial tone. Apparently the details surrounding the sudden death of thirty-five-year-old Eric Braun were of no interest to his father.

"It was as if I'd called to offer Braun a tip about the stock market."

Hank figured Braun at somewhere around his own age, late sixties. In the final video, he looked at least ninety.

"Sebastian does indeed think Viktor is using Braun as a test subject for the prion disease," Evan said.

Lindsey and Rich locked eyes, each thinking some version of, *Okay, we're in. We can't walk away from this one.* Lindsey permitted herself a brief sigh as she thought of her peace-filled days working with her beloved Dobermans. But for Rich, the now prescient words of Father John rang in his mind: "You and Lindsey had done so much in your lives before you met one another. Separately you'd fought many wars: injustice, betrayal, and even the loss of dear family members. Each battle was unique and waged the way the most important ones are—in the dark and alone. Your battlefields have varied from Lindsey's, but you've both been battling a long time. It's all warfare."

The two men had been talking at the Pismo house, at a combination housewarming and birthday party for Rich back in June. Father John had frowned as he scanned the room, landing on Lindsey. "Watching a young man die in front of her eyes and being powerless to stop it? Then participating with you in a battle against what sounds like pure evil? This is big stuff. You beat him…for that round, anyway." His intense gaze met Rich's. "Make no mistake, though, these affairs get the attention of the Evil One. I think the war is just beginning,

Rich. And it will require more from each of you then you may believe you possess."

Rich suppressed a shudder as he recalled the prophetic words of the priest. "Okay, then. Tell me what you want me to do."

Until that moment, Evan had kept his expression blank, as if to say, "*Help us or not, it means nothing to me.*" But at Rich's words, both he and Demitri breathed out long sighs of relief.

Rich couldn't help it. He had to ask, "So, guys, what was your backup plan if I had refused?" To his credit, Evan's gaze never left his own. But Reardon and Dimitri fidgeted, obviously uncomfortable. No one said a word for a moment.

Finally, Evan said, "We didn't have one, Rich."

Groaning, Rich murmured, "Why am I not surprised?"

CHAPTER TWELVE

Lausanne, Switzerland

"Cairns here."

"Joe, this is R—"

"I'll be there in forty-five minutes, maybe thirty, the traffic is thinning out."

"Be where?"

"Lausanne. ASL parking lot."

"But how did you—" Rich shut his mouth when he realized that Cairns had hung up. He glared at Lindsey who was closing her overnight bag.

As she turned toward her husband, she smiled. Lindsey had listened carefully to that non-conversation and filled in the blanks with ease. This wasn't anything she could help Rich with, she knew. Not with words, anyway. So she opted to pretend that she wasn't as worried as he was, with hardly any memory of the events of the previous June. None of that chatter would help him. So she merely stated the obvious. "Well, the good news is you'd been worried about how to talk him into coming here, and you hadn't wanted to discuss FedPol's proposal on the phone. So that's no longer a problem."

"Right. But how would Cairns have known to come here,

that we needed to meet? Or even that I was going to call? How is any of that possible? He says he'll be at the ASL parking lot in half an hour!"

Lindsey regarded her husband and willed her expression to show nothing but love and understanding, thinking hard as she did so. The Rich Jansen she knew—and loved more than life itself—was a man who seemed to fear nothing. She was understandably astonished at times like these, when he behaved like a normal human. Her mind raced as she sifted through the possibilities. *Joe Cairns. Rich does have sympathy for him…understands how he ended up going from patriot to paid killer. And he doesn't know what he'll do or think when he sees him again.*

Her mind flashed back to the day they'd figured out that Cairns had been hired by Diedrich Braun; that Braun had artfully and deceitfully crafted a background for the ex-soldier that would make him a perfect fit for Liisa Reardon's Director of Corporate Security.

"Rich, if I tried to understand all the impossible things that have happened to me—to us—I would go crazy." She walked over and tightly hugged him until she could feel the rigid muscles in his back begin to soften. Leaning back while still holding her husband, she looked at the clock in the guest house bedroom. "If Cairns is planning to be at ASL headquarters in thirty minutes, you'll need to leave soon. You won't have time to take me to the airport. I'll ask George or Hank if they have time." Checking her phone, she said, "Yeah, there are hourly flights from Zurich to Paris between eight am and five pm."

At the knock on the door, both she and Rich started. Humorously singing a, "We're not jumpy, not us," refrain, Rich opened the bedroom door to see Hank Reardon standing there in a blue denim shirt and khaki trousers—Reardon's idea of dress clothes. He looked more like an average woodsman than the CEO of one of the top pharmaceutical companies in the world.

"Lindsey," Hank started in without bothering to say hello, "you and I are flying to Paris together. We'll take my company plane, which will get us there in a little over thirty minutes. I called Liisa and Ariana to let them know we'll be there in time for dinner." Reardon grimaced as he studied Rich. "There is nothing more I can say to you, Rich. You were just here a few months ago, risking your life for your Lausanne family and friends, and all you got was a 'thank you.' The least I can do now is take Lindsey to Liisa's Paris research facility so that they can catch up on their latest Longevive research."

"Right, dinner at one of the finest bistros in Paris, along with some fine merlot. Right, Hank. Tough work, but someone has to do it!" At the widening of both sets of eyes looking back at him, Rich knew his sarcasm had been a bit over the top, and he faked a big smile. "Look, I know there is nothing either of you can do right now. I've got this. I do...but I would be a damn liar if I told you I wouldn't rather be getting on that plane with you two."

The snowfall the night before had dumped close to a foot. Unaccustomed as he was to driving a car as big and cumbersome as Hank's Bentley, it took Rich forty minutes to get to the appointed meeting spot. Aside from his four undergraduate years at Harvard, he had limited experience driving in snow. At another time, the drive would have seemed magical, but this evening, Rich was consumed by memories. And fear.

It's not as if this the first time he'd been afraid. On the streets of Houston, on the beach at Lebanon, in the courtroom in Amarillo, he'd felt the bite of fear before. But Joe Cairns was a professional assassin—not just Marine Force Recon, but a mercenary. Barely noticing the snow-laden aspen and birch trees lining each side of the broad two-lane highway, Rich kept repeating variations of the same thought: *Joe Cairns didn't kill you or Reardon back when he'd been ordered to. There is no logical reason he should do it now.* He worked hard to ignore a fact that he knew all too well—plenty of people get killed for no good reason at all.

Suddenly, he was pulling up to the parking lot facing the fifteen steel buildings of various shapes and sizes that comprised the ASL campus. Except for a black SUV with its headlights on, the lot was vacant—which made sense, since it was six in the evening a few days before Christmas.

Cairns. He's here.

Rich breathed slowly in and out, suddenly aware that his fear was gone.

Bring it on, I'm ready.

Relieved, he winged a quick prayer of gratitude to the God he knew was there with him.

The two men simultaneously opened their car doors and stepped outside into the cold.

"What did you want to talk to me about?" Cairns said, standing in the light of his headlights, his arms dangling loosely at his sides.

Sure, skip the 'Hey Rich, how's it hanging?' or any explanation of why he left Reardon and me in the emergency room last June. No mention of anything. Fine.

Rich got right to the point—the whole crazy thing. "Fed-Pol wants you to go back to work for Diedrich Braun. And them. But there's a problem—a big one. A problem that could threaten the population of the entire planet." He quieted for a moment to let that sink in, then said, "And Joe, just to satisfy my curiosity, why are you here? How did you know to come back here?"

They stood about six feet apart and were dressed in a similar style, in jeans and long-sleeved black t-shirts. No jackets. No jackets to hide the bulge of a Glock. Rich wondered if they looked as ridiculous as he felt, two ultra-macho guys standing outside in the freezing cold, each acting like he was perfectly comfortable. Were they also both unarmed? Rich was, and he was feeling increasingly vulnerable by the nanosecond.

Cairns stood as if posing for an ad for GQ. As if he had all the time in the world. *He's in good shape,* Rich mused. *I bet he's about my age, maybe a few years older.*

"Are you planning to answer me, Joe?"

"You would never believe me if I told you. The whole story is just too bizarre." Cairns shifted his stance so that most of his body weight was supported by his right leg. For the first time, he looked cold. He blew on his hands then rubbed them together. "Hey Rich, how about us going somewhere warm? We could sit in one of the cars, or, even better, hit a bar...that is, if you have time for a beer?" He could barely see Rich as he squinted into the bright headlights of Hank's Bentley. Cairns was just winging it at this point, and it looked like he would need to tell Rich about David. The visions, the commands, all of it. He felt nervous, an unfamiliar feeling for the man.

Well, David, this is a bit more complicated than just listening to what Rich has to say, isn't it? He wants to know about you. If there is a prayer of making him believe me, I'll need to tell him the whole story. I hope you're planning to hang around for the conversation, because my credibility with the guy must rank at somewhere below zero—sort of like the air out here,

He stomped his feet on the frozen, snow-covered ground, wishing he'd had the presence of mind to buy boots, or at the very least a jacket.

"Warm sounds good. So does a beer. You don't look like you want to kill me—at least not yet—so sure, let's go somewhere."

Rich followed Cairns' SUV into Lausanne's Old Town. Cairns had lived in Lausanne for a few months and knew the bars. Rich hoped he'd find a quiet one. Chuckling to himself in relief, he replayed Cairns' words, and wondered. Cairn had sounded tentative...as if Rich, not he, held the upper hand. Strange. But then again, maybe not.

Old Town could be touristy, but there were just a few folks out braving the cold. Traffic was light and there were plenty of parking along the quaint main street, which was lit up in storybook Christmas fashion. Stars, wreaths, and assorted colored lights sparkled over the doorways, lighting up the night.

Fifteen minutes from the time they'd left the frigid parking lot, the two men sat across from each other at a small restaurant and sports bar on Rue Madeleine called The Great Escape. The exterior was whitewashed concrete with both British and Swiss flags affixed to the roof, reminding Rich of pubs he had seen in Cornwall, England.

It was a guy's bar. The décor was plain. The large open room had a wooden floor, tables along the sides, and a variety of sports posters alternating with at least six huge television screens. To the left of the long bar was a good-sized stage, now dimmed. To the right of the stage stood the sole nod to the season—an anemic-looking evergreen adorned with a handful of ornaments.

They must have worked very hard to find this pathetic excuse for a tree among the thousands of towering alpine firs around here, Rich thought sardonically as he followed Joe through the mostly empty bar. Cairns grabbed a chair at a table near the back and pulled it out so that he faced the door, the position favored by most men who had been in combat. Never turn your back to an entrance. There were couples scattered throughout, but the bar was subdued on this Monday before Christmas.

Along with beer, they ordered hamburgers, a specialty of the house. Rich hoped that Dimitri had gotten his text and was headed here to take over the explanation of Cairns' new "assignment," since he knew just enough to be dangerous. He certainly didn't know enough to brief Cairns on the details. Still bemused about how all this had happened—the fact that he hadn't needed to say a word to get Cairns to meet with him—Rich asked, "So, what wouldn't I believe, Joe?"

"That I'm here because *he* told me to come here. To listen to what you had to say."

"He?"

Who is he talking about? Listen to what?

With a sigh, Cairns just said it, staring out the window at the night. "King David."

"King David," Rich repeated. *King David. Right. He couldn't possibly be referring to the Israeli king from the bible—could he? Well, he warned me that I wouldn't believe him. There's no reason this miserable excuse for a former Marine should be believed—about anything. And yet... he came back. He was free, of us, of his psychotic boss, of the murder charges. With his background, he knows how to disappear better than most, and he could comfortably live on the money he has stashed away. And he didn't kill Ari. She said he had the gun pressed to her head, yet chose not to pull the trigger. Why? It made no sense at all. None of it.*

The silence stretched into minutes—or it seemed to, anyway. Cairns continued staring out the window while Rich looked fixedly at the assassin, as if the force of his concentration would reveal answers.

He couldn't help himself. "Why didn't you kill Ari? She said the muzzle of your gun was squarely on her temple and she knew she was about to die. But you didn't shoot. You walked away."

Still studying the people hurrying by on the sidewalk outside, bundled up against the cold and on their way to somewhere, Cairns replied, "He told me not to."

He. Meaning King David again?

Rich decided to humor him, as he would the schizophrenics living on the street back in Houston when he was trying to get some information about a homicide. "King David told you not to shoot Ariana?" Listening to his own voice speak the outlandish claim had a curious effect on Rich. He found himself beginning to consider the possibility that Cairns was telling the truth. After all, Ariana had told them she believed her prayers had touched Cairns. Her prayers had not been for herself, but for him; she had begged the Lord to forgive the man she thought was about to kill her. Was it possible that her prayers were answered in this most miraculous way?

Impassive, Cairns turned to regard Rich. Shrugging, he said, "Yes, he did. In fact, he grabbed my hand so hard that I couldn't have pulled that trigger if I'd wanted to. His hand felt like an iron band over mine."

Just then, Rich became aware that Madonna's "Like a Prayer" was blasting out of the large speakers over the bar. *Life is a mystery, everyone must stand alone.* He reached for his beer, grateful for the distraction. *Leave it to a pop singer to nail it.* "I'm listening," he said. And he was.

"There is absolutely no reason you should believe a word that comes out of my mouth, Jansen, I am well aware of that." Waiting to see if Rich would reply, Cairns nodded slowly into the other man's silence.

"Okay, here goes. When I was a kid of about six, he started showing up a few times a month. From then until high school, he always had on that loin cloth, you know the thing they show him wearing when he took on Goliath?" A thoughtful expression passed over his face and his eyes were unfocused. He was seeing someone other than Rich.

"He was really short, like me. I didn't start to grow until I was a sophomore. He seemed to know—to understand—that I was a wimp, too short and skinny for football or basketball."

Just then, the story was interrupted when a cute college-age girl brought their burgers. Quickly scrutinizing their faces, she asked, "You did order these burgers, yes?" Her hair was boyish, eyes huge—a twenty-first-century Audrey Hepburn. Her English was heavily saturated with French as she asked again.

Smiling at her, Rich said, "Yes, we did. Thank you." He took the big platters from her and placed them on the table.

Cairns continued as if there had been no interruption. He'd never told this story before, to anyone, and now that he'd begun, there was no stopping. He had to get it all out.

"My Irish Catholic mother worked two jobs, but by God, she made it to Sunday mass and made sure that I did, too. My dad was never home. I never knew if it was because he was at the bars or with another woman. Mom never complained, though—about him, about me, about the work. Not once." His voice caught, and he covered it with a cough. "When she was barely fifty, she dropped dead in the middle of the night, working her second job." His voice dropped to a whisper. "Fifty. That's just three years older than I am now."

Against his will and better judgment, Rich could feel himself being reeled in. He wanted to despise this man and all that he stood for, to believe he was a lying menace who should be thrown in prison for life. But he knew Cairns wasn't lying. There were too many details. No matter how good a liar the man might be, visions of King David since childhood were too eerie to be made up. And then there was that most unfathomable fact of all: *he'd come back.*

Rich was a devout Catholic who believed in the community of saints, intercessory prayer, and the sacraments. However, looking into the eyes of a killer who claimed to have biblical visions was something wholly outside his experience. It was equal parts terrifying and beautiful. *If this were true, then...*

"If you're not going to eat that burger, I am," Dimitri said, as he slid in beside Rich, picked up the untouched meal and took a huge bite. Setting it down carefully, he smiled at Cairns and Rich as he chewed.

"If Braun or one of his goons' doesn't kill me, and I manage to get out of this alive, you'll let all charges against me drop." It wasn't a question. Cairns had eaten everything on his plate while listening to Dimitri describe a complicated and profoundly flawed plan. The point of which was to get Cairns back into the good graces of Diedrich Braun.

Blinking a few times, the Swiss cop hesitated, then nodded.

Unsatisfied with the halfhearted reply, Cairns pushed. "I'm talking about *all* charges: murder, kidnapping, attempted murder, and all felonies associated with the attempts to steal the anti-aging drug. You will erase all traces of my 'activity' on behalf of Braun from your records."

"Yes," Dimitri said, with all the force he could muster. "Once you agree, you're an agent of FedPol. Everything else is expunged from our database."

Just as Cairns started to reply, Rich spoke up. He had listened carefully to Dimitri's ideas for close to thirty minutes. He liked the guy, but realized that his actual experience with operations was limited, and he suspected that Dimitri had never been involved in anything remotely resembling this situation. Most of what Dimitri had laid out was theoretical, and for the third or fourth time, Rich wished McAllister were here. Pointing at Dimitri's phone, he asked, "Do you have the videos your guy Sebastian sent before he disappeared?"

Dimitri glowered at Rich. Apparently, he hadn't wanted Cairns to know about the missing agent, or the perilous situation he was walking into.

Rich waited him out. Cairns, realizing that the FedPol agent was holding back information, looked at, then tipped his head to Rich in appreciation and surprise. Then he sat back and sipped his beer, watching Dimitri scowl at Rich. *Well, Rich Jansen, Semper Fi to you. Thanks for watching my back. I get the feeling there's a whole lot more to this caper than just getting re-hired by the twenty-first-century version of Adolf Hitler.*

After several seconds of silence, Dimitri shook his head at Rich. "Commander Pierre was right. The Marine Corps must instill some kind of loyalty in you guys." Sardonically, he added, "Semper Fidelis and all that, right? Even for a man who went over to the dark side?"

Rich said nothing in reply and his steady, calm gaze never left Dimitri's. Cairns would do this, Rich knew. Now that he had shown up, he had no choice but to agree to be a double agent for FedPol, then head to Berlin and manipulate the primary decision-makers at Diedrich Gruppe into hiring him. He could get it done, too. A guy that experienced? He didn't need the stupid theorhetic ideas of people who had never done anything like this. But the likelihood of his getting killed before this was over, Rich calculated, was close to a sure thing. Cairns would know that far better than he. That was why he deserved to know every single thing they knew.

This prion thing, this weaponized version of mad cow disease, sounded like something out of a science-fiction movie. Soldiers and cops accept the risk of getting killed; it comes with the territory. But dying like Braun was dying? The brain and spinal cord basically rotting away? That was more horrifying than any bullet or bomb, and Cairns would be walking right into the maw of the monster. He had to know the extent of the evil he would be facing. Alone.

Watching the Ukrainian-born Swiss cop struggle with his own conscience, Rich reflected on the many times he had used confidential informants. There was always a temptation to treat them like scum, but good cops refused to do so. And he figured Dimitri for one of the good guys.

Finally, Rich quietly said, "Dimitri, whatever you think of this man, you guys are sending him into the exact situation in which your last operative was killed... or horribly wounded, at best. That level of risk earns him full disclosure."

Studying Jansen and then Cairns, Dimitri shrugged and smiled. He weighed the costs of showing the videos and transcripts of Sebastian's communications. His boss had expressly forbidden him to do it, and for good reason. Once he understood the real danger, Cairns would make a run for it. Like most people, he would quickly calculate his odds of getting through it without being shot or—worse—infected, and that would be that.

And then what? The last thing he and Pierre needed was more media attention on Tigris. Which is precisely what would follow if the sleepy town of Lausanne were to witness a high-speed chase.

I have to give it to Jansen. He knows how averse we are to publicity at Tigris.

Reopening the canvas bag, Dimitri frowned as he inspected the contents, then withdrew a thick file along with a second phone, the one with the videos. Clearly, he had won the battle with himself and now regarded Cairns neutrally, as he would a colleague. His annoyance at Rich was gone, or seemed to be at least. Taking a swallow of the beer just placed in front of him, Dimitri handed the file to Cairns.

While Cairns scanned the pages, Dimitri explained who Sebastian was and what he had been doing before he'd disappeared. He then turned on the phone, fiddled with it, and set it on the table in front of Cairns. His voice a low whisper, he narrated the various videos of Diedrich Braun, revealing the horrific deterioration of the man. Just as Dimitri started to explain FedPol's suspicion that Braun's protege was poisoning Braun, Cairns cut him off.

"What do you know about Viktor Dragovik?" he asked, his face expressionless in spite of having gotten an eyeful of the devastating footage. The only indication it had affected him at all was a subtle deepening in his eyes, from dark-brown to black.

Those are the eyes of a killer, thought Rich, to his own surprise. *His eyes look exactly like those of the Force Recon Marine who tried to recruit me for Recon during my first tour.*

Surprised by the question, since he hadn't yet mentioned Dragovik, Dimitri asked, "Do you know him? From before?"

"Yes." Cairns recalled clearly the man he had met at Braun's "tea party" at his summer villa the previous June. That was in Konigston-Taurus, a small resort town in the state of Hesse, Germany. It was a command performance for Cairns, one of the newest Diedrich Gruppe employees at the time.

Dragovik was the replacement CEO for Matt Adams. The first of the assassinations that Cairns' had undertaken at the behest of Braun had been carried out the week before, in Chicago. After spending just a few minutes making small talk with Dragovik, Cairns had smiled, made his excuses and wandered off. Joe Cairns had worked with some severely damaged and corrupt men in his life, but this guy seemed to personify evil. Although it was a warm sunny day, the air around Dragovik was chilly.

Cairns revealed none of this to the FedPol cop.

Realizing, after a couple beats of silence, that Cairns planned to say no more, Dimitri decided to continue following

Jansen's lead and treat this guy well—like a colleague.

Reopening the battered canvas carryall, Dimitri pulled out a second file, opened it, and began to read. "The man known now as Dr. Viktor Dragovik was born Hasan Milak in Yugoslavia. In 1995, at the age of twelve, Hasan was the sole survivor of two massacres. The first eliminated his entire family—parents and three brothers, one of whom was his twin. Pausing for a moment to study something on the page, Dimitri added, "Milak had been wandering alone in the woods trying to survive on roots and berries. He was picked up by a Bosnian family fleeing to Srebrenica—"

"Fleeing to Srebrenica," Cairns echoed. His next words were barely audible, but both Dimitri and Rich heard him whisper something that sounded like, "running to Fallujah in 2004."

Of course, he would have been deployed to that fiasco. Force Recon would have been the very first to go. Once we finally decided there was no choice, the US had to jump into the middle of the insanity, and we would naturally send the Marines first.

Neither Dimitri nor Rich asked Cairns if he had been there; the expression on his face said it all. Cairns grabbed his half-full pint of beer and drained the mug. Carefully placing it back on the table, he wiped his mouth, looked at Dimitri, and asked, "Then what?" His tone was almost devoid of emotion, but just almost. Underneath it was dread.

Dimitri had been drinking also, but at the question, he put down his mug and picked up the file again. "The next several years get muddy. Evidently, he ended up in one of the makeshift orphanages set up once the war was over, but ran away and somehow ended up in Berlin. He managed to survive until he met up with Braun, and that's when he became Viktor Dragovik. Braun paid his way through the Swiss Federal Insitute of Technology, where he had aced every undergraduate course plus a graduate course in inorganic chemistry by the time he was twenty-two. He then got his doctorate in Organic Chemistry at the Technical University of Munich. Took him only two years." Dimitri glanced at Rich. "Your wife nailed it when she called him a 'mad genius.' He worked for a couple of years at Porton Down in Wilshire, England, under one of Braun's former chemists, then returned to Braun to head up Adams and Adams."

Rich recognized the name of the 100-year-old British military science complex, Porton Down. He began to recoil inwardly at the enormity of the menace facing them.

"And now, he's using the man who gave him his life back as an experimental rat." Cairns laughed grimly at the irony of it. Not waiting for a response to his comment, Cairns asked Dimitri, "Why hasn't this guy been recruited by ISIS? He seems to have all the requisite qualities, doesn't he?"

Rich was suddenly cold despite the warmth of the bar. He envied Lindsey's sojourn in Paris where she was doing the work she loved while he sat her listening to a biography of depravity. Looking across the table at Cairns, he was once again overcome by a sense of foreboding for him. But this feeling was more specific than the one he'd experienced that morning. It was so tangible that he could almost touch it, almost hear it like a voice inside his head. *He will not survive this mission.*

Aware of Jansen's stare, Cairns smiled back. It was a genuine, even loving and sympathetic smile, as if he could read Rich's mind. Strangest of all, his eyes had changed, lost their blackness. They were... almost loving. There was no fear in them, but rather a profound peace.

Nodding in agreement with Cairns, Dimitri answered the question Rich had forgotten about. "ISIS? They poked around. They sent one of their top guys to meet with Dragovik while he was finishing his doctorate in Munich. One of our people had eyes on the whole thing. We were just starting to record their conversation when the connection was lost."

"Your guy must have been made. Did ISIS make contact through a mosque?"

"Not that we know of. We don't think Dragovik's religious." Waiting a beat, Dimitri added, "But he is a prolific writer."

"Scientific stuff, right?" The spell broken, Rich's question was perfunctory. He needed to say something to dispel the lingering effects of a communication that had been extraordinarily unsettling. Anyway, he assumed that someone with Dragovik's education would be well- published in his field.

"No. In fact, 'Malthus Revisited' was the name of his last article," replied Dimitri.

Both Cairns and Rich echoed Dimitri. "Malthus? The population guy Malthus?"

"Right. That's the one."

"We done here?" Cairns pushed back his chair to stand.

Startled, Dimitri glanced at Rich as if seeking help and said, "I have three wireless communication devices, directions to our safe house, IDs, tickets for a flight to Berlin, and—"

Cairns leaned forward across the table and cut in. "Look, I don't want to sound like an ass, Dimitri. You and your bosses have been fair. More than fair and I thank you. But I've collected more IDs than I could ever use in one lifetime." His mouth twisted to the side in a mocking smile. "When you've been in the places I've been, you get good at creating fakes. And I'm not about to use any of your high-tech wireless gadgets—they're way too easy for the wrong ears to intercept these days." Without any trace of arrogance, he added, "I guarantee you that Sebastian got made during one of his check-ins with you guys."

Pretending not to see the rise of color in Dimitri's cheeks,

Cairns turned to Jansen and said, "Thank you for your help just now. And for listening to the story of… my friend and me. I've never told anyone but you, and probably never will." Holding Rich's gaze for another moment, he added, "I'll bet you were one hell of a Marine. I would have been proud to serve under you."

With that, Cairns stood and said, "If Sebastian is alive, I'll find him and get him back to you." Turning to leave, he continued, "I know the way to Berlin. You'll hear from me within three or four weeks. Or you won't."

CHAPTER THIRTEEN

Pismo Beach, California

"'Malthus Revisited?' Really?"

Lindsey was seated on the edge of the couch out on the deck. With her hair pulled back in a ponytail, and her mouth open in a perfect O, she looked more like a medical student than a forty-something-year-old researcher.

Rich drank a large gulp of celebratory Cava, wriggled his eyebrows in a decent imitation of lasciviousness, and said, "Dr. McCall, may I suggest a far more fitting way of celebrating our being home for Chrismas than discussing the possible end of the world?"

Two hours later, clad in bathrobes, the pair was back out on the patio waiting for two of Rich's perfectly cooked New York steaks to come off the grill. "I forget what I wanted to talk to you about, "Lindsey said dreamily. Half a bottle of Cava and a glass of cabernet were working wonderfully to slow down her usually racing brain.

"Good," Rich responded, testing the steak by making an okay sign with his left hand and comparing the feel of his flesh with the feel of his right index finger on the steak. "Almost done." Turning to the Caesar salad, he added the dressing he had made earlier and and tossed. After tasting a small portion, he added a few more squeezes of fresh lemon. Staring out at the sun setting on the ocean, he said, "Hard to believe that just twelve hours ago, we were in Switzerland."

"What's even harder to believe is that we ended up with our romantic Christmas after all." Lindsey followed her husband's gaze and murmured, "We have over a week before LJ and Morgan get back from Texas. Why does it feel like we've been gone four months instead of four days?"

Later, as they were finishing dinner, Lindsey said, "Okay, so back to 'Malthus Revisited.'"

Stretched out with his feet up on the firepit, Rich smiled. "I knew you hadn't forgotten. Yep, 'Malthus Revisited.' Go."

"While you were sleeping on Hank's flying hotel, I did some research."

"Of course you did."

"Remember Paul Ehrlich?"

Rich nodded yes, but suspected she couldn't see him in the fading light. "Yes, Paul Ehrlich and that book, *The Population Explosion*, right?"

"Yes, that one. I had assumed that Malthusian theory had been invalidated by all the advances in farming, genetic engineering of crops, and the like, but apparently, it's alive and well. The Pope invited Ehrlich to a Vatican conference on 'Biologic Extinction.'"

"Really? Ehrlich is still alive? That book was written in the sixties, wasn't it?" Feet down and sitting up, Rich was suddenly alert.

"Yes, really. Ehrlich is alive and vigorous at eighty-three, and is not bothered by the fact that his doomsday predictions of world famine never happened. He remains adamant that compulsory mass sterilization and forced abortions, especially of females, are acceptable ways to manage the population."

"I bet Ehrlich's presence at the Vatican caused more than a little consternation. I wonder why the Pope would invite such a controversial personality?"

"Because he's an academic Jesuit. Or is that redundant?" Lindsey smiled at her own joke.

"What does that mean?"

"I've read enough about this Pope to understand that contentious ideas don't frighten him, even—or maybe especially—when they directly oppose his own." She took another sip of the wine she'd been playing with then set it down. "It's actually an ingenious thing to do; welcome all views, particularly those of your sworn enemies. That way you know first-hand what they are thinking and feeling. But I doubt the majority of Catholics see it that way."

Rich had to agree with her. He thought, not for the first time, how powerful Lindsey would be if she were ever to go into politics. While he sometimes thought of her as a bit of a 'quant' because of her computer-like analytic skills, it was that detachment of hers that pulled him up short. There was scientific objectivity and then there was Lindsey McCall. Although he had not received the rigorous training Lindsey had, Rich considered himself superior to most in his ability to bounce from side to side of very controversial arguments. But he lacked her disengagement... her 'Ignatian indifference.'

"I found Dragovik's paper, 'Malthus Revisited.' It was the dissertation for his doctorate in organic chemistry—which is kind of strange in itself, because completion of the degree doesn't require a paper. Organic chemistry is like medicine, a technical doctorate. But he wrote one anyway," Lindsey paused, thinking.

"And?" Now intrigued, Rich prodded her.

"And... the Pope and Viktor Dragovik have a few things in common."

Leave it to Lindsey to find similarities between the spiritual leader of close to two billion Catholics, and a man attempting to decimate the world's population, quite literally. He waited for an explanation.

"While we were on the plane, I also read the Pope's encyclical on the environment. He writes radically. He affirms that global warming is real, worsening, and affecting the poorer countries already. He calls for an 'ecological conversion' for the developed countries. And he lays the blame for much of the earth's condition on multinational corporations and their reprehensible pillaging of third-and fourth-world countries."

Listening to his wife, Rich's mind began to wander as he calculated the number of hours she had been awake. It had to be close to thirty-six, since she and Reardon had taken Liisa out for dinner before they left Paris. No wonder that brain of hers was in overdrive.

"The speakers at the Vatican Conference were unanimous in their dire predictions of vast biologic extinction within the next fifty years. Paul Ehrlich is now being quoted as a supporter of Pope Francis, even though Ehrlich says he is an atheist. Dragovik sourced Ehrlich for many of his own arguments, including the ones for forced sterilization, female infanticide, and abortions. One of my favorites—an observation made by Ehrlich, and expanded on in Dragovik's paper—is this one: 'You can be aborted as a conceptus, you can be killed at birth, or you can be sold into slavery and die in a slum someplace. It would be interesting to know how many females you're keeping out of hideous situations—the ones who are not killed or infanticided but nonetheless not valued.'"

Rich knew Lindsey couldn't see his half-smile in the waning light. Her ability to memorize and retain particular facts and then repeat them never failed to astonish him. Most of the time, she didn't even think about it... her nearly photographic memory was second nature. "But I thought the birth rate had fallen to the point of zero population growth."

"Yes, in the western world, but not in India and Africa. Augmenting his arguments for a 'human extinction,' Dragovik includes global warming and the industrialized nations as causes for the coming mass biologic extinction, just as Pope Francis predicts in his encyclical."

Deciding to ignore the basic odiousness of the comparison, Rich stared at Lindsey. "*Human* extinction. Good God in heaven. What is Cairns supposed to do about a madman like this?"

Suddenly sober, Lindsey picked up her second glass of wine and rotated it slowly, watching the legs of the substance adhere to the sides of the glass. She figured that Rich would tell her about his conversation with Dimitri and Joe Cairns when he was ready. As she waited for him to elaborate on his rhetorical question, she wondered what any of them was supposed to do about a madman like Dragovik. This was just the beginning of a long and pitiless war, of that Lindsey had no doubt. It was just a matter of when the first battle would start. Unless Joe Cairns was already fighting it on his own.

Watching the viscous cabernet trail slowly back down her glass, Lindsey thought once again about the friendship between her husband and Gabe McAllister. Although Gabe was close to twenty years younger than Rich, he had become a close friend. Both were former combat Marines, though in different wars. McAllister had done four tours in Afghanistan. Their shared understanding of Cairns becoming a hired killer surprised her, but it shouldn't have.

It was a brotherhood, the Marine Corps, appreciated only by the Marines themselves. This wasn't all that different, she thought, from the sense of loyalty forged in medical schools, residencies, and among working physicians. The fields of battle of medicine and combat looked very different, but only superficially. Once you removed the sterile drapes and gloves, it was blood and viscera you saw; and lives you held in your hands.

This would be neither a relaxing nor a romantic Christmas holiday, and they both knew it. But for this one night, it was fun to maintain the fiction. Reasonably confident that her partners would be willing to put aside their suddenly trivial tasks in light of this almost unimaginable peril, Lindsey decided she would wait until the next day to tell her boss and Jodi of the horror about to be unleashed on an unsuspecting world. She'd pretend that all was well for one more night.

CHAPTER FOURTEEN

Wissembourg, France

Joe Cairns exited the freeway. It was over 600 miles from Lausanne to Berlin, a straight shot on the A-9. It was now two in the morning, and he'd nearly fallen asleep at the wheel twice. The last time he'd slept a full night had been back in Delphi, close to thirty-six hours ago. It wouldn't do to get himself killed before he even got there. He was in the northeastern corner of France, not far from the German border. The exit said Wissembourg, population a little over 8,000. Driving slowly, he was relieved when he saw a hotel sign with the 'vacancy' light on.

He parked and got out of the car. As he walked toward the front door, he worked to compose a question in understandable French.

"Avez-vous un chambre-libre?"

The kid looked up dully. "Huh?" Trying to stifle a laugh, Cairns noted that he looked just like a bored American teen—wholly indifferent, acne scattered on both cheeks and chin, and not even bothering to hide the yawn.

In English, this time, Cairns said, "Do you have a room available?"

"Yeah. Seventy-five Euros. Sign this."

When he opened his eyes later, Cairns fought a sense of dislocation. *Where the hell am I?* Lying in a formulaic motel room with the weak wintry sun peeking through the curtains, he thought he was back in Delphi. But no, the room was too ugly. Remembering, he jumped up to check the time and was startled to find it was close to eleven.

Well, that was probably my last chance to sleep for a while, so good for me.

Ten minutes later, he had showered, donned clean clothes, and headed back onto the A-9 with a cup of surprisingly good coffee that he was practically inhaling. As he drove, Cairns considered his options. He could go to Braun's Berlin residence, or bypass Braun completely and head directly to Dragovik. Berlin was where the cops had suggested he go. The last two transmissions from Sebastian had emanated from areas near the Diedrich Gruppe research labs there. But something about that idea had been fluttering in his brain for hours now. There was a memory at the edge of his mind, but he couldn't quite grab hold of it.

In any case, there was no point in going to see Braun. From what he saw in the last video, Braun was dying, and may already be dead by now. It was Dragovik that Cairns would need to see.

Strangely, he was not worried about the danger to himself. Cairns had expected to die many times during operations gone bad. There were several where he had been the only survivor— an outcome that isn't all it's cracked up to be. He had no illusions about his chances, but he would not avoid doing what needed to be done in order get out of this alive.

His mission was simple. The FedPol agent Dimitri had winced, but reluctantly agreed when Cairns had cut through the euphemisms and pretense of what they wanted from him. *Stay alive long enough to find Sebastian. If the agent is alive and coherent, get him back home to work with Lindsey and her gang of scientists for an antidote for this thing.*

If Sebastian was already dead, Cairns had to get his hands on a sample of Braun's tissue, secure it, and get it to Lindsey McCall. Then, at least, she and her team would know what they were fighting.

What troubled him now was the lack of a strategy.

On the radio, a French rendition of the Beatles song, "Yesterday," played softly. It wasn't bad, and in French, sounded more melancholic. Fitting. As Cairns hummed along to the tune everyone over forty knew so well, he thought about Braun and Dragovik. Suddenly, he knew exactly where he needed to go. He was confident the timing would be perfect as he accelerated and continued on to Berlin.

Right at five thirty, Cairns walked into the seedy bar on Bei Schlawinchen. *It looks exactly the same,* he thought to himself as he looked around.

In most large cities, maybe even the rural ones too, there is one bar frequented by the local cops. Generally, no one knows the reason for the affiliation, a choice made by someone so long ago that no one questions it. This was the place where the German Federal cops hung out. Cairns could bank on it.

There was a Playboy-type calendar hanging behind the cluttered bottles of scotch, gin, vodka, and assorted other liquors. Staring at the pin-up page that claimed the month was February and the year 1984, Cairns wondered if that guy Hugh Hefner was still alive. *If so, he must have done okay since these calendars have been selling since—when? The sixties?*

The same weird combination of old bicycles, musical instruments, and toys was hanging from the walls. Could this place exist in Manhattan or Philadelphia, he wondered? He thought it could. There was something universal about seedy bars and their appeal to cops and soldiers.

Cigarette smoke hung so heavily in the air that Cairns felt as if he'd smoked four cigarettes within the first five minutes, as he looked around for a familiar face.

Spotting the guy he was looking for, Cairns walked over to a table occupied by three men and extended his hand to the big blond man finishing a beer. "Can I buy you one, Horst?"

The man's broad face was a study in surprise and delight. Jumping up so quickly that his chair fell over, he grabbed the extended hand and pumped it up and down enthusiastically. "Joe! No, I buy you one! In fact, I buy all your drinks for the rest of your life!"

Horst Mueller looked more like a country farmer than a twenty-year veteran with the Federal Intelligence Service, Germany's version of the CIA. With his rosy cheeks, sky-blue eyes and broad smile, he was no one's idea of a cop.

Cairns recalled the undercover job in Berlin where two German cops were killed. It could have been three. Horst Mueller would have been killed along with his two buddies had Cairns not taken out the target's last bodyguard. Using the doorjamb as leverage, the wounded terrorist had aimed his HK 416 at Mueller's head. Cairns just happened to spot the muzzle of the gun and he dispatched the man swiftly.

After taking the proffered seat and accepting the beer, Cairns made small talk with Mueller and his three associates. "Horst, where is Stefan tonight? Home with the new baby?" He feigned surprise when Mueller replied that the former Captain had quit the Intelligence Service to head up security for "some billionaire."

So, Stefan is working for Braun.

Cairns merely nodded and said, "Probably got an offer he

couldn't refuse." Finishing his beer, Cairns slapped Mueller on one muscled shoulder and left, thinking hard as he walked to his car.

Just as the motor purred to life, that earlier fluttering suddenly cohered into memory. Finally, he was able to focus on what had been niggling at him for hours—an overheard conversation in German the previous summer.

Last June, as Cairns had walked away from his non-conversation with Dragovik, intending to thank his host, Diedrich Braun, for the afternoon soiree at his villa in Konigston-Taurus, he'd heard something. It was just a few words of whispered German, but the furtive demeanor of the two men standing apart from the rest of the goup had caught his attention, and he had slowed down slightly as he passed by. One of the men had caught his eye and pulled his confidant back into an isolated part of the patio. *Wir testen die neue CJD Formel heute Abend an der Frankfurt Lab.*

At the time, Cairns had dismissed what he'd heard pass between the two men of indeterminate age. He'd been eager to leave the stupid tea party and return to Lausanne. So why now—six months later—did that snippet of meaningless German man float to the top of his consciousness and suddenly become comprehensible?

David, of course.

Although he was anything but fluent in German, Cairns pondered the men and remembered their words: *neue CJD Formel der Frankfurt Lab.* Spontaneously, he understood their meaning. A new formula for CJD—Creutzfeldt-Jakob disease—would be tested at the Frankfurt lab. This wasn't hard to interpret, in light of what Dimitri had told him. Dragovik had started working on this months ago.

As he'd expected, Mueller had bought his story about wanting to ask Stefan for a job. Happy to be of help, the cop even called his sister in Jena to ask if she had a room for the "man who saved my life." He had drawn a crude map on a cocktail napkin with the directions to Berlin by way of Jena, a charming university town, pointing out that it would be a perfect place to stop and get a good night's sleep. Frankfurt was over 350 miles southeast of Berlin, and it was close to eight in the evening, so Cairns eagerly accepted his kindness.

When he lay down in the wonderfully comfortable bed at the more-charming-than-promised B&B, he expected to crash into a deep sleep. He was as tired as he had ever been, but suddenly, his brain was in overdrive. He was scared, and couldn't manage to talk himself out of the feeling.

What's the difference, facing Dragovik now rather than Braun? They're the same, those two. Crazy. You've dealt with wacky people for the last twenty years.

Having resigned himself to laying awake, Cairns was surprised when he opened his eyes six hours later. But his thoughts continued as if they had never been interrupted. There *was* a difference between the two men. His fear returned as he lay thinking about Viktor Dragovik. Sure, Diedrich Braun was a lunatic, but the images from the video that the FedPol agent had sent Dimitri had seared his brain. Braun's neurologic deterioration was terrible on its own; he had no control over his extremities or facial expressions, he was seizing constantly, and undoubtedly was mere hours from death. But even more macabre had been the expression on Dragovik's face as he watched his former mentor convulse. It was as if Dragovik were looking at a specimen, with an almost reptilian curiosity. He exhibited no feeling of any kind for this man who had saved his life. Cairns knew he was about to meet Grendel's mother—the monster of all monsters.

Jumping out of bed, Cairns showered, shaved, and was out

the door of his room in under ten minutes. At six-thirty, he thought he could sneak out without waking Mueller's sister, but as he crept quietly through the small foyer, he heard her call out.

"Herr Cairns, please eat some breakfast before you leave."

Cairns gazed at the array of pastries, each one a work of art. Typically, he didn't allow himself the calories. After forty, sweet desserts turn to fat. Perhaps just one… to be polite.

Sitting at the simple dining table and chewing carefully, Cairns pictured the delight of his high school English teacher, Mrs. Blake, at his "Beowulf" analogy. Smiling, he said to a female version of Horst Mueller, "So, what is your suggestion for one who is about to kill Grendel and his mother?"

The heavy set woman looked embarrassed and apologetic. "Grendel… who?"

"Never mind. Thank you very much for your trouble—and for the delicious pastry."

After a passionate disagreement about payment, Joe managed to pay Mueller's sister, complimenting her on the cleanliness and charm of her B&B. "Such quality and hospitality should not be free," he said, and left with a bag containing another fruit pastry and a chocolate eclair. In his other hand, he carried a large container of rich coffee.

He would be in Frankfurt in just under three hours. Fortified by the sleep, sugar, and caffeine, Cairns realized he was no longer frightened. He had walked this path many times before, eyes wide open, striding toward those who might kill him.

Okay, let the games begin.

CHAPTER FIFTEEN

San Luis Obispo, California

The silence in the conference room was deafening. Father Blaise and Jodi were, quite naturally, overwhelmed and dealing with information overload of the highest order. First, Lindsey had reviewed the high points of Viktor Dragovik's doctoral dissertation. Then she had distributed the text copies of all transmissions from Sebastian to FedPol. The narrative outlined Dragovik's success in creating the prion in short bullet points, made all the more chilling by bland phrases such as, "September 25th, test mice sick… October 20th test mice dead." One of the last posts, from early December, noted the time between infecting the mice and death to be less than twenty-four hours. And to top off the fun, Lindsey had played the video comparing the fit, healthy Diedrich Braun of early December with the dying man just one week later.

"'An even higher form of killing,' who would have thought it possible?" The expression on Father Blaise's face as he spoke was a study in distress. His bushy eyebrows were drawn together to form a hairy slash across his forehead. Lindsey looked over at Jodi inquisitively. She had no clue what the priest was talking about either and just shrugged, too absorbed in the grim reality of what they were facing to take in anything else.

The priest answered Lindsey's unspoken question. "Fritz Haber was a Jewish chemist. One of the most baffling figures in scientific history, Haber was primarily responsible for preventing the disaster that Malthus predicted when he published his 'Essay on the Principle of Population.' Nodding at Lindsey's raised eyebrow, he murmured, "Everything is connected," under his breath. Then in a normal voice, he continued speaking. "Haber won the Nobel Prize for his discovery of a way to synthesize ammonia from hydrogen and nitrogen under high temperature and pressure. The Haber-Bosch process is credited with saving half the world from starvation early in the last century. Over fifty percent of the food production in the world relies on the Haber-Bosch process." He paused and narrowed his eyes. "Just five years later, Haber achieved another honorific. He became the father of chemical warfare for the country that would use his process for the Final Solution."

By that point, both Jodi and Lindsey were staring at the priest, wide-eyed.

"It was Haber, the Jew from Poland, who oversaw the deaths of more than 4,000 allied soldiers when chlorine gas was released into the trenches. And it was Haber's process that resulted in the creation of Zyklon B, the gas that killed six million Jews, some of whom were his own relatives. In his excitement after the bloodless extermination of the soldiers, Haber wrote, 'In no future war will the military be able to ignore poison gas. It is a *higher form of killing*.' He was using his God-given genius to do the unpardonable—and then had the gall to justify it."

Studying the list of FedPol bullet points, the priest repeated, "And now, we are facing the prospect of *an even higher form of killing*, if you will. A new mad genius who hopes to annihilate humanity."

The priest paused to let that sink in, then continued. "You said Liisa Reardon had read the transcript and seen this tape?" Without waiting for a reply, he checked his watch and said, "It's four thirty in Paris. We should be able to reach her in her lab, right?"

After Liisa, Jodi, and Father Blaise spoke via Webcor for over an hour, Lindsey's mind was spinning. She was a researcher, but not at the level of these hard-science double-docs. Within fifteen minutes of listening to all the dizzying acronyms such as PrP, PrPsc, TSE's, MM, and MV, Lindsey decided to do something useful. She made some coffee. Today was definitely a cowboy coffee day, she thought as she put beans in the grinder, then poured the fragrant grounds into the Cuisinart.

"This coffee is delicious. Where did you say you get it?"

"Mystic Monks in Wyoming."

The priest smiled. "Leave it to a bunch of monks to make spectacular coffee."

Jodi nodded and smiled as she drank.

"Can someone translate what you all were talking about please?" Lindsey said.

"Of course, Lindsey," said the priest, nodding so vigorously that his several chins wobbled.

Watching him narrow his eyes as he looked at her, Lindsey could tell Father Blaise was considering the best way to explain concepts that were both complicated and controversial. She had grasped enough of the conversation of her colleagues to understand that the transmission of prion disease was poorly understood, even by those who had been studying it for decades. The Jesuit could be somewhat pedantic, even about matters that seemed trivial. This reminded her of basic science profs back in medical school. She knew to just wait patiently for his oration.

"For decades, researchers have assumed that transmissible prion diseases like the spongiform encephalopathies are caused by an infectious agent consisting only of proteins. In the late nineties, Prisner at UC San Francisco won the Nobel Prize in Physiology or Medicine for his work in identifying the infectious protein, logically calling it Prion Protein or PrP. The infectious protein is resistant to radiation and most other typical methods for eradicating microbes. And it is difficult to study due to incubation periods that can last for several decades." Staring at Lindsey, he waited.

She did not disappoint. "That makes it the perfect bioweapon! It's radiation-resistant… hell, it's resistant to most everything normally used to kill the little bastards!" Her eyes widened as she realized what she had said. "Sorry, Father."

"No need to apologize, my dear, I might have come up with an even more colorful term myself." Shaking his head, the priest continued, "But here's the thing, despite the award of the Nobel, no one has been able to reproduce any of the encephalopathies in test animals following direct injection of PrP. Not Creutzfeld-Jacob, it's variant, or any of the other diseases now categorized as transmissible spongiform encephalopathies." Noting Lindsey's frown, he said, "Right. That makes no sense at all. Ergo, the controversy. You know, I am sure that the name *spongiform* derives from the sponge-like holes seen in an infected brain on autopsy. The infectious prion causes multiple folds in the tissue, eventually destroying the integrity of the cell. Although it acts like a contagious virus, it is believed not to be."

Both of his bushy eyebrows were raised as if waiting for a reply, so Lindsey dutifully nodded in agreement, although she remembered only scant bits about the disease from medical school. At the time, it had seemed too arcane to worry about.

She tried to catch Jodi's eye, but the vet was working out something on her laptop and raised her index finger in a silent, "Wait a sec."

Laboriously rising from his chair, Father Blaise waved Lindsey away when she attempted to help him. Grunting, he mumbled, "I'll get there my girl. One day, they'll need a crane, but not yet—thank you, Jesus—not yet." Chuckling, he shuffled over to the coffee pot and poured himself another cup. "My daily exercise, ladies. Don't deprive me of it."

As the priest added cream to his coffee, he watched Jodi's fingers flash over her keyboard. Nodding like an avuncular uncle, he stood there, sipping and waiting, far more patient during the wait than Lindsey. Finally, Jodi looked up triumphantly and declared, "If a microbe does not fulfill Koch's postulates, it cannot be the causal agent!"

Lindsey knew she was referring to the third of the famed German physician's Heinrich Koch's four criteria for determining a causal relationship between an organism and disease: The microbe must produce the disease when introduced into a healthy subject.

Father Blaise merely asked, "And so?"

Jodi's sense of elation seemed to vanish. "So… we know Dragovik has found a way to shorten the incubation period from years to days. He did this in Braun and must have embedded this indestructible prion into a virus so that it can become transmissible—right?"

"Yes and no," said the priest, helping himself to more coffee. "Yes, we can assume he has shortened the incubation period because of the stunning decline of Braun. But, we know it's not infectious. Not yet."

Lindsey and Jodi both stared at the priest. "How do we know that?" asked Jodi.

Shaking his massive head, looking remarkably like a graying Bull Mastiff shaking off after a dip, the Jesuit grimaced. "The last thirty seconds of the video shows Dragovik holding Braun. He practically carries him to his bed. If Mr. Braun were infectious, our Dr. Dragovik would not have risked getting close to him like that."

Ignoring the '*duh, of course*' expressions on the women's faces, Father Blaise mused thoughtfully, more to himself than to his colleagues, "He's got two more phases before he is ready. First, he's got to test this thing on a population of people—preferably a contained one. Assuming it works—and kills most, if not all of those unfortunate souls—then he needs a way to embed the prion in a virus, just as you said, Jodi. This is no easy thing." His glance darted to Lindsey, "Liisa Reardon said she would attempt it, but she did not sound hopeful. Lindsey, you said it was Rich who met with Joe Cairns and set up the meeting between him and the Swiss Police. We could sure use whatever details he can recall of that meeting."

CHAPTER SIXTEEN

Frankfurt, Germany

Cairns had been on a few operations in Frankfurt in recent years, so knew the city reasonably well. There were just a few areas that would fulfill the criteria for a man like Diedrich Braun. On instinct, he headed for downtown, and the Commerzbank Tower. He had turned onto the A-5 a while back, and the Garmin was showing that it would take just under twenty minutes to get there. He only hoped his hunch proved correct.

Like most of Germany's larger cities, Frankfurt am Main, or Frankfurt on the Main River, had been nearly destroyed in the war. Unlike her sister cities in the European Union, Frankfurt had restored only a very few of the old buildings and, over the previous few decades, had erected an American-style skyline, earning it the local moniker "Mainhattan." Frankfurt prided itself as a global center for transportation, education, commerce, tourism, and culture.

Cairns turned right onto Taunusanlage and found himself mired in mid-afternoon traffic. He was not far from his destination, and could see it now, just a few blocks away. Spotting a hole, he managed to cut off a Mercedes-Benz and head toward the Japan Center, where he hoped to dump the SUV and walk to the Commerzbank Tower.

Mildly surprised that his plan had worked, Cairns walked alongside a young German couple pushing a baby carriage. Christmas was just days away now, and he caught phrases floating toward him in the gusts of cold wind; "… *erster Weihnachts,*" "*geschenke.*" He smiled at the beaming parents and said, "*Frohliche Weinachten.*"

Where did that come from? I don't know how to say Merry Christmas in German! Amused at himself, he trudged ahead into the wind. And suddenly, there it was. As the largest building in Frankfurt, Commerzbank would suit Diedrich Braun's grandiose view of himself, Cairns mused, as he trotted up the many steps to the foyer of the building. *Diedrich, I hope I have assessed your megalomania correctly. There are an impressive number of humongous skyscrapers in this city, and I sure don't want to have to search every one of them for you.*

Cairns looked around at the glass atrium, impressed by the light in the less than optimal conditions of a diluted mid-afternoon sun and in the midst of winter. He recalled reading somewhere that this was one of the first "green" skyscrapers and saw one of the reasons why as he looked upward. Dense vegetation was visible along the edges of the glass-walled building at intervals of ten or twelve stories.

Cairns spotted a directory of the corporate offices in the building, and sure enough, Diedrich Gruppe was alone on the 56th floor. *Of course you would have purchased the entire floor.*

Wondering if there would be anyone working up there five days before Christmas, Cairns stepped over to the appropriate bank of elevators, pushed the *up* button, and stepped inside the first of several whose doors opened immediately. Alone in the enclosure, he eyed the glass wall. Like the Hyatt hotels, the elevator was open on one side to the atrium. The explosive ride up was dizzying, and within a scant ten seconds, the doors opened to reveal a sign—in an ostentatious cursive script—reading *Diedrich Gruppe-Adams and Adams Pharmaceuticals.* Adjacent to the six-foot by four-foot mauve-colored wall holding the sign, sat a young woman behind a mahogany receptionist desk.

"May I help you?" Her English was perfect, without even a trace of an accent.

"Yes, I have an appointment to see Diedrich Braun." He saw no need to add that the meeting had been scheduled for last June.

Losing her exceptional poise for just a moment, the blonde blinked twice, then said, "I think you must be mistaken. Mr. Braun is not here." The cool, blue gaze did not waver.

Adopting a perplexed expression, Cairns said, "Well, that is certainly odd." He held her look without blinking until she looked away.

"Perhaps Dr. Dragovik could help you, sir? He is in today. If you wish, I can ask if he has time to speak with you?"

"Thank you, I would like that very much."

Picking up the phone, she spoke in low, rapid German. Cairns could not understand a word she said. Placing the phone back in its cradle and turning to him, she said, "Dr. Dragovik asks if you are able to wait for no more than ten minutes. At that time he would be happy to help you." Pointing toward a grouping of overstuffed leather chairs, she suggested, "Please take a seat, Mr., uh, what did you say your name was?"

"I didn't," he replied, and sat down to wait.

CHAPTER SEVENTEEN

Friendswood, Texas

"Are you ever going to tell me?"

"Tell you what?"

"Morgan, sheesh! You're staying up until all hours, and then when you do finally crash, you wake up screaming. Something is wrong, way wrong." LJ looked at her best friend, scrutinizing the dark shadows under eyes that were usually sparkling, but now seemed dull and lifeless. "I'm really worried about you, Morgan," she said, softly. "But I don't know what to do or say if you keep giving me the silent treatment."

The girls had been at LJ's home in Friendswood, Texas, for a week and had one more to go. LJ's mom was on vacation from school and had been cooking up a storm for them and her other three children. In front of her and the other kids, Morgan acted excited, curious, reverent, or whatever else the occasion called for. Only when she and LJ were alone in the bedroom they shared, did she drop the pretense. And just when she went to sleep, did she let out that terrible scream.

Morgan wanted to tell LJ, to tell someone about what she was seeing. But how could she explain what she could not understand herself?

"MOM! Please come in here, now!"

It was just after three in the morning and LJ was holding a hysterical Morgan. If the sound of the young woman's sobs had not been so heartrending, it would have been a comical tableau, as the lanky Morgan outweighed LJ by more than thirty pounds and was at least seven inches taller.

Julie raced down the hallway and into her oldest daughter's room. Morgan was crying so hard that the word *keening* popped into Julie's head. She'd never heard a sound like it and she hoped she never would again. The anguish seemed to be erupting from deep within Morgan's psyche, each of her sobs seeming to be tearing away pieces of her heart and flinging them from her body.

Julie was much taller than her adoptive daughter. She motioned for LJ to get out from under Morgan. The interruption of disentangling arms and legs slowed down the tears a bit, and by the time Julie could sit down beside Morgan on the king-size bed the girls were sharing, Morgan was shuddering and hiccupping.

"Honey, go get Morgan a glass of water, will you please?"

As LJ hurried out of the room to get the water, Julie placed her large, gentle hands on either side of Morgan's face, and stared into her eyes. Slowly and firmly, she said, "Tell me."

The shuddering started again and Julie moved her hands from Morgan's face down to her shoulders. Gripping her tightly, she commanded, "No, Morgan. Tell me. Now."

The girl's eyes were huge—terrified. Her pupils were so dilated that Julie could barely see any brown in her eyes. *Deer in the headlights—literally,* she thought. More than anything, Julie wanted to help this girl find peace. Although LJ had said nothing until now, Julie had heard Morgan's terrified screams each night. As had everyone else in the house.

Julie Grayson had taught high school math for over twenty

years, and had some experience with students "on the spec-trum," back in the days when autism was largely misunder-stood and misdiagnosed. Like many excellent teachers, Julie had assessed each of the two students in question herself, re-jecting labels like "retarded" or "mentally incapacitated." After getting permission from their distraught parents, she had worked with the boys after school and on Saturdays. The stu-dents and the teacher had taught each other. They'd helped Julie understand the onslaught of pain and distress that could be triggered by certain types of sensory stimulation—bright lights or loud noise, for example. Not a touchy-feely gal herself, Julie could empathize with the boys' intense discomfort with accidental touching. Her instincts told her that these kids—and others like them—thought differently. Rather than learn-ing concepts in words, they learned them in images. She knew that, although the boys had been told they were stupid from an early age, they were anything but. In fact, she was convinced that one of them was a math savant. That young man was now completing his Ph.D. in physics at Rice University.

Perhaps as significant as her instinctual understanding of autism was Julie's complete lack of fear of it—which set her apart from most of her colleagues. To Julie, it was merely an unusual manifestation of the God-given and unique dignity of each person.

Watching her mother with Morgan, LJ was overwhelmed with love and gratitude. Her trust in Julie was wholehearted. If anyone could help her best friend, it was her mom. Quickly, LJ checked that thought. Was she being disloyal to her *real* mom, the one she had never met until last June? Smiling to herself, LJ thought, *Nope, they're entirely different women. And how blessed am I to have the genes of the genius and the personal example of Julie Grayson?*

She jumped at the otherworldly sound of Morgan's voice.

"*B ngzhù w , b ngzhù w , b ngzhù w .*"

Julie's arms and hands were killing her, but she had not let up on the downward pressure of her hands on Morgan's shoulders. She had been holding the position for at least five minutes and was exerting as much force as she possibly could. Since she was also a soccer and tennis coach at the high school, it was a lot of weight on the thin frame of the young girl.

Morgan's eyes had closed, and she was falling asleep, still whispering the foreign phrase into the silence of the bedroom.

"She's saying, 'Help me, help me, help me.'"

Both LJ and Julie jolted at the sound of a male voice. Julie's husband Ted stood at the door and translated the Mandarin Chinese Morgan had spoken before she fell into a deep sleep.

These aren't just nightmares, Julie realized with a start. *This is some kind of warning. This girl is being used, which makes sense because she so totally lacks guile. That makes her easy to be used, right?*

CHAPTER EIGHTEEN

Cal Poly

"King David."

They had listened to Rich talk about Joe Cairns for more than sixty minutes. He began with a reprise of the assassin's background and his employment by Diedrich Braun and then Liisa Reardon. Leaving nothing out, Rich covered Cairns' murders of the two kidnappers, and the attempted murders of investigator Toni Martinez, and Chief Animal Tech, Ariana Dumas. He ended with their recent meeting and the agreement by Cairns to serve as a double agent for FedPol—if and when he managed to get rehired by Diedrich Gruppe.

The tale sounded more like one of those Netflix thrillers than real life. When he was done speaking, the room was silent for several minutes. Finally, his bushy eyebrows rising to their maximum elevation, Father Blaise seized on the last thing Rich had said, adopting a scathing tone.

"King David? Really?"

Quietly, and without a trace of irony, Rich said, "Really."

"Don't tell me you believe him, Rich."

Unable to suppress a smile, Rich replied, "But I *do* believe him. Why is it impossible to believe that the spirit of King

David befriended a skinny, poor Irish kid—a child destined to be a warrior? That this benevolent spirit taught and consoled him? And that years later, when he saw his fellow soldier going off the rails, he returned once again to protect him from the worst kind of evil—the loss of his soul?"

As Rich heard the words coming out of his own mouth, he realized that his feeling for Joe Cairns was not pity or sympathy, or even empathy. It was far more profound—though he could not label it. Until that moment, he had not admitted to himself that he believed Cairns and his entire zany tale. But he did.

Lindsey, Jodi, and Father Blaise were seated around a conference table in the central research area of the Animal Research Center. Out of the corner of her eye, Lindsey watched the priest and wondered if he was angry, embarrassed, or both by Rich's passionate defense of Cairns. But he seemed neither. Instead, he seemed amused, or perhaps curious. Jodi seemed the most uncomfortable of the group, by far. Watching her right leg jiggle faster and faster, Lindsey thought her colleague might explode if she couldn't interject her thoughts. Which she did, just a few seconds later.

"Am I missing something here, gentlemen? Can one of you explain just why we care whether this guy is hallucinating or is merely a pathological liar?" Jodi had placed both her feet firmly on the floor and was leaning forward with her elbows on the shiny table. Her eyes sparked with impatience, though she was careful to speak softly so that some students nearby wouldn't overhear. The effort it took to do so was readily apparent in the rigidity of her spine.

Placing both hands over his ample belly, the priest replied, "It doesn't matter all that much, Jodi." All trace of amusement gone from his face, he then regarded Rich. "I pray you are right, Rich, that Cairns is neither mentally ill nor a liar. From the bottom of my soul, I do." Then he turned back to study Jodi quietly, and as he did so, her agitation and tension seemed to dissipate, replaced with something like exhaustion. She had worked through the night, he knew, searching for ways that a prion could be converted to an infectious agent. Jodi had spoken with colleagues working on the One Health Initiative in Europe, South America and Japan. She had even called her former mentor, Dr. Joel Wallach, to seek his help. All to no avail.

Under the scrutiny of her boss, Jodi finally smiled.

Both Rich and Lindsey waited to see if the priest would elaborate. After another moment, he continued. "I pray that we do have a divine intervention here. Because if the solution to stopping this madness rests solely on our shoulders, God help us all."

So it's come to that, thought Lindsey.

The more the priest talked, Rich's fear that Cairns was on a fatal mission grew stronger. Strangely, though, he did not fear the possibility that Dragovik's fiendish plot would succeed. Braun's protégé was most assuredly an agent of the Evil One—there was no other explanation—but Joe Cairns was a servant of God. Somehow, Cairns would prevail. He would get the information that Lindsey and the research team needed. Of this, Rich was wholly confident.

He decided to keep these thoughts to himself. His wife's boss was not a man he wanted to take on, and Jodi Tamarack would undoubtedly think him naïve or foolish. Lindsey, he realized, was no longer with them, and she was wearing that expression he had seen only a few times since he had known her. The energy that emanated from her felt like a current that Rich could almost touch. It was precisely the kind of intense focus and determination that had resulted in the creation of the Digitalis molecule.

CHAPTER NINETEEN

Frankfurt, Germany

Exactly ten minutes had elapsed when the door opened and Viktor Dragovik strode out from behind the reception desk with his hand extended, as if he were greeting one of his oldest friends.

"Joe Cairns. What a most pleasant surprise!"

Camera. There's got to be a camera. No way could he remember me from our twenty-second meeting. It's either in that sign where visitors step out of the elevator, or somewhere on the desk. Most likely the sign.

"Thank you for taking the time to see me, Dr. Dragovik. Especially only four days before Christmas. I wasn't sure there would even be anyone here."

A chuckle. "Call me Viktor, please. Come in, do come in." Graciously directing Cairns back behind the desk and into the hallway, he called over his shoulder, "No interruptions, please Gretchen. Just take messages."

Cairns suppressed a smile. *Of course the perfect blonde's name really is Gretchen—what else could it be? Then, David, I sure hope you are with me. I'm winging this. I have no clue what to do next.*

Dragovik stood to the side of his open office door to permit Cairns to enter first. Instantly, Cairns saw why.

Rather than stare at the business end of the Walther PPK pointed at his chest, Cairns smiled into the face of the former Captain of the German Federal Intelligence Service, Germany's equivalent of the CIA.

Well, that answers that. Dragovik knows I worked for Braun, and probably what I did—and didn't do.

"Guess the new baby made Braun's offers irresistible, huh Stefan?" It had been this man who had introduced Cairns to Braun back in the spring after a joint operation between Joe's former Force Recon unit and the German Feds. Stefan had arranged a post for Cairns in a protection detail for the European Economic Summit meeting.

Mind racing, Cairns thought to himself. *This isn't a bad thing. He owes me. That whole op would have blown up had my guys not taken over. Unless, of course, he hates my guts for showing him up.*

With a start, Cairns noticed another guy standing in the corner of the office, mirroring Stefan's posture, even down to the two-handed grip on his revolver. The only difference was that guy' gun was pointed at his head rather than his chest.

Willing himself to focus on anything but the guns, Cairns scanned the office, one of the most tasteful he had ever seen. There were beautiful Impressionist paintings on the walls— Monet, Renoir, Degas—that looked like originals from where Cairns stood. Dragovik's desk was a square glass block positioned in the corner opposite where the ex-soldier stood, a contemporary black-and-chrome chair poised behind it. The whole scene emanated the ideal Feng Shui. Three of the four walls of the room were floor-to-ceiling glass, revealing the onset of dusk through a flurry of wet-looking snowflakes.

Taking a seat behind his desk, Dragovik nodded once to

Stefan. Instantly, the two gunmen approached and flanked Cairns, and with a surprisingly gentle hand, escorted him out of the room.

CHAPTER TWENTY

Friendswood, Texas

"Merry Christmas to you as well! Hope you enjoy your skiing trip!"

Julie clicked off the call and turned to see Morgan standing in the open doorway of her bedroom. Smiling, Julie moved toward her, stopping about a foot away. "I was just speaking with your Mom, Morgan. She asked me to tell you that she'll call tomorrow night when she gets to Aspen."

Julie knew Morgan had been attempting to listen in on the call, but saw no need to call her on it. Anything she'd have overheard was complimentary of her, as Julie had sensed how anxious Morgan's mom must be about her daughter's behavior.

Morgan nodded slowly, her face revealing no expression. "Did you tell Mom about the nightmares?"

"Of course not, Morgan. That would be your story to tell, if you decide that's what you want to do." *But why wouldn't you tell her? Lack of trust? No, that's not it. Maybe because you know she worries. Anne Gardner had clearly worked very hard to help this young woman cope with her differences, and from the looks of things, done a spectacular job.*

Morgan stared at Julie for a few seconds longer, and was greeted with an unwavering stare in return. *Her eyes are quite lovely!* Julie thought with surprise. Hidden behind enormous black plastic glasses and hanks of long straight hair, those two concentric circles, dark copper surrounded by amber, were usually hidden.

Julie was no fan of heavy makeup on anyone, but she found herself imagining Morgan with a good haircut, a touch of eyeshadow and mascara, and a more flattering pair of glasses. Voila! She could be a beauty.

"Most people can't do it back."

"What?"

"Stare." The edges of her mouth tipped up. It must have taken considerable effort to contain a smile.

"Is staring a good thing?"

"Well… it's not bad."

Julie laughed. Morgan reminded her so much of those two young men who had taught her what it was like to be autistic.

"You act like you like me. Almost as much as Mom does, even."

Because I do, Morgan, very much. Julie knew better than to say this aloud and simply smiled and looked away. "What about Lin— LJ?" Julie was still getting accustomed to her daughter's new name. Oddly, though, she and Ted agreed that it suited her very well. The last few years had cost LJ her childhood, so why not a nickname befitting a CEO or writer?

"She's my best friend, so… of course she likes me."

Time to end this.

Careful not to touch Morgan, Julie edged around her as she casually said, "Well, Morgan Gardner, I've enjoyed talking with you very much—and with your mom, too. But please excuse me because tomorrow is Christmas Eve and I've got lots to do to get ready."

Earlier that morning, Ted had argued that Julie should tell Morgan's mother about the strange nightmare. The pleas of "help me" in Chinese—you don't get much weirder than that. But Julie had disagreed. Something told her the disclosure would be a grave error. Morgan would talk with them about the nightmare, she knew. And soon. For now, it was a relief to sleep soundly again.

"I'd like to help, Julie. May I help?"

Julie nodded, smiling. "Of course you can help! You see that pile of gifts over by the closet? How about you start wrapping them and put them under the tree?"

As she watched the young woman hustle down the hall to get the wrapping paper and tape, she called out, "Morgan, the gifts are in piles with each person's name on top. Please be sure to tag each gift."

"Okay, Julie. Got it."

Humming "Away in a Manger" to herself, Julie thought about Morgan's mother, Anne. She sensed they could be friends, good friends, if they lived closer together. It had actually been Anne who had called Julie—to see how things were going. She imagined that was code for, "How is Morgan behaving? Has she thoroughly upset your house yet?"

It had taken Julie a few minutes to calm Anne's concerns, and finally, she'd said, "Look, Anne, Morgan is not the first person with ASD I've encountered." When this elicited only stunned silence, she followed up with, "She's a great girl and we are loving having her with us for Christmas. And honestly, LJ adores her. After all the 'girly girls' of high school, Morgan's direct frankness is a welcome relief!"

Once she'd put Anne at ease, the two women had so enjoyed getting to know each other that Julie invited Anne to stay with them when she came to Houston the next year.

Recapping the conversation in her head, Julie marveled

that it seemed as if they'd known each other a long time. Clearly, the fact that she understood Morgan's condition and didn't sentimentalize or shrink from it was what opened the door. Though she hadn't gone into it with Anne, Julie had dealt with her own "problem child" during the horrendous period of LJ's alcoholism. She understood—perhaps better than anyone—that sometimes parents have to trust themselves above any professionals.

At first, Julie and Ted had put their faith and hope in one therapist after another. Even the most trivial of decisions was taken to one of the "team" treating the Graysons.

The therapists had been emphatic that there be no liquor in the house, but it would take the couple some time to summon the heart to dispose of their stash, so they'd simply hidden it. Sleepless one night, they decided to sneak a glass of wine. As they enjoyed it, LJ discovered them giggling in the dark. They were mortified, but she begged them to enjoy themselves—not to let her destroy one of their pleasures.

That was the night that Julie and Ted reclaimed their parenthood. She bet Anne Gardner had had similar experiences with autism experts.

CHAPTER TWENTY-ONE

Cal Poly

The small team's division of labor was designed to capitalize on each researcher's specialty. Liisa, a developmental biologist, worked with yeast because there are several proteins in the substance that can undergo a prion-like conversion of their structure. Specifically, she was studying a translation termination factor involved in the metabolism of nitrogen. The prion conversion was transmissible, and so provided generations for study. If Liisa could identify the configuration of abnormal protein folding in the yeast, then the others could replicate it in their animal models.

As department head, Father Blaise had procured close to 500 transgenic mice in order to test out a variety of mathematical models for the enzymatic sequence of the diseased prion. The mice and their associated models were divided among Lindsey, Jodi, and himself.

The priest had been eager to try out the CRISPR-Cas9 system, but had needed a complicated problem to warrant it. Mapping the PrP molecule fit the bill perfectly, but even with the revolutionary gene splicer on the case, cutting the time to modify the molecule to under and hour, Father Blaise had not been able to induce neurologic symptoms in his experimental mice.

"So… we're nowhere. We cannot even create a prion that shows symptoms—any symptoms—never mind causing neurologic collapse in just hours." Jodi had stated the obvious to Liisa, and watched her colleague's usually bright-blue eyes cloud over. Lindsey, Father Blaise, and Jodi had been comparing notes for about thirty minutes via WebCor conference. No one wanted to admit their lack of progress until Jodi finally stated it. They had all been working eighteen-hour days for over a week.

Lindsey had not even been home for three days. After over 150 failed models of the diseased prion molecule, she believed she was close. She could feel the right formula sitting at the edge of her brain, could almost see it... but only almost. Unlike her two colleagues, Lindsey's approach was intuitive rather than linear. She could visualize each of the molecular configurations and painstakingly recorded the seemingly endless list of failures. She sensed that the answer lay in the amyloid aggregates that collected in the abnormally folded diseased protein.

The three scientists were, of course, trying to do the impossible. In spite of decades of study, the mechanism of prion diseases remained a mystery. Just as Father Blaise had explained, scholars were divided even about the most fundamental aspects of prion disease.

In spite of the thousands of reasons she had to let despair and hopelessness claim her, Lindsey *knew* that they were close. Their eclectic team—Evan Pierre, Dimitri Vlasov, Joe Cairns, Sebastian, Liisa Reardon, Father Blaise, Jodi, Lindsey, Rich and maybe even King David—would beat Dragovik at his loathsome game. They *had* to.

Trying to suppress a flash of annoyance at Jodi's negativity,

Lindsey smiled and said, "We'll find it Liisa. We've already found hundreds of configurations that *don't* work; we only need to find *one* that does."

When the conference call ended, Father Blaise looked at both women and declared, "It's Christmas Eve. Go home. Have a celebratory drink or, better yet, go to midnight mass."

Lindsey started to object, then thought better of it. He was right. She remembered all those years of searching for the new Digipro molecule. It had taken her years to grasp the delicate balance between persistence and obsession. It was time to walk away for a few hours. Without thinking it through, she smiled and said, "Hey, you guys, why don't you join us for Christmas dinner at the house?"

Jodi's tired face lit up. "Are you sure, Lindsey? You've had even less sleep than we have!"

"I am positive, Jodi. The boss is right. We all need to get some distance from our obsession with saving the world." Lindsey had no idea what her friend's religious beliefs were— or whether she had any at all—but she put an arm around her shoulder and said, "It's Christmas. We need to celebrate."

"Sold! What time and what can we bring?"

"Nothing! Just bring your weary selves around 3:00. We'll start with drinks and appetizers, then eat around 4:00. I figure we'll all want to make an early night of it."

CHAPTER TWENTY-TWO

Hesse, Germany

Cairns could see nothing. Sitting handcuffed in the back seat of his own SUV with a black hood tied over his head, he carefully considered what had happened, what it all meant, and what his options might be when they got to their destination.

While Stefan and his steroid-overdosed pal were escorting him out of Dragovik's office, Cairns had said, "Hey Stefan, I'm just looking for some extra work here, buddy."

"I know, Joe. And we have just the perfect job for you."

Stefan had smiled at Cairns when he had said it. Not quite a sneer, but close. They had known he was coming. Although Horst Mueller had claimed that he had no contact number for Stefan, he had evidently called his former boss to tell him that Cairns was coming to Frankfurt. And why.

Don't burn your bridges… you never know when you might need something.

Cairns understood how essential CYA was among the heavily bureaucaratic military organizations. Mueller had provided Stefan with the most valuable commodity of all, information. Stefan, in turn, had informed Dragovik.

All of it made more sense than hidden cameras, or the possibility that Dragovik had remembered a twenty-second conversation with Cairns six months earlier. Stefan must have explained to Dragovik who he was and what he used to do. And he probably added that it had been he, Stefan, who had introduced Cairns to Diedrich Braun. *That still leaves the possibility that Dragovik doesn't know how or when I quit,* Cairns thought. *So that's something.*

Once all three men were in the SUV, Stefan plucked out a black hood from the pocket of his loose pants. "Sorry, but we can't risk you knowing the location of the lab, Joe. Not until you've proved yourself." This time, the sneer was full blown. "Can't be too careful these days, when so many seem to work for more than one interest." As he pulled the hood over Cairns' head and secured it, he directed Albert, the other man, in rapid German. The only part of it that Cairns got was "Konigston-Taurus."

Stefan ignored Cairns' attempts to make chit-chat, saying nothing until the car began to slow and take a wide right-hand turn onto a very bumpy gravel road. Cairns' teeth snapped together as he bounced up and down on the back seat, unable to balance himself with his hands cuffed in front of him. They were reaching their destination, and Cairns thought about his options. He presumed he was about to meet Sebastian, a traitor known to be working for FedPol. Clearly, the "perfect job" Stefan had in mind for Cairns would be a test of loyalty. Kill the scientist.

Cairns figured he'd have twenty, maybe thirty seconds to disable these two. Albert would be easy. He was one of those guys who load up on steroids and overwork their upper bodies in pursuit of perfection. That much heavy muscle hampers the rapid movement necessary for fighting every time, and steroids dull the mind and reflexes. The former captain of the Federal Intelligence Service of Germany was a different story.

Tall and lean, Stefan was a good fighter, but too cautious—perhaps because he had a family. Stefan played it safe, and Cairns figured he could use that to his advantage.

The German ex-cop sat to the right of Cairns, which meant that his shoulder holster was about a foot from Cairns' right hand. It had been a mistake to handcuff Cairns' hands in front of him. Albert had done it while Stefan was talking to someone on his cell, probably his wife.

Stefan's cell phone rang again. This time, his side of the conversation was composed largely of single words, yes or no between blocks of silence, assumably while the caller was speaking. Cairns figured it must be Dragovik.

If Cairns couldn't get to one of the guns worn by his escorts, he hoped to reach his own Strider SMF, which was strapped to his left thigh. A titanium folding knife went everywhere with him as well, and had saved his butt on several occasions. He hoped he wouldn't have to kill these two, especially Stefan, who had four kids and a new baby. He didn't consider the alternative.

CHAPTER TWENTY-THREE

Pismo Beach, California

"She saw thousands of dead bodies in a Chinese prison?"

Rich's hand stopped in midair when he heard Lindsey's stunned question. He had been pouring coffee into their cups. Midnight mass had not ended until early morning, so they had slept in and were discussing whether to eat breakfast or save their appetites for their early Christmas dinner with Father Blaise and Jodi. In spite of Lindsey's protests, both had insisted that they'd bring a dish.

LJ had called to wish them a Merry Christmas, and after they had spoken for a while, Julie took the phone and told Lindsey the details of Morgan's strange recurring nightmare. She'd had the dream again on Christmas Eve, but this time she hadn't wakened the entire household.

On Christmas morning, at breakfast, Julie and Ted had listened quietly as the young woman narrated a far grimmer and more detailed nightmare. While the girls cleaned up the breakfast dishes, Julie and Ted concocted a story about needing fresh cranberries and ginger, as an excuse to go out for drive. They both felt the need to have a conversation away from Morgan and LJ.

As soon as he closed the car door and started the car, Ted said, "I don't see how we can keep all this from Morgan's mother, Julie. Something very strange is going on with that kid. Maybe she has some kind of brain tumor or something. Sudden spurts of fluency in a foreign language can be a sign of a tumor."

Ted glanced over at his wife, who watched him thoughtfully but said nothing. He decided to pull over at a local park so they could focus on the issue at hand.

He pressed. "If this were happening to LJ or any of our kids, wouldn't you want to know, honey? Don't we have an *obligation* to tell Anne Morgan about this?"

Julie nodded slowly. "Yes, of course. But I don't think the dreams or the fluency in Chinese indicate pathology." Watching her husband's face darken, she quickly touched the hand still resting on the steering wheel. "Ted, I cannot tell you why I think this, but these nightmares have something to do with Lindsey, something she and Rich have gotten themselves into. The dreams are… I don't know… some kind of *warning* or premonition or something. It sounds a little crazy, I know, but *I'm sure of it.* We have to talk to them first. We'll tell them about the dreams—in confidence—and see if anything rings a bell. If not—or maybe even if so—I promise, we'll call Anne."

Ted looked at Julie in amazement, his annoyance instantly replaced by unabashed admiration. He had experienced examples of his wife's strange intuition too many times to dismiss it. He had learned to trust these flashes of insight.

"Apparently, Morgan has had this recurring but progressively worsening nightmare for several months, Lindsey. She has told no one, not even LJ. The only reason she decided to tell us was that she woke up the whole house screaming in Chinese a few nights ago."

Lindsey put her phone on speaker so both she and Rich could hear.

Once he'd caught up with the conversation, Rich murmured, "Morgan speaks Mandarin?" He'd intended the rhetorical question only for Lindsey, but Julie heard him and said, "Right Rich. So does Ted. He has worked with Chinese physicists over the last several years. I kidded him about taking Mandarin when we were both in grad school at Rice, but now I see the foresight in the man... one among many of the qualities I love."

Lindsey and Rich were out on the deck overlooking a calm, sparkling Pacific Ocean and Rich was pacing. He was starting to make some associations that seemed crazy, but somehow felt right.

"Julie, this prison in Morgan's dream—does she have any idea where it is? Did she say?"

"Actually, yes. She says it's in Qinghai. I looked it up online, and it's the most sparsely populated province in China, in the northwest, very close to Tibet. It's mountainous there, and apparently loaded with nuclear testing sites, labor camps, and prisons."

When Rich didn't reply, she continued. "The first time we were aware of the dreams was last week. Morgan was shouting 'HELP ME' at three-thirty in the morning—in Mandarin! Ted was able to translate for the rest of us non-polyglots." This last comment elicited grins from both Lindsey and Rich, but their smiles faded at Julie's next question.

"Linds, are you working on something related to mad cow disease? Or—you know—Creutzfeld-Jacob?"

"How could you possibly know that? Surely not from Morgan!" Lindsey's expression was a study in incredulity. Rich's, not so much.

"Exactly what did Morgan say, Julie?"

"Ted and I spent the last couple of hours with her, trying to get the whole story. Apparently the nightmares are changing. For months, they were just terrible images, stuff of the worst kind of horror movies. No context. No voices or locale. She couldn't have talked about them if she'd wanted to, because she didn't know what she was seeing. But once she came here to Texas, she began to see faces of individual people and hear what they were saying. She was so scared when she woke up from a bad one a few nights ago that she told LJ about what she saw. LJ convinced her to talk to us. Telling you exactly what she said is challenging, because she kept switching from English to Chinese and crying, of course, because these aren't just dreams to her.

"What? What do you mean?"

"They're *visions*. I wrote down what she was saying because, for some reason—I'm not even sure why—I thought it might be important. A hunch I guess. I thought it might somehow be connected to you and your research."

Rich spoke this time, quite calmly under the circumstances. "Go on."

"She said that she had seen a man dressed as a soldier. He was preparing something in a huge vat. It looked to her like powder. The man wore a mask, and after he had mixed the powder to his satisfaction, he poured it into big containers. This all took place in a huge room that she thought was a kitchen."

Rich was starting to realize they were dealing with something supernatural. Although a former soldier and cop, he possessed one of those rare brains in which the right and left hemispheres were almost equal in size. So-called left-brained people are thought to be analytical, while their right-brained counterparts lean more toward creativity and synthesis. Rich had a healthy dose of each—which had proven to be a godsend in an unusual situation like this one.

Lindsey was left-brained all the way, so Rich was not surprised that she didn't sense the otherworldliness of what was happening here. Besides, she wasn't exactly herself. Looking at her now, he saw dark circles under her usually vibrant green eyes. In the past week, he calculated, she'd slept maybe twelve hours. He was thankful to the priest for ordering Lindsey to come home last night. Up until now, this whole damnable battle was being waged by her and her team—plus Joe Cairns, of course. This revelation—the particulars of Morgan's dream—provided him with some insight, and ideas about how he could help as well.

CHAPTER TWENTY-FOUR

Konigston Um Taunus, Germany

The SUV rolled to a stop. Cairns did not move, but tensed every muscle. Stefan was whispering in rapid German again, and all Cairns could make out was the name Sebastian. *He is here—and alive! Just long enough for me pass my employment test by killing him, I guess.* He heard Albert climb out and then open the door to the back seat. The ex-cop pulled hard on Cairn's left upper arm, forcing him to slide to the edge of the seat or risk a shoulder injury. The guy's grip was iron. He heard Stefan get out then, and come around to where Albert was holding him. Each taking one of Cairns' arms, the men hoisted him to his feet and all but dragged him along the gravel road. Neither German said a word.

This is bad, really bad. Cairns thoughts were racing, and he was as close to panic as he had ever been—not because they were going to kill him, but because he knew that the mission he was embarking on was the most important of his life. *Yo, David, are you around? Do you know what's happening here? Please tell me that you didn't drag me into this just so I could get popped before I could save Sebastian… or at least help Lindsey figure out what kind of bug this lunatic Dragovik has created.*

Suddenly they stopped and Cairns heard the sound of an overhead door opening. Now, only Albert walked him, but had adjusted his hold and was pulling his charge by the handcuffed hands. The strongman yanked off the hood.

Blinking furiously, Cairns could see only bursts of light and shade. He heard Stefan laughing derisively, but could see only his shadow. "Come on, oh great Force Recon soldier. Time to show us you're workin' the right side."

For the first time, Cairns heard a slight slur in Stefan's words. He sounded nothing like the guy he'd spent seventy-two hours with six months earlier. As his eyes adjusted, he could see it—Stefan's pupils were tiny pinpricks. *Stoned. Is that why you left the intelligence service, Stefan? To support your habit?*

Cairns struggled to remember if the former cop had acted stoned while in Dragovik's office, but couldn't. But then, Stefan had not opened his mouth in front of his boss.

They stood in a cavernous space—about the size of a football field, Cairns estimated—with thick walls. It seemed old. A bomb shelter? In the middle of the floor sat a man strapped to a metal chair. There were straps across his chest, each arm, and each leg. Three spotlights, like those in surgical suites, illuminated his battered, bruised face. His bare torso looked badly injured, with massive contusions along his rib cage.

Sebastian. Too far away to tell if he's breathing. But if he's got broken ribs, his breathing would be shallow anyway. If he's alive, he's not conscious.

"Well, Joe boy, are you ready to show your stripes? Albert, assume the position."

Assume the position, what the—?

The ever obedient muscleman strode behind Cairns and placed a Glock into his handcuffed hands. He wrapped his own huge hands around both of Cairns' and pointed the gun at the battered man in the chair.

"Shoot him, Master Marine Man. Now!" Stefan was screaming, eyes wild.

Sebastian didn't stir.

May as well go out fighting, thought Cairns. *Crazy Stefan will shoot me as soon as I move, but it beats standing here waiting for him to figure out that I'm not about to kill Sebastian. I can't reach the knife but I sure as hell can create some nasty problems for Albert.*

His plan was pretty shaky, but Cairns began to tighten every muscle in his body until he was rigid like a coiled spring. He would use each of his 185 pounds as he sprang backward into Albert's unsuspecting core. With some luck, he could stamp on the German's instep, then try to topple him with his left foot.With a little more, he could reach the knife strapped to his leg and take the goon out before Stefan killed him.

Just as Cairns was about to make his move, a small red dot appeared in the center of Stefan's forehead. Followed by the loud crack of a gunshot. The German wavered, then collapsed, without a sound. Albert loosened his grasp on Cairns and backed away in shock. All of this gave Cairns the opportunity to make his move on Albert.

Once he had the large man facedown on the ground, Cairns looked up. He was dazed, nauseated, and trembling from the after-effects of the massive amount of adrenaline coursing through him. "Where the hell did you come from?" he managed to direct at Horst Mueller. "How the hell—? Why did you kill Stefan?" His voice sounded weak and tinny, even to his own ears.

The big blond German Federal Intelligence Officer smiled. "You saved my life. I owed you. Now I saved yours." He shrugged as if it were nothing, then reached out and unlocked the handcuffs.

Mueller held up the key so Cairns could see it, then pocketed it again. "Universal key."

"But how did you know I was coming here? You must have followed us from Frankfurt!" Cairns was breathing hard, trying to calm himself down. Still kneeling next to Albert's inert body, he took a couple of deep breaths and shakily rose to his feet.

The cop's smile was replaced by a frown. "When I called Stefan to tell him you were coming in for a job, he sounded off, strange. Said some things that made no sense. He hasn't made much sense ever since he started working for these guys." Horst's accent thickened with emotion as he explained. "Stefan left his wife and kids last summer." He shook his head as if to clear it. "Walking away from your family… it's not right." He grimaced, then continued. "Stefan had gotten hooked on cocaine. He claimed he could control it, but that's what everyone thinks. First, it was just on his days off, but then he couldn't stay away from it. I believe he took this job to pay for his habit."

Horst glanced over at the body off his former boss, then back at Cairns, who could see the sadness in his eyes. "He was a good cop, you know."

As he listened to Horst's story, Cairns was regaining his composure. "Yeah, he was, Horst. But once the dragon gets hold of you, you disappear into pure need." He had seen it over and over. Figuring they were done with that topic, he asked again, "Why did you come here?"

"I got worried after that weird conversation. I have a bunch of vacation time, so I decided to take some to see what was going on with Diedrich Gruppe. I'd heard some strange stories—nothing specific, but enough to nag at me. I wanted to satisfy my curiosity. "Stefan tried to recruit me for the company a few months ago, so I knew where the Frankfurt office was. I got there just in time to see Stefan and this other brute loading you into your SUV. It didn't look friendly. I decided to follow you. Anyway," he said, nodding toward Sebastian, "I think you'll need some help with that guy. He looks pretty bad. There's a doc we use for the service not far from here. We can take him over there."

Then he glanced over at Albert and Stefan. "You'll need some help with them, too. Let's face it, your German's kind of—"

"Non-existent?" Overwhelmed, Cairns tried to continue talking and couldn't. His throat was thick and tight with emotion. He looked at the big German who had just saved his life and finally croaked out, "Horst, how do I thank you? What can I say?"

CHAPTER TWENTY-FIVE

Kornberg, Germany

"Ja, Cairns wurde versorgt. Aber Cairns hat Alfred getötet, bevor ich ihn bekommen könnte. Ich werde Alfred in Kronberg begraben und hier für die Nacht bleiben. Das Wetter wird hier schlecht." Horst paused, listening, before he replied, *"Ja, der FedPol-Agent ist auch tot."* Then he nodded and said, *"in Ordnung."*

When he'd clicked off the call, Horst turned to Cairns and said, "I bought us a day, probably not much more. Dragovik sounded distracted, as if I was interrupting him."

So Dragovik had bought the act. He'd called Stefan's cell and had accepted Horst's voice as Stefan's, just as Horst had predicted he would. Now Dragovik thought that Stefan had succeeded in killing both him and Sebastian—and knew nothing of Horst's involvement.

Looking out the window of Horst's big, black Ford truck, Cairns noted that the weather was getting worse by the second. The freezing rain would soon turn to snow. Horst and Cairns had loaded Stefan's body onto the open truck and left Albert, still unconscious, tied up with the shackles that had held Sebastian. Horst had insisted on bringing Stefan's phone with them, assuring Cairns that Dragovik would call for a progress report. "There's no way that you could fake being Stefan," he'd said, but I can." Sure enough, the phone had rung right on cue, and the guy had pulled it off. Even after Cairns had explained to him just how insane Dragovik was—about the mad cow disease and everything else—he insisted on sticking with him.

"Joe, you need me. You can't do this by yourself. We're going to get this guy to my doctor friend, so just get over it. Besides," he said, his smile making him look almost cherubic, "I gotta tell you, Joe. It's entertaining working with you again. You bring out the Schwarzenegger in me."

Listening to Horst's impression of Arnold's famed, "I'll be back," cracked Cairns up.

"Okay, Horst, but don't blame me if we both end up with our nervous systems rotting away, foot by foot."

Now, staring at the driving sleet, Cairns thought about his desperate plea to King David during what he thought were his last seconds on earth. Miraculous was the only way to describe that fact that he was alive... but it had been an experienced cop who saved him. *So you work through us all, is that it? This man is here because you worked your magic on his mind, right?*

Dr. Franz Peterson strode out to where Horst and Cairns had been waiting in the foyer of the doctor's home. The tall, sixty-something surgeon was clad in blue scrubs. "In another day, or maybe just hours, this man would have been dead."

"Any idea when we can talk to him, Doctor?"

"In a few hours, as soon as the pain meds wear off a bit." He peered through half-glasses at Cairns. "You work for Fed-Pol? The Tigris Unit?" He was understandably surprised that another American would be working for the Swiss.

Nodding, Cairns replied, "It's kind of a long st—"

"Joe is the Special Forces Marine who saved our butts—and my life—in that screwed-up op in Berlin back in April, the one where we lost two good men."

Dr. Peterson trained a cool gray gaze on Cairns, then grinned broadly and extended his hand. "Well then, American Force Recon Marine, thank you for saving the life of one of the finest policemen in Gemany."

More than a little chagrined at the over-the-top welcome, Cairns took the proffered hand and pumped it. "Sir, I don't know how to thank you for helping Sebastian." He hesitated and glanced at Horst, wondering how much to tell the doctor about his injured comrade and Dragovik's demented plan. Horst nodded almost imperceptibly, but his meaning was clear: *You can trust this guy, He's one of us.*

After nearly a minute of reflection, which is a long time when standing in front of a stranger, Cairns said, "Sebastian is a scientist, Dr. Peterson, a virologist. He has been working at Gruppe Pharmaceuticals as an undercover agent for FedPol. He uncovered Viktor Dragovik's plan to unleash a modified version of prion disease—mad cow—on the world, which would kill off most of the population.

The doctor didn't say a word, so Cairns continued.

"Someone, probably the head of Dragovik's security team, must have learned that Sebastian was working with FedPol and planned to kill him. But first, Dragovik needed Sebastian to tell him how to make the prion infectious—to weaponize it—by embedding the thing in a virus."

The doctor's gray gaze was no longer calm, but horror-stricken. "Horst, was Stefan aware of what Dragovik was planning?"

This guy is really tied in with the Intelligence Agency. I wonder if he works for them. He asked about Stefan in the past tense, does he know the guy is dead? I don't recall Horst telling him so...

"Dr. Peterson," Horst replied, "Stefan had to have known what Dragovik was planning. He was trying to force Joe to kill Sebastian when I stopped him."

The surgeon nodded. "Stefan was high?" Before waiting for the obvious answer, he turned to Cairns and said, "Joe, you should know that I'm also a major in the German Intelligence Service. I have worked with Evan Pierre and Dimitri Volkov frequently."

Aha! For the first time in days, it seemed, Cairns smiled. "That is excellent news because I'm sure they'd like to know that Sebastian is alive and recovering. Could we call them and let them know? Everything I own is in the SUV we left back at that bunker."

Well David, I apologize. You are apparently in control and are having a great time pulling all the strings. Next time, though, maybe you could think about not cutting it quite so close?

CHAPTER TWENTY-SIX

Pismo Beach, California

"Yo, Rich! Merry Christmas!"

From the minute I met you, Hank Reardon, I liked and trusted you. You are the quintessential everyman who just happens to be a billionaire. Rich was thinking about the anguish Reardon had suffered when he'd had every reason to believe that his daughter was dead. And his chief tech as well. For a while, a short while Rich had thought the stress would kill Reardon. Hearing that vibrant, joyful greeting was a wonderful Christmas present.

Without waiting for a reply, Reardon continued, "I was just getting ready to give you a call. They must have called you, too."

How many cups of coffee have you had Hank? It's only six am your time! But then Rich remembered that Hank was usually up and working by four. Smiling at the phone, he said, "Who? Who must have called?"

"Dimitri and Evan Pierre! They're on their way to Kronberg to debrief Sebastian and Joe Cairns. Joe not only found Sebastian, but got him out alive! How's that for a Christmas present, my friend?"

Thank you, thank you, thank you. Knees suddenly weak, Rich sunk to the bed he'd been standing beside.

Emerging from the bathroom where she'd been getting ready for bed, Lindsey looked worried. *Are you okay?* she mouthed.

Raising his thumb at her, Rich said, "Hank, I'm going to put you on the speaker phone. I want Linds to hear what you just said."

Both Lindsey and Rich smiled ear to ear as Reardon repeated what he had just told Rich. Joe had done the impossible: He'd found and extricated Sebastian.

"Hank, do we know how he altered the prion? Has Sebastian been able to explain what Dragovik was doing—or anything about his plans to weaponize it?"

"Not yet, Lindsey. I've told you everything we know so far. When Dimitri called me, he and Pierre were in the air on their way to Germany. Apparently, Joe hooked up with someone he'd worked with before, a German Federal Intelligence Officer by the name of Horst Mueller, and—oh, hold on. Rich and Lindsey, can you wait a sec?"

The two could hear muffled conversation in the background, then Reardon came back on the line.

"Stella has Dimitri holding on the other line. Let me call you back."

After hanging up, Rich took Lindsey's hand and led her out to the deck. He gently pushed her down onto an overstuffed lounger, and said, "Sit. I'll be back out here before Hank calls again."

"But we were going to go to bed, and maybe get another eight hours of sleep like last night!" Although mild, it was a protest.

"Linds, do you really think you could go to sleep now? If so, go for it, and I'll tell you what Hank has to say in the morning. But I'm going to get something to drink."

"Yeah, you're right. I guess sleep is just a pipe dream at this point."

As promised, Rich returned in under than ten minutes with a tray containing the rest of the cab from dinner, an assortment of cheeses, and some chunks of sourdough bread. As he was filling their wine glasses, the phone chirped.

"Lindsey and Rich, we have everybody on speaker from Dr. Peterson's clinic in Kronberg. Joe, Horst Mueller, Dimitri, Evan, Sebastian and Dr. Franz Peterson—he's a surgeon and major in the Federal Intelligence Service of Germany."

Lindsey motioned to Rich to talk since her mouth was full of bread and cheese.

"Joe! Man am I glad to know you're still with us!" Rich's enthusiasm was infectious. He heard several male voices agree in German and English.

"Thanks, Rich, appreciate it."

With all this happening, there's no way Reardon will remember that I called him. May as well jump into Morgan's strange nightmares now.

"Hank, this is going to sound off the subject, but I assure you, it isn't—so bear with me. I called you earlier with information which could be relevant to Dragovik's plan. Now, can I ask each of you if you know anything about people dying at Gonghe Prison in Qinghai, China. Maybe from some variation of Creutzfeld-Jakob disease?"

"How could you know about Gonghe? There's no way that Dragovik let his plan be known to anyone." The voice was faint but American—it had to be Sebastian.

"Sebastian? Good God, man, I'm glad you made it out of Dragovik's clutches!" Rich waited for a beat to see if anyone else would comment. He heard someone speaking German—possibly the surgeon—in an attempt to make the injured scientist more comfortable.

When he finished, Sebastian continued, his voice slighly stronger. "You have no idea. I'm still trying to get my mind around the fact that I'm alive. I hurt like hell everywhere, but evidently, nothing major is lacerated or broken. Dr. Peterson tells me I'm a lucky man, which is an understatement if I've ever heard one." His attempt at a laugh came out like whoosh of exhaled air and a groan. Then he said, "Can you hold a minute while I get another dose of morphine? These damn broken ribs are playing the devil with my breathing."

Lindsey raised an eyebrow. Although she'd never experienced it, she knew the pain from this kind of injury could be incapacitating.

"Rich, Dimitri here. I'm going to go ahead and help Sebastian out, because I think he'll be out cold in just a few minutes."

Lindsey muttered *Good!* under her breath.

"Gonghe Prison, Quinghai, China. Tell us."

"A gifted young girl we know—a friend of our daughter's named Morgan—has been having vivid nightmares about men screaming for help in Mandarin Chinese for over two months. Recently the dream has intensified in frequency and more details have emerged. Her last dream included masses of writhing, dying bodies. Rather than the expected screams, she heard maniacal laughter. Which was, of course, even more horrifying than the screaming. The girl also saw a man, maybe a soldier, spreading a powder into the food fed to the prisoners. Is it possible that this powder contained Creutzfeld-Jacob disease?"

CHAPTER TWENTY-SEVEN

Xining, China

Lieutenant Wang Jianjun signed out for the last time. His twelve-hour tour of duty at Gonghe Prison was over, and he had become a wealthy man. The twenty-eight-year-old soldier took the train back to Xining, then rode the bicycle he'd left at the train station back to his apartment, just as he did each week in preparation for his one day off. Dodging carts, cars, and other cyclists, the soon-to-be ex-soldier showed no emotion as he traveled through the smog. No one watching him would think this day any different from hundreds of other dreary days. The air quality in Xining was even worse than that of Beijing, and many citizens wore masks when working or walking outside. Jianjun could not be bothered.

As the youngest of three, in a country where almost no families had three children, Jianjun had learned to live as if he were invisible. His mother had died in childbirth, and his miner father had claimed that Jianjun was an orphan to keep the boy. China's one child per family rule had been relaxed in the last few years, but in remote sections of China, the "family planning policy" was still enforced. The Chens had received an exemption for their second boy by promising he would begin work in the mines at the age of twelve, as his father had. Another exception was impossible. But a small bribe to a local official provided the false documents Jianjun's father had needed to keep him. All of Jianjun's paperwork listed his surname as *Wang* rather than *Chen*, like his two brothers and father.

Each year on his birthday, Jianjun received a beating from his father with a bamboo cane—one lash for each year of his life. *I paid good money for you, boy! You show me no gratitude for my sacrifice.* That is, until his sixteenth birthday.

On that day, when his father returned home from the mine, Jianjun was waiting behind the door, holding a basball bat. His father never knew what hit him. From then on, there were no more beatings, and the People's Liberation Amy was eager to believe him when he said he was twenty-one.

Maintaining his neutral expression, Jianjun nodded at the elderly woman who lived in the apartment below his. Once he'd closed his door behind him, he removed the uniform he had worn for over ten years and carefully opened the envelope. Only then did he reveal any emotion. His eyes widened, but he remained quiet.

Fifty-thousand dollars.

Quickly crossing the small room, he lifted his mattress and removed another envelope. This one was very thick. It contained his savings from twelve years of working for the PLA: 34,085 yuan. Exactly 50,000 dollars. *That's what ten years of scrimping will get you.*

Jianjun was a soldier. He followed orders and never entertained thoughts of right or wrong, fairness or injustice. These were not concepts that made sense to him—which is exactly why his name had been brought to the attention of General Tan Zheng. As his final responsibility, Jianjun had spent one full hour mixing up the powder as he was instructed and adding it to the single meal served to the Gonghe prisoners each day. They were probably eating it right now.

The voice on the USB had explained his mission carefully. It had cautioned him not to inhale the dust or eat the food once he had mixed the powder into it. When he'd asked what the powder was, he was told that it was the result of a significant scientific breakthrough—the first-ever oral contraceptive effective for both men and women. It had not yet been tested on humans, and that is why it was being given to the prisoners first—to determine any potential side-effects.

Although he knew he was not supposed to do so—and that it could be dangerous—Jianjun had left a little of the powder in the box, then carefully closed the lid and slipped it into the upper pocket of his uniform shirt, intending to bring it with him on the train. A powerful contraceptive might come in handy in his new life.

When he got home, he took off the shirt, folded it regulation style, and left it in the center of the bed, forgetting the box in his breast pocket.

Very carefully, Jianjun arranged his few belongings in the backpack that would serve as his only luggage. He shoved his fortune to the bottom, under the clothes.

Now dressed in black jeans and a black T shirt, Jianjun walked back down the stairs and nodded once again to the elderly woman. He cycled the five miles to the train station to catch the Quinhai-Tibet train to Lhasa and on to Katmandu. He planned to be in India in two days time.

He would have made it—*if* he had obeyed orders and not eaten the poisoned food. But while in the prison kitchen, Jianjun had realized this would be the last free meal he could get from the prison kitchen. As it turned out, it would be his last meal of any kind. Jianjun would be dead before the train reached the county of Gonghe, in Qinghai Province.

CHAPTER TWENTY-EIGHT

Konigston am Taunus, Germany

Viktor Dragovik wandered through the cold, depressing rooms of the villa that had been the summer refuge for Diedrich Braun. The old man had died four days earlier and had left everything to Viktor—an estate valued at twenty-two billion dollars. Braun's lawyer had executed the will the day before, even though it was Christmas Eve, hoping, no doubt, to be kept on to manage the estate.

The restored castle was in Konigstein um Taunus, known as the "Spa City" from the days before World War II, when it had been a charming summer haven for Jewish artists and musicians.

Viktor had no interest in taking part in the Christmas festivities of the small town. He knew no one and planned to guard his anonymity, just as Braun had done for twenty-one years. From the very first, the billionaire had schooled his young protégé in the art of detachment and indifference to people and their tedious concerns.

As he walked through the villa, Viktor thought of the first time he had seen it. The day he had first met Diedrich Braun. He was fourteen. Feral. Survival had always been a ferocious battle. One late October morning, he had been so desperately hungry that he'd followed an obese middle-aged woman into a fragrant Berlin coffee shop, hoping for a chance to snatch something to eat.

The boy strolled into the warm shop, redolent with the scents of coffee, sugar, and many other irresistible things. Sticking his hands in both pockets, Viktor walked by the woman, looking everywhere but at her. Feigning nonchalance, he smiled and nodded at a young mother with an infant in a stroller completing a purchase, then at two men in line for coffee. Out of the corner of his eye, he saw the heavy-set woman seated at a small table for one, devouring a chocolate éclair, one of the three succulent pastries sitting in front of her. When she turned her head to smile and say something to the lady with the baby, Viktor saw his opportunity. In less than five seconds, he'd grabbed a chocolate croissant and sprinted out the door, down the street, and into the alley on the next block.

Just as he was about to take a giant bite of his treasure, a tall, gray-haired man in a long black wool coat, black trousers, and a white silk scarf appeared in front of him.

That man was in the shop, second in line for coffee. He saw me steal the pastry!

Dropping his prize on the filthy ground, Viktor darted past the man and almost made it—but not quite. A long, powerful arm ending in a black leather glove reached out and grabbed Viktor by his bony shoulder. Viktor kicked, spat, and flailed uselessly. Easily pinning both of his arms behind his back, the man smiled.

I know what he wants... what they all want...

The boy hung his head. All hunger and fear drained away. He had been here before. As he reached for the zipper on the man's black wool trousers, he heard a shocked "Nein!"

This gave Viktor the second he needed to run—but after

a few steps, he stopped.

If he didn't want that, what DID he want?

The man—Diedrich Braun—approached the boy again, but this time he did not strong-arm him. He merely stood behind him and waited for the irresistible combination of curiosity and hunger to compel the starving kid to turn around.

When Viktor did turn to face the tall silver-haired man, Diedrich smiled and said calmly,

"You have nothing to fear from me, son." Looking down at the croissant on the ground between them, Diedrich added, "The lady had far too much on her plate. You probably saved her from another insulin shot when she gets back home. I admire your finesse."

The kid had moved so fast that no one had noticed the theft until the woman turned back to her plate and yelped. Diedrich had handed ten Euros to the alarmed store owner, saying, "This should take care of things, Ernst. I'll go find the boy and make sure he won't bother your customers again.

Viktor just stared. He spoke rudimentary German, enough to get by on the streets, but he had no idea what this man was saying.

Diedrich studied the vacant look on the boy's face, momentarily puzzled. This kid was smart, perhaps brighter than most. *Must be a refugee from Serbia, Muslim maybe. A survivor. Against all the evil thrown at him, he's figured out how to stay alive.*

Although skeletal now, the teen had almost perfect features. Given a chance, he would become a handsome man. And he was apparently able to control his hunger and fear, even while being scrutinized by an obviously powerful man. Impressive. *This boy will be my son. He is everything Eric will never be.*

Putting aside his typical High Franconian German, used

to convey his lofty social status, he repeated what he'd said to the boy, this time in standard German.

The boy understood. The corners of his full mouth cautiously tipped up, a faint echo of boyhood smiles from long ago. "My name is Hasan Milak."

"Hasan Milak, your name is now Viktor. Viktor Dragovik, the determined conqueror."

Remembering Diedrich's patience, kindness, and generosity on that day, Viktor smiled. Had anyone been watching, they would have been struck by his deep brown, almost black eyes. But his smile might have confused them, contrasting as it did with the coldness in those eyes, which seemed bottomless, emitting no light. They would have been afraid.

Standing outside the house, Viktor stood watching the snow collect on the four turrets. It would snow all night, apparent by the accelerating pace of the flakes and whipping of the wind.

He thought about the events of the previous week. The guy who had answered Stefan's phone was not Stefan. Viktor did not know who he was, just that he was a German and he was very good. But not good enough.

The first time Viktor had called Stefan's cell phone, something had felt off, but he had filed the suspicion away to deal with later. There was too much to deal with in China. General Zheng had upped the ante. Rather than a payment of two million, he had raised it to three. Claiming that he was risking his entire reputation in the PLA, he was compelled to request another million. After all, the General claimed, Gonghe was one of China's model prisons. Viktor had been impressed by the faked sincerity on the General's face as the two men regarded each other across cyberspace. The General willed himself to stare back at the scientist. Although a weak man and a coward, he had no desire to inflict harm on anyone, even enemies of the state. Choosing his words very carefully, he said, "Your medication may have consequences, Dr. Dragovik. Consequences different than the intended sterilization of our prisoners." Something told him to stop there.

Waiting calmly for the question that never came, Viktor thought cynically, *Model prison? General, the whole world knows about your country's irrational desire to eradicate Falun Gong. You've made a career out of imprisoning your citizens because of their adherence to an innocuous spiritual and meditative regime. Your "re-education camps" are really brainwashing centers.*

Viktor said none of this aloud, of course. He merely nodded and said, "Yes, I understand. The additional money will be wired to your account as soon as we work out the final details." Studying his fleshy countenance and the chubby fingers on the General's crossed and manicured hands, Viktor merely asked, "Is there anything else, General?" He pretended not to notice the sudden sheen of perspiration on the forehead of the Chinese official, or the telltale rapid blinks of his small dark eyes.

"No, there is nothing else, Dr. Dragovik."

Regardless of country, these people are all the same: greedy, pompous, and overfed—if not with food then with praise. They care for nothing and no one but themselves and their bottomless appetites. How deserving they are of extermination.

Viktor had just hung up from his second conversation with the man posing as Stefan. What he'd suspected before, he now knew for sure. The man had tried too hard... and said too much.

"With this snow, you and Albert are surely planning to stay in Kronberg throughout the day," Viktor had said, not asking but assuming. He had purposely mentioned Albert in passing, not caring if he ever saw the man again. Albert was not a smart man—not even average. Plus, his inability to control himself was creating a problem for Viktor. Viktor had asked Stefan to fire him as soon as he could be replaced.

The whole situation was somewhat ironic. Viktor had almost believed he was speaking with the real Stefan—he'd convinced himself that he was just paranoid—until "Stefan" had explained that Albert was down with the flu and too sick to travel. Stefan would never have told him anything like that. He'd have known better.

Somehow, Cairns had survived. With the help of this mysterious German ally, whoever he was, the two men had managed to kill Stefan and Albert and had probably freed Sebastian.

How much damage could they do to the plan?

A lot. Sebastian knew about the proposed test of the altered prion at Gonghe Prison. He knew about the money paid to the Chinese Major General. The idea had been his, after all.

"If you needed to test a new drug that may have severe side effects, including death, where would you do it?"

Dr. Sebastian Cameron was smart. Within three days, he had identified the precise process for changing the incubation period of the prion from years to days. Stefan believed his story about converting to radical Islam and wanting to destroy western civilization. Viktor had been cautiously optimistic about his sudden appearance during the summer. He trusted Stefan's judgement of the American's motives and hired him. Sebastian's suggestion to test the drug at Gonghe prison had been pure genius, as had his prediction that finding an official to bribe would be simple. It had been.

Viktor murmured to himself, "Always have a backup plan. Regardless of how certain you are of success; no strategy is immune to betrayal or simple error." The words had been Diedrich's, and Viktor had committed them to memory. Sixteen years under his tutelage; the study of those crazy Nazis; the pretense that he agreed with their magical thinking. But not all of these long-dead men were silly dreamers. One was a prophet.

Eager to school his protégé in the subtleties of the Thule Society and Dietrich Eckart, Diedrich had provided access to his extensive library, where Viktor had been introduced to the Mastermind and the broad group of German scientists who created modern chemical warfare. Viktor had not faked his fascination with Fritz Haber. Quite the contrary, the teen had found in him a mind with which he could identify. Haber's ability to separate his work from all moral codes appealed to this child of bloodshed and violence. To Viktor, Haber was the quintessence of the scientist. He agreed with Haber that chemical warfare was a higher form of killing—a far more humane way to wage war than what he had witnessed as a child. By the age of sixteen, the nearly illiterate Serbian had been transformed into a pampered German scion. Or so it seemed.

After he'd devoured Haber, Viktor had moved on to the research of Gerhard Schrader, the German scientist who created the deadly neurotoxins known as tabun and sarin during the late thirties. Diedrich had proudly encouraged young Viktor's fascination with chemical warfare by paying for the boy's education all the way through to a doctorate.

After wandering about the rapidly darkening snowscape, Viktor allowed himself a rare indulgence and permitted a sense of pleasure to warm him. Although the ground was frozen, he could feel the power surging up from the earth. He had conceived this dream just about twelve years earlier, and now it was becoming a reality. The process had begun... there was no turning back.

Walking back into his new home, Viktor decided he would start a fire and sample some of Braun's splendid supply of single malts. And maybe play some Wagner. Surely, Diedrich would approve.

CHAPTER TWENTY-NINE

Pismo Beach, California

After Reardon, Lindsey, and Rich had talked with their FedPol friends for about forty-five minutes, Lindsey suggested switching to WebCor, since it was clear that they would be at it for another couple of hours. That way, they could share documents visually, if necessary.

Dr. Peterson's computer sat on a table in front of the bed where Sebastian lay sleeping. Cairns, Horst Mueller, and Dr. Peterson were seated around the table. The subject under discussion was what might be happening at Gonghe Prison and how they could quietly get to Xining. How could they sneak into Chinese air space without creating an international incident, getting shot down, or—worse—causing worldwide panic?

The men were speaking quietly in an attempt to let Sebastian sleep, when Lindsey interrupted the conversation by shouting, "Dr. Peterson! Check Sebastian! I think he's flailing!"

Lindsey carefully watched the injured agent breathe, seeing that a condition known as "flail chest"—in which the right and left sides of the chest move in opposite directions— was evident. His lips were dusky and his nostrils flaring, denoting cyanosis.

Startled, the German surgeon erupted from his chair and stood over his patient, looking puzzled. "Sorry, Dr. McCall, I…" Ashamed that he hadn't caught the condition himself, Peterson looked away from the camera.

Lindsey had been concerned about the status of the scientist-spy ever since she'd heard him talk. He had been beaten severely and had suffered several broken ribs. Although Sebastian needed the intravenous morphine Franz had given him, Lindsey was worried about the respiratory depression caused by the opiate. She also feared the possibility of a tension pneumothorax—punctured lung—from one or several of the broken ribs.

While Peterson was experienced in general surgery, he'd clearly missed the subtle signs that Lindsey, trained in both cardiology and emergency medicine, readily picked up.

"He has a tension pneumo, Franz. Get a chest tube now! Hurry!"

The surgeon glanced at Sebastian, then raced out of the room. Within seconds, although it seemed much longer to Lindsey, he returned and quickly inserted the chest tube. The loud sound of air escaping from Sebastian's chest could be heard over the computer's microphone.

Awake and now breathing normally, albeit painfully, Sebastian squinted at the computer, but could not see the image. He gave up and peered at Peterson. "Did I hear someone ordering you around, Franz, a woman? Or was it merely an auditory hallucination?" Looking at Cairns, he began to laugh, grimaced from the pain, and took a shallow breath before speaking, "Was I as close to dying as I felt? For the second time?" Sebastian's attempt at light-hearted banter left him winded. He closed his eyes.

The surgeon took a deep breath and put a hand on the bed

to steady himself. "Yes, to both questions, Sebastian. Meet Dr. Lindsey McCall, from America. She just saved your life."

The others in the room had watched the life-and-death battle in shocked silence. The first to speak was Horst Mueller. "Dr. Peterson?"

"Yes, Horst?"

"How about we take a break and have a few beers? Or if you want your scotch, I remember where you keep it."

"Hank, why don't you call Sam Wong?"

"You mean the CEO of that Chinese version of Amazon? *That* Sam Wong?"

Rich chuckled at the sight of Dimitri's dilated blue-eyed gaze and said, "Yep, that's the one."

The suggestion was so simple and brilliant it was comical. Rich had offered a solution to Joe and Dimitri's problem of how to get into China and get a look at Gonghe Prison. Joe's astonishing rescue of Sebastian had forged a bond between the Swiss cop and former assassin. Truthfully, Rich was pretty impressed by what Cairns had pulled off, and by his unlikely partner, Horst, who looked like nothing more than a big, dumb muscleman was apparently anything but.

Reardon was quiet. Thinking. Wondering how to handle his reservations about the call to Sam, about the stipulation of complete disclosure for his cooperation. Nodding in agreement at Rich's suggestion, he finally said, "I'll do it. Happy to, and this may well be the only way to find out what's going on. But here's the thing. Sam Wong is among the smartest men I know. He's going to want the *entire story* from the beginning." Looking directly at Dimitri and Evan Pierre, he continued, "Sam sleeps maybe two hours a night, and I know for a fact that Christmas is meaningless to him. So here is what I suggest—patch him into this WebCor conference call. I suspect we'll find he'll be eager to help. In fact, I'm pretty sure he'll consider it his duty."

The expressions on the faces of the Swiss cops were priceless. Understandably, they were reluctant to add additional people to their circle, knowing the consequences if the news were to leak. But what choice did they have?

Reardon waited for a response.

Finally, Evan spoke up. "Okay, Hank. Let's patch him in."

CHAPTER THIRTY

Lausanne, Switzerland

Andrews, Sacks, and Levine, was the only American pharmaceutical company that had been able to establish a presence in China and make money while doing so. There were two reasons for that. Digipro, which had been created by Lindsey; and Sam Wong's willingness to coach Hank on avoiding the many pitfalls of doing business in China.

Billionaire Sam Wong represented the iconic American success story—born poor, self-taught, driven, and ultimately unstoppable. What set him apart was that he wasn't American at all; he was Chinese. His rise would have been impressive had it occurred anywhere in the world. That he had become the richest man in Communist, anti-capitalist China in less than twenty years was nothing short of miraculous. His early life was marked by failure at just about everything he tried, but his core values of persistence, fortitude, risk-taking, and personal responsibility never wavered.

Hank Reardon and Sam Wong had met at a Bilderberg meeting in 2010. Both men had accepted the invitation to the controversial conference with reservation. Sam was convinced that as a successful Chinese businessman among the economic heavyweights of Europe and America, he was a bit like a circus sideshow. Hank had initially refused the invitation because he feared bad publicity from the online talk shows, which had grown fond of concocting conspiracy theories about the Bilderberg Groups. Although he hated to admit it, he thought they might be right about a few of their claims.

"Well, if it isn't the social media you fear, why won't you attend, Mr. Reardon?"

Because of your snarky British attitude!

The current chairman of the steering committee for the Bilderberg Group was a senior member of the British Parliament, a Life Peer in the House of Lords. Whatever that meant. Hank realized that the man's accent and haughtiness had been bred into him from birth. He was Earl of something or other, and it showed. Hank's negative response to the man arose from his typically American allergic reaction to snobbery.

"If I told you that Sam Wong is attending the meeting because he hopes to meet you, Mr. Reardon, would you be willing to participate?"

"Hey everyone, it is my distinct privilege to introduce Sam Wong." After presenting the group still in Kronberg, then Lindsey and Rich in Pismo Beach, Reardon handed over the lead to the Chinese entrepreneur. Wong smiled broadly and engagingly into his screen. "I am so sorry for the long delay. I know our time is limited. But sometimes things move more slowly in my country than in all of yours."

Wong looked nothing like a mega business man. His open-necked chambray shirt and jeans looked as if they had come from Walmart—which made sense, considering one of his many enterprises was the Chinese version of Walmart. With his unusually high forehead, close-set eyes, and head that seemed a bit large for his body, he looked almost deformed.

That is until he smiled and opened his mouth to speak. His spirited delivery had a way of seducing listeners even across cyberspace. When Sam Wong smiled, everyone else did as well. Even the resident stoics. Evan and Cairns.

A week had passed since the group had last spoken. Dimitri and his boss, Evan Pierre, were back in their office in Zurich, while Cairns, Mueller, and Sebastian remained in Kronberg, at the home of Dr. Peterson.

"Mr. Wong, have you been able to confirm the outbreak of disease at Gonghe Prison?" Dimitri's usually brilliant blue eyes looked dull, and there were dark smudges underneath, revealing sleepless nights.

Sam's smile tightened and his right index finger extended upward as he nodded. "Yes, Mr. Vlasov. All but 32 of the 2,500 inmates are dead, as well as 200 PLA soldiers."

"Sir," Sebastian chimed in, "have your people been able to determine the specific cause of the deaths? Is it definitely prion disease? Has it infected anyone outside the prison?"

Just a week after his brush with death, Sebastian looked like an entirely different person. His facial bruising was now faint and looked more like shadowing on the computer screen. He looked hyper alert, restless. If the group had all been together in one room, he would have paced and talked at the same time. As it was, he was tethered to the screen.

"No, Dr. Cameron. They have not. There is extensive disagreement among the few medical personnel who have been allowed in Xining. And the citizens of the city are under quarantine until more is known. Evidently, a few insist it is mad cow disease but several claim this to be a prion not seen before."

There were nine known types of prion disease, and six of them were potentially infectious. But, because of the high mortality rate in this outbreak—with over ninety-seven percent of the exposed population dead in under twelve hours—the Chinese believed it to be a prion they'd not seen before. They were right.

He knows how close he came to death, thought Lindsey as she watched Sebastian. *The first time, he was saved from Dragovik's goon by Joe. Then the tension pneumo.* She'd done some research on him and found that he was boarded in Infectious Disease with a doctorate in Epidemiology. He'd done a stint at the CDC as an emergency response doc, which had taken him to many of the hot spots in Africa. Studying him, Lindsey decided that Sebastian resembled an African American Ichabod Crane. He was not lean but scrawny, and his Adam's apple stuck out at a forty-five-degree angle from his throat. His nerdiness was accentuated by the frameless glasses he wore. *He must be around my age—late thirties, early forties. He's certainly driven, almost as if he believes his time is limited. Then again, based on what we're dealing with here, that is true for all of us.*

Lindsey had a gift for pushing that kind of thought out of her head, pretending that life was normal. The night before, Sunday, she'd made dinner for Rich, LJ, and Morgan, and they'd chatted and laughed like it was just another family night. As she continued to watch Sebastian, she thought, *He cannot get away from what he knows. Of all of us here, he's the only one who has looked into the face of the beast.*

"Sir?" Cairns cut in. "Would it be possible for our team to get in there? To obtain specimens from your doctors so that we could help identify what we are dealing with and start working on an antidote before we have another two thousand victims?"

Leave it to Joe Cairns to ask the questions no one else dared to, thought Hank, who practically held his breath during what felt like a long silence that followed.

Wong had been prepared for it, so there was no surprise in his face. "Yes, we'll get you in, but send no more than six people—and I need their names now, because the window of time I have been promised to get them in safely is just seventy-two hours. Which of you will go?"

For the first time, Evan Pierre, Commander of the Tigris Team, spoke. "Sebastian, this is your op. You've earned it. Pick your team."

The scientist spy smiled in relief. "Thank you, Evan. Dimitri, Joe Cairns, Horst Mueller, Dr. McCall and Rich Jansen—you guys are my picks. Are you all willing to go?"

Lindsey was so absorbed in her thoughts, she did not hear her name.

"Linds?" Rich prodded, touching her arm. When she remained silent, he answered for both of them. "We're in. Thank you, Sebastian." There was no hesitation in his voice or thoughts. For Rich and for his wife, he knew, it was far better to be at the center of this thing and working to solve it, than to be "safe" at home.

One by one, they all assented to the mission, then agreed on a time and place to work out the details. "Sam," said Reardon. "I'd be happy for the team to take my private Lear out of Lausanne if that would be okay on the other end. Sorry Rich and Lindsey, this means that you two need to get on a plane tonight."

"That'll work," Wong said. "My contact in the PLA has assured me that as long as the six of you are in and out of China within the next seventy-two hours, your identity as World Health Organization personnel will be preserved. I will get all the paperwork you need to Hank's office by tomorrow morning." He blinked a few times. "I have known the General for over twenty years. His fondness for cash cannot be overestimated."

CHAPTER THIRTY-ONE

Pismo Beach, California

"You and Rich are flying to China? Now?" LJ's voice was pitched so high it was cracking.   Dismay, fear, and shock were written all over her face. "You are going to that prison where Morgan saw all those dead and dying people, aren't you?" Ignoring the two fat tears slowly trailing down the sides of her face, she pleaded, "At least talk to Mom before you do this. Please!"

Before Lindsey could say no, LJ had dialed Julie Grayson's number and handed over her cell to Lindsey.

"Honey, are you there? What's wrong?" It was close to one in the morning and Julie had back-to-back classes starting at eight. But she'd been wide awake when her phone rang, and was almost relieved at the interruption of her chaotic thoughts. She glanced over at Ted, who was still sleeping soundly. *An earthquake wouldn't wake that guy.*

"Julie, I'm so sorry to bother you at this time of night." *Would it sound childish to tell Julie that LJ insisted she call?* Instead, she said, "LJ wanted me to call and let you know that Rich and I are headed to China, to the prison in Morgan's dream." Lindsey paused and gulped, astounded at what she was saying. *We're heading to a remote prison in 'Middle of Nowhere, China,' where we hope to stop a madman from weaponizing mad cow disease.*

Julie whispered, "Lindsey, this call is such a relief, you have *no* idea. You all have been on my mind for hours." As she spoke, she slipped out of bed and crept into the long hall of the second floor, closing the bedroom door behind her. "I asked LJ to let me know if you and Rich were going to jump into the middle of this evil scheme. Of course, I'm not surprised that's the case, Linds. I understand if you feel you have no choice. And to be honest, I'm grateful you are going! I know you can do some good out there, so long as—" Julie interrupted herself to ask, "Are you… leaving soon?"

"Tonight. In less than an hour, in fact. Julie, I really need to get off this phone and—

"Don't say no to what I'm going to ask you to do. Not until you hear me out. Promise me."

Abruptly Lindsey's best friend had undergone a transformation. Her tone commanded obeisance.

Puzzled now and curious, Lindsey replied cautiously. "Okay Julie, I'm listening."

"Good. I think Morgan should go with you. She knows more than you or anyone else about what is happening. She can help you. I am sure of it."

Lindsey listened openmouthed while Julie expressed her conviction that Morgan was being used in a most mysterious way—used to stop these maniacs from accomplishing their goals. *Used by whom?* the scientist wondered, but there was no getting into that for the moment. Time was of the essence, and there was no interrupting Julie in any case, now that she'd begun to talk.

"I know it sounds crazy, but I honestly believe that Morgan's presence on this… mission—or whatever you want to call it—it might mean the difference between success and failure. And we all know that failure isn't an option here. One last thing Lindsey, whatever you do, don't question Morgan about how she knows what she knows, or ask for more detail than she gives you. You *must* understand she is telling you everything she can. If you push for more, you'll confuse and scare her, and possibly stem the flow of information she's receiving from… wherever it comes from. And for God's sake, don't let anyone else interrogate her!"

After she'd reassured Julie that she'd follow her instructions to the letter, she clicked off and handed LJ's phone back to her. Lindsey searched her daughter's earnest, wet face, wiped the tears from her cheeks, and kissed her forehead. "I love you, LJ. Thank you for coming here to live with us." Then she hugged her hard. As she released the girl, she said, "Moments like these show me just how little I understand about myself, this world, and the people I love most. The physicists remind us that we are capable of seeing less than ten percent of reality. The rest is dark matter and dark energy. Thank you, LJ, for calling the wisest woman on this planet. Not listening to your mother is a mistake I will never make again."

Lindsey was well aware that Morgan had been listening at the door. "Morgan, why don't you, Max, and Gus come on in," she said evenly.

At the sound of their names, Morgan and the dogs appeared in the doorway. If it's possible for a dog to frown, that's exactly what Max was doing. He'd seen the suitcase on the bed and knew what it meant. Gus, on the other hand, was oblivious, wagging his tail furiously. With each rightward swipe, the inverted question mark end of it brushed Max's eyes, making him blink.

Staring at the threesome, she sat down on the bed beside the suitcase. In a flash, Gus tore across the room, jumped onto the bed next to her, and splayed himself out for a belly rub. Max followed, but far more sedately, and sat down in front of Lindsey. He lifted his right paw and plopped it in her lap.

Dogs... it's impossible to stay in a bad mood around them. How do people make it through their days without these fantastic creatures?

Morgan interrupted her reverie. "When do we leave for China?"

Let's not pretend we need to ease into the conversation, right Morgan?

Morgan stood next to LJ but about a foot closer to the bed where Lindsey sat. Her feet were almost touching Lindsey's bare toes.

Although Lindsey had read six books explaining autism spectrum disorder and understood that flat affect and little respect for personal boundaries were characteristic, she was occasonally unhinged by Morgan. Like now. Lindsey replied, "Within the hour, Morgan, but first, I need to speak with Rich about some things, can you give us some space please?"

Rich entered the room and stopped short at the sight of the crowd, tightening the towel wrapped around his waist. He had just showered, intending to throw some clothes on, stick a few more in the suitcase, and get to the plane. Taking in the body language of his wife and the girls, he asked lightly, "Hey ladies, what's going on?"

"Morgan, back up, I can't move."

The girl moved back but not a lot.

Puzzled, Rich waited, wondering what was happening, but said nothing more.

Now standing pratically toe to toe with Morgan, Lindsey noticed what Julie Grayson had the week before. The young woman had striking eyes with long, curly lashes. Hidden behind those ugly glasses and swags of hair was a genuinely lovely girl. *If we make it back alive and the population of the world is no longer in immediate danger of extermination, Morgan, LJ, and I are going to spend an entire day at that swanky spa in San Luis Obispo. Maybe we can drag Jodi along as well!*

But all she said was, "Morgan wants to go with us Rich, and… LJ and Julie think it would be a good idea." She smiled at Morgan, "Your fluency in the Mandarin language may be the secret weapon we need. Run and grab some clothes now! We need to be in SLO within the next twenty minutes."

At Hank Reardon's suggestion, they had leased a private jet and crew which would leave from San Luis Obispo and fly directly to Lausanne, thereby reducing their flight time from twelve to less than eight hours.

CHAPTER THIRTY-TWO

Lausanne, Switzerland

"Did you say you're going to Diedrich Braun's funeral in Berlin? You, Liisa, and Ariana? Seriously, Hank?"

Sebastian, Cairns, Horst, Dimitri, Rich, and Morgan had just filed into Reardon's Learjet 85. The fastest and longest-ranging plane in the Learjet fleet, the 85 would get the group into Xining in a little over ten hours. Lindsey lingered behind to talk with Hank.

"We are indeed," Hank said. "In fact, we're leaving within the hour. "I cannot *wait* to hear what Dr. Dragovik will have to say about the sudden death of his beloved mentor, Diedrich Braun, in his eulogy."

Shaking her head, Lindsey said, "Hank, they tried to kill you! They came damn close to killing Liisa and Ariana!"

"Actually, Lindsey, the 'they' who tried to kill us is on that plane... on your flight to one of the most remote places on earth. So maybe you shouldn't be schooling me about danger!"

The two friends stared at each other, each thinking of the years they had been friends. Lindsey had barely been out of her Cardiology fellowship when she had convinced Hank to fund her quixotic attempt to improve on the digitalis molecule. There had been a lot of strange twists and turns in that enterprise, but there had never been anything like the immensity of the task that lay before them.

"Lindsey! We have to get going!" Sebastian broke in, shouting over the din of the plane's engine. "Sam Wong promised us seventy-two hours and we're down to sixty."

Viktor Dragovik climbed the two steps to the altar, turned left, and walked over to stand behind the pulpit. He waited while the members of the orchestra and choir, who had just finished a stunning rendition of Mozart's Requiem in D-minor, settled themselves. He slowly raised his head and gazed out at the more than 1,200 people who had gathered to remember Diedrich Braun. As he began to speak, he was the very picture of quiet grief.

"Most, if not all of you know the story. Or at least parts of it. Were it not for Diedrich Braun, I would have undoubtedly died on the streets of this city. My family had been killed in the Bosnian Wars, and the family who tried to help me was also executed."

The Kaiser Wilhelm Church was filled to overflowing. One of the famous landmarks of West Berlin, the church had been severely damaged in an air raid in 1943. The architect in charge of the restoration had preserved the ruined west tower at the insistence of the locals, who now called it "the hollow tooth." The new part of the church was built to the west of the ruins and consisted of concrete, glass, and steel. The walls were a honeycomb filled with more than 20,000 stained-glass inlays in colors similar to those at Chartres Cathedral, blue with a sprinkling of emerald green, ruby red, and yellow.

Although it was cold, the sun lit up the stained-glass walls, creating an ethereal blue hue in the church and across some of the faces assembled. A fifty-foot metal figure of the risen Christ was suspended from the ceiling over the center of the altar, back lit in a way that it gave off a kind of glow from the head and torso.

The twenty-four members of the Diedrich Gruppe Board filled the first two rows of the church. Heddy Schmidt, the German Finance Minister, appeared captivated by the beauty of the altar, or perhaps by the man standing there in the quintessence of quiet remorse. With his olive skin, black hair, and those dark blue-black eyes, the new CEO of Diedrich Gruppe looked more like a film star than a businessman and scientist. His features were of mixed ethnicity and he appeared refined, elegant and aristocratic. Viktor Dragovik had become the impressively handsome man Braun had predicted he would be some fifteen years earlier.

Dragovik had begun his address in German, but interrupted himself after a just a few sentences to apologize in English to the "several Americans, although pharmaceutical competitors, who were kind enough to honor Diedrich Braun's life and legacy with their presence today." As he looked directly at Hank, Liisa, and Ariana, everyone in the crowded building turned curiously to regard the Americans.

It had been staged, Hank was sure of it. Dragovik had expected them and had given orders to the ushers to seat them directly behind the board members. But the delicacy with which it was orchestrated was uncanny. As he watched the young man's performance, Hank decided that, for someone like Dragovik, everything was calculated, and had been for most of his life. Otherwise, he would not have been able to pull off such a splendid facsimile of spontaneity.

Dressed in a Bruno Cucinelli form-fitting dark gray suit jacket with a lighter gray turtleneck underneath, Dragovik managed to look appropriately attired for the somber occasion, while carefully drawing attention to the perfection of his face and athletic build.

Hank was almost sorry they had come. Perhaps Lindsey had been correct in her concern. It wasn't that he feared for his life or those of the two women with him. No, Viktor Dragovik was far too self-aware to do anything but play the aggrieved stepson today. It was a role he seemed to have been born for.

This man was far more formidable than his mentor had been. Braun's imperiousness had been so overt, his German fanaticism so impassioned, that he seemed almost pathetic. Viktor Dragovik was something very different. His subtle use of emotional manipulation exceeded anything Hank had ever experienced. He found himself working hard to resist the intense personal magnetism of the man, continually reminding himself of what they were dealing with. *This guy murdered Diedrich Braun—his savior—with his own weaponized prion disease. His next move, if he gets away with it, will be to decimate the population of the earth.*

Even Reardon's daughter and his chief tech were riveted. Neither woman had taken her eyes off Dragovik.

It had been many years since Hank had believed in a God who cared about the trivialities of human existence, but the power of the man in front of this crowd was one of the most frightening things he had ever experienced. He recalled the definition of *evil* from grade school catechism class: *All that is not Good—the total absence of God.* Years ago, Hank had dismissed the Christian notions of good and evil as simplistic and primitive. But now, he felt the clear and present danger of pure evil and it made him shudder. For the first time in his life, Hank wondered about the spiritual wars in Revelation, the terrors of the apocalypse, and the existence of an anti-Christ. As he sat there, he did the only thing he could think of…he prayed.

Lord, have mercy on us.

Hank knew beyond the shadow of a doubt that Dragovik was aware of their plan to foil him. And that meant that the team arriving in China was in profound peril. He had not shed a tear when his beloved wife Peg had finally succumbed to ovarian cancer, but he felt the sting of tears now, along with a fear that approached despair at the fate of his seven colleagues on that plane.

Had Hank looked more closely, he would have seen that Ariana was not transfixed by the man on the pulpit. Rather, she was clutching the crucifix she always wore around her neck. Had he leaned a bit to the left, he would have heard and understood her whispered prayer. Ariana had recognized evil, too. She had looked it in the face before, and knew it was back in a far more potent form.

CHAPTER THIRTY-THREE

Somewhere above the Ukraine

Rich stretched, yawned, opened his eyes, and was instantly disoriented. Automatically reaching for Lindsey, he felt only empty space. Looking around, he remembered where he was.

The others had insisted that Rich and Lindsey sleep in the master bedroom of the luxury jet, while they made do with the plush leather seats that converted to surprisingly comfortable beds. Rich hadn't argued. He remembered refusing any refreshment from the steward, and just grabbing Lindsey and stumbling back to the remarkably large bedroom. He had closed his eyes and been asleep for... how long?

A long time, apparently. The plane dipped and Rich sensed they were getting ready to land. Sitting up on the edge of the bed, he looked at the spacious surroundings—the Berber carpet, dark mahogany headboard, and generous pile of pillows. *Jansen, you've come a hell of a long way since pounding the streets of Houston as a homicide detective.*

Rich went into the attached bathroom, where he brushed his teeth and ran wet hands through his hair. He pulled on a pair of trousers and a T shirt, then walked out into the main cabin.

A chorus of voices greeted him, but the only one he could distinguish was Lindsey's.

"Hi handsome, come join us." His wife was seated in a grouping of three white leather chairs surrounding an oak table, which was covered with legal pads and laptops. Next to her was Sebastian, and Morgan was beside him. Further down the aisle were Joe, Dimitri, and Horst. None of the six looked as if they had slept a wink during the nearly eleven-hour flight, but all looked alert, and excited. Even Morgan.

At the sound of a soft chime, the steward appeared from the front kitchen cabin. "We are making our final approach and will be landing in Xining within the next ten minutes. Please turn off all computers and cell phones." Smiling at Rich, the only one looking remotely refreshed, the heavyset forty-something man added, "At least one of this group is ready to tackle the trendy night club scene in Xining." He checked his watch, "Just eleven pm, local time, the bars should be rocking right about now."

"Why are you talking about night clubs in a Communist city best known for its prisons? You know what you are saying isn't true, right?" said Morgan, ever punctilious about the facts.

Rich opened his mouth to run interference, but happened to catch Lindsey's eye. The shake of her head was barely perceptible, but Rich knew she wanted Morgan to fend for herself. He remembered Morgan's aggressive insistence on coming along and figured, *so be it.* He walked silently over to Lindsey, Morgan, and Sebastian to grab a seat behind Joe and Dimitri.

Aware that he was on his own with the young girl, the steward approached Morgan, but stayed a respectful couple of feet away from her. "Yes, I know what I said was not true. I apologize if my joking offended you."

Morgan merely stared mutely at him.

"See…" the steward continued, "I have never been to China—not even to the cities the tourists see, like Peking. So, coming here to Xining makes me nervous. And when I'm nervous, I kid around." He held Morgan's stare for another moment then asked, "Maybe you have done that before?"

"No, I have not. I'm not good at jokes. But thank you for explaining what you were doing."

Lindsey smiled, first at Morgan and then at the steward, impressed with both of them.

The soft chime sounded once again, the 'fasten-seatbelt' sign illuminated, and the plane nosed toward the ground.

CHAPTER THIRTY-FOUR

West Berlin, Germany

"Will there be anything else, sir?"

Viktor had broken away from four of the most influential board members and was headed toward another group of prominent West Berliners when his assistant Gretchen snagged him.

She was quite lovely, Viktor thought. Diedrich would have called her a perfect Aryan. Tall, slender, and hair so blonde that it looked white—and she had unusual eyes, silvery blue, like a glacier. The gossips among the female employees at Diedrich Gruppe were divided into two camps—those who were convinced that Gretchen was a lesbian, and those who claimed she was in love with Dragovik. The latter group would have been certain of their position if they were watching her now, as she rested her long white fingers on the dark gray of Viktor's suit jacket.

"You must be very tired. This was a grueling afternoon," she said, with a gaze appearing almost tender.

Viktor placed his left hand over hers, clasped and held it for a moment, then gently dropped it. "Thank you for all your hard work, Gretchen. Your idea to hold the reception here in the Memorial Hall was brilliant. I don't know how many city officials you had to sweet-talk to gain permission to use it, but I genuinely appreciate your meticulous management of the details."

Well aware of the effect he had on the young woman, he smiled and extended his arm in a sweeping motion. "My dear, this has been a most sophisticated and tasteful reception. Diedrich would have loved it."

The company Gretchen had hired to cater the affair had arrived during the memorial service. They had set up a small open bar near the entrance and close to fifty small tables were distributed discreetly throughout the space, where guests could gather or leave their unfinished drinks and canapes.

More than seventy-five men and women dressed in black trousers and white silk shirts glided effortlessly through the crowd of close to 1,200 guests, offering fresh glasses of wine and delicate hor's d'oeuvres.

Viktor and Gretchen happened to be standing on top of a detailed mosaic of St. Michael engaged in his final battle with Lucifer, just before the moment when Satan and his followers were expelled from heaven. Neither one noticed the terrible beauty of the scene, but if Hank Reardon had been watching, he'd have seen this placement as a purposeful one. For her part, Gretchen was utterly dazzled by Viktor and drank in his rare praise.

"You've done quite enough for now, Gretchen, thank you again. Feel free to take your leave."

The young woman blinked rapidly, visibly disappointed, then turned and disappeared into the crowd.

Viktor was aware of Gretchen's affection for him. Her porcelain skin flushed each time his gaze met hers, and her "accidental" caresses had long amused him. But Viktor had neither the time nor the inclination to advance their relationship beyond that of employer and employee. Viktor did make use of women and enjoyed the experience of physical release. But these liaisons were exclusively with women in the business of sex; never with an innocent like Gretchen.

Glancing at his phone, he saw it was nearly time.

CHAPTER THIRTY-FIVE

Xining, China

"Mr. Reardon's orders are to wait here." Glen Spencer had been flying for Hank Reardon for more than twenty years. A former Air Force helicopter pilot, he looked the part. Although he was close to Hank Reardon's age of sixty-eight, he looked younger.

Sebastian and Dimitri stood talking with Spencer outside the cockpit of the Learjet, which was now parked near a hangar in the Xining Caojiabao Airport. Evidently, Spencer disliked what he heard from the FedPol cops; his weathered, rugged face was a study in furrows. Glancing back into the cockpit at the clock on the instrument panel, he tried again. "Look, I take my orders from Hank Reardon, and he was clear. All three of us—me, my co-pilot, and my steward—stay here on the plane while you do your thing at the prison. We have clearance to be in this airspace for fifty-one-and-a-half more hours. We need to be in the air by eleven pm two days from now...give or take ninety minutes. And we will be."

"What's going on?" Joe Cairns was distracted by an ambiguous statement Morgan had made to Lindsey and Rich as they were getting their gear together.

"We need to find Lieutenant Wang Jianjun," she said—as if suggesting that they get some Chinese food. When she went on to explain that she had seen this Chinese man in a dream, Cairns had wanted to ask more questions—but the altercation in front of the cockpit had stopped him.

Dimitri was in full cop mode, "Joe, we'll handle this. Please stay out of it."

Glen Spencer repeated his statement for the third time, re-wording it slightly as Cairns approached. "We work for Reardon, not you. Mr. Reardon's instructions were crystal clear. We stay until all of you complete your work. Then we leave. To-gether."

"So, what's the problem with them doing what they were told by Reardon?"

The effort of staying in control was apparent in the muscles on each side of Dimitri's tight jaw.

I've seen that look before, Cairns mused, *back in Switzerland when he "hired" me. He hates being trumped—especially by me of all people. He's worried about the safety of the pilots. He and Sebastian have more than enough to handle without these three civilians added to the mix. Get over it Dimitri, Spencer isn't going anywhere.*

CHAPTER THIRTY-SIX

Frankfurt, Germany

"He's dead, Sir." Viktor's new head of security stood at almost military attention, his somber gaze reflecting the horrific manner in which the man had died.

Viktor nodded, unsurprised. Albert's death was no loss, and Viktor cared nothing about how he had died. "Were you able to locate all the scientists?"

"Yes, sir."

"And they will each be in the conference room in one hour?"

"Yes, sir."

"Good." Turning his back to the man, Viktor picked up the phone and began to dial. But when he did not hear the sound of his door closing, he turned around. The man was still standing there.

Stephan had always known when he was dismissed. The death of Stefan was costly. He hoped to repay Joe Cairns in kind.

"That's all. Please go now."

Nodding curtly, the guard made sure to close the door silently behind him.

"Has the plane landed?"

"Yes, about fifteen minutes ago."

"And?"

"No one has exited the plane."

General Chen Cheng's "fondness for cash," as Sam Wong had so delicately termed the Chinese General's notorious gambling addiction, had driven him to call upon another of his virtual ATMs following another massive loss at a Macau blackjack table. New Year's weekend had left him over half a million short.

The gambling revenues of the resort city of Macau surpassed those of Las Vegas and Atlantic City combined, making it the supreme "sin city" of the world. Only a few miles from mainland China, the former Portuguese colony had a unique legislative situation. Aside from matters of defense and foreign affairs, the little property was autonomous from the Chinese government, though close to 700,000 people lived in its eleven square miles—making it the most densely populated area on earth.

Fully aware of Macau's allure to Chinese citizens, the government had imposed restraints. Mainlanders were allowed to visit the tables only four times per year. The jobs disdained by Macau residents, such as pouring tea at the blackjack tables and building hotels and casinos, fell to foreign workers who were easily bribed. The whole situation made it quite easy for General Cheng to cut through the restrictions imposed on "ordinary" citizens.

"How many people have you sent?"

"Enough, Dr. Dragovik. Enough to get the job done." General Cheng's chuckle sounded forced.

"General."

Viktor could see that the man was perspiring heavily. He

waited another twenty seconds, then repeated his question, this time in Mandarin. "General, how many do you have waiting for them?"

"Three. I have three, but they are my best—" The General was speaking to the dial tone.

Checking his watch, Viktor knew he was early but opened the door of his office, turned right down the long hall, and walked into a large room. Fifteen men and five women stood nervously, waiting.

"Good morning, ladies and gentlemen. Thank you for being early."

Quickly scanning the group, Viktor eyed the three hopefuls he was familiar with from reviewing their employee files. Dr. Yves LeClair, a biochemist from the Louis Pasteur Institute in Paris; Dr. Boris Sladikin, a molecular biologist from the National University of Science and Technology in Moscow; and Dr. Farah Jabbour, a developmental biologist and virologist from the University of Science and Technology in Tehran. All three looked unobtrusive, geeky. Perfect.

"Do you know why I asked you here this morning?"

Dr. Peter Andersson, the head of the Diedrich Gruppe Clinical Research Department, stepped forward to speak, but before he could open his mouth, Viktor waved him back. Embarrassed by the public rebuke, the Norwegian chemist stepped back into the line of people, cheeks flaming.

I have never trusted Andersson. I should have fired him, but Diedrich liked him—liked his ingratiating ways and those Aryan features. He could be Gretchen's twin brother, with that platinum hair and those light blue eyes.

The silence in the room was heavy. Most of the scientists stared resolutely at the floor, as if deep secrets could be learned from the subtly luxurious blue-green and gold Persian rug that lay under the mahogany conference table. None of them wanted to be here. It was a command performance for a new position no one wanted anything to do with. It had been Sebastian's project—and look what happened to him. The head of the department had been Diedrich's pick. They all knew it was only a matter of time until Andersson was canned, and all avoided looking at him—their boss—or at *his* boss, Dragovik. All but one.

"You are interviewing for the creation of an antidote for CJD." Raising a thick black eyebrow, Dr. Farah Jabbour added, "Dr. Sebastian Cameron used a modification of the vCJD-variant Creuztfeldt-Jakob molecule to shorten the time for onset of symptoms from years to days. Thus, making it possible to study the mechanism of the disintegration of the prion and creation of amyloid aggregates. But his work was interrupted." Dr. Jabbour's expression revealed nothing. Viktor was mesmerized by the ease with which the woman spoke about Sebastian's sudden, unexplained disappearance. Ignoring the muffled coughs, and heightened anxiety flooding the room, she continued speaking. "A mechanism for the transmission of the altered prion must be devised, preferably viral, so it will be airborne."

Her words resonated in the silence of the room. Minds raced, attempting to process what she had said. Although everyone there knew that the stated goal of the prion project was bogus, none of them had admitted it to themselves. Until now.

Viktor had seldom worked harder to contain an emotion. Jabbour was perfect—a devout Muslim who bore abysmal hatred for the west. Her entire family had been collateral damage when a drone blew up most of her village during the first Desert Storm. Just fifteen years old at the time, Jabbour had been away at school when she learned that her six siblings and parents had been blown to bits. Just about the same age that Viktor had been when he became an orphan.

As always, Viktor maintained a calm outward appearance and merely nodded. "Excellent, Dr. Jabbour, outstanding. Please remain here with me. I would like to speak with you further about this matter."

Viktor nodded at the head of the research lab, who still seemed shaken by Viktor's earlier rebuke. "Thank you, Dr. Andersson, for arranging this meeting. I appreciate your efforts. I have made my decision and you can all get back to your duties." The remark about appreciating him was a lie, but necessary to assuage Andersson's fragile ego.

As the group began to file silently out of the room, Viktor said, "Everyone, please remember the confidentiality agreement you signed upon employment with Diedrich Gruppe. This meeting and what has been said here is proprietary. Any leaks will be dealt with immediately and with severity."

Everyone knew the meaning of *severity*.

CHAPTER THIRTY-SEVEN

Xining, China

"We've got to move. The prison is a four-and-a-half-hour drive. Joe, Dimitri, and I will take the Jeep and head out there. How about if the rest of you take the smaller car and see if you can find the Lieutenant's apartment?"

The pilots had won their case. They were staying in the jet. Cairns persuaded Dimitri and Sebastian to follow Hank's wishes. Although the FedPol cops had a point about the safety of the cabin crew, Glen Spencer had trumped them when he showed the men his arsenal of two revolvers and three shotguns and insisted that he and his team were proficient in their use. Cairns' muttered prediction that the group would likely need to make a fast take-off did not go unnoticed. Lindsey, who had been uncharacteristically distracted ever since she and Sebastian had been interrupted in their discussion of their alternatives. Her mind kept returning to a sardonic comment she had made, like a sore tooth.

The seven stood in a surprisingly long queue at the Xining Europcar rental agency at eleven in the evening. Sam Wong's people had rented two cars for the group, demonstrating the thoroughness of the help they were receiving.

When they finally reached the front of the line, a bespectacled, harried-looking agent babbled incomprehensibly. Morgan stepped up and spoke quietly to her, at which point she smiled and nodded vigorously, then turned to point out at the parking lot.

"What did you say to her, Morgan?"

"That Mr. Sam Wong had reserved two automobiles for my party, a Jeep Cherokee and a Honda. I asked her if we needed to complete any paperwork, or whether we could just take the cars."

"What did she say?"

"She said the paperwork had all been taken care of and the cars were in the parking lot with their keys inside."

Rich and Lindsey shot amused glances at each other, but Sebastian's eyes were as big as saucers. "Is she some kind of child prodigy?" he asked Lindsey.

Having overheard him, Morgan said, "Actually I have been diagnosed with several condtions, including autistic spectrum disorder, Asperger's syndrome, autistic savant—those are the ones that come to mind now. But—"

The Europcar woman asked Morgan another question, and she turned to reply.

Cairns approached them and quietly said, "You four take the Honda as soon as you get cleared away here with Morgan. We'll stay behind to see if you pick up a tail."

"Four?" Lindsey asked. And then she saw Horst materialize from nowhere.

"Yes, four," Horst confirmed. His eyes moved down the line of people waiting for their cars. He was on high alert.

"You're carrying, aren't you?" Cairns asked Rich, and when Rich nodded, he murmured "Good." He turned to Mueller and said, "See anything?"

The German shrugged. "There's a couple of guys at your six who haven't taken their eyes off us. And there's another standing at the top of the escalator. Looks like a clone of those two. I think it's just the three."

Suddenly Lindsey felt hollowed out—as if a drain had been unplugged. *Of course, Dragovik must have people watching us here. What if this is all...* She forced herself to stop.

The People's Liberation Army was the largest in the world, with 2.3 million soldiers serving on the ground and in a steadily growing naval force. In the previous five years, the Chinese government had increased the military budget by fifty percent. One of the chief obstacles to modernizing the Chinese militia was corruption, a fact that could be exploited. Men like General Zheng tended to get their jobs by buying them. Such unwarranted rank did not inspire allegiance from the troops, but rather, prompted them to look for ways to enrich themselves—just as Wang Jianjun had done.

Three guys following us," thought Cairns. *How the hell did they know we were here? Dimitri is confident that all of the video and audio equipment was removed from Hank's offices and home. And the plane was cleared.*

"Can we talk for a second?" Cairns caught the Swiss cop's concerned gaze at Horst's revelation and pulled Dimitri aside. "Unless Hank's crew is dirty, you have a leak at FedPol." Dimitri's answer was a tight nod and grimace. "We'll need to give them some false info to get them off our track."

"How are we going to do that?"

"I honestly don't know. I'm sure Sebastian will come up with something."

The men watched as the small Honda disappeared into the night, heading for Lieutenant Wang Jianjun's apartment.

CHAPTER THIRTY-EIGHT

San Luis Obispo, California

"Well hello there, LJ. What brings you here? Are you finished with classes for the day?"

Father Blaise Roderick peered up over his half-glasses at the young girl standing beside him shifting her weight nervously from one leg to the other.

"I'd like to help." LJ wished she had ignored the urge to stop in at Lindsey's lab on the way home from school. The priest looked at her as if he had no clue of what to say to her. There were papers strewn all around his office, and he looked harassed. His mouth made a perfect O, but he said nothing, merely stared at her.

This was not one of your brighter moves, Grayson, what did you think you could do to help these people? A double doc like Lindsey and a vet? You're a freshman in college...

Just as she began to backtrack, literally backing up while mumbling," Gosh, I'm really sorry to interrupt. I… I guess I better get home to take care of the dogs," Jodi Tamarack raced breathlessly in to the center. "I've been working on the animal-to-human species barrier for prion transmission and wonder if— "Hi, LJ!! What are you doing here?"

"She'd like to help us," Father Blaise said, exerting considerable effort to get his massive body out of the chair. "I can only imagine how difficult it would be to get along without the frenetic activity that keeps our minds off the danger that Rich, Lindsey, and the rest of them are in. Perhaps we should share some of it with LJ, here."

Thoroughly embarrassed now, LJ could feel the sting of incipient tears. The priest had nailed it. LJ was as overwhelmed as she had ever been—well, aside from those months of therapists probing her about the personal stuff that had turned her into a teenage drunk. The questions were never phrased that way, of course—they were far more subtle—but that was the gist. She'd been pretty freaked out back then, but this was far worse. Now she was flat-out afraid, not for herself but for people she loved dearly. Three people she had not known existed until just six months ago were now in grave danger. LJ knew it would be a miracle if Lindsey, Rich, and Morgan, along with others she'd probably never meet, lived through this trip to the other side of the world. But LJ believed in miracles. At least she was valiantly trying to convince herself that she did.

Jodi looked at LJ, then at Father Blaise, then back at LJ. "Want to share our craziness? We could use some computer research help, big time."

LJ's eyes shone while Jodi explained the task at hand. Grabbing a blank legal pad and ballpoint pen off Father Blaise's desk, she began to jot down notes as Jodi talked about her need for studies specific to the aggregate of amyloid in prion disease, any prion disease. The researcher had a theory, but she'd need confirmation from the most obscure sources: studies of PrP. With an incubation period of years and an incidence of less than one case per million people, the study of prion disease attracted very few researchers—so LJ's search would be a painstaking one, requiring more than 100 search terms.

CHAPTER THIRTY-NINE

Frankfurt, Germany

"Less than forty-eight hours."

Viktor was pleasantly surprised by Dr. Jabbour's answer. Pleasure and surprise were foreign sensations to him and he disliked both. Surprise signified a loss of control, and enjoyment conjured up memories of his happy early childhood that he preferred to keep suppressed.

He walked away from his employee to stare out at the bustling streets of downtown Frankfurt, battling a vivid flashback of his ninth birthday party. Willing the extinction of the memory, he focused on the thousands of people, seemingly the size of ants, scurrying around sixteen floors below. None of them would live to see next weekend if the woman was telling the truth and not simply what he hoped to hear—that in two days, the engineered prion would be transmissible by a virus. Airborne.

Is it possible that all these years of planning, preparation, experimentation have borne fruit? Has this nobody of a Muslim scientist—a female—actually done it?

The tide of excitement rising within him had an almost erotic potency. *Do not let her in. Do not lower your defenses.*

Not to this woman. Stomp on this. Think of religion, the stupidity of religion. The fanaticism it breeds.

"Why don't you wear a hijab?"

Dr. Jabbour said nothing in reply to Viktor's question which had come out of nowhere. It was none of his business. She held his dark gaze, unblinking.

Viktor moved closer, so that his face was just inches from hers. "I have seen you making Salaat. Why don't you cover yourself if you are so devout?"

Calmly, as if this explosive tirade from the CEO of the company for which she worked made perfect sense, Dr. Jabbour replied, "I don't find the hijab to be anything but an affectation." Without shifting her gaze from his, she added, "I have never claimed to be devout."

Although she must have wondered when and where he had seen her prostrate in prayer, she did not ask.

Viktor was the first to blink.

CHAPTER FORTY

Route G6, Xining

"Rich, we're being followed." Horst Mueller spoke quietly, hoping he would not be overheard by Lindsey and Morgan, who were sleeping in the back seat.

Rich looked in the passenger-side mirror. It was dark. Streams of traffic entered and left the airport. All Rich could see was a sea of headlights.

"Are you sure?" *I hope you're wrong, Mueller. The last thing we need is a tussle or worse in a country where our presence is barely tolerated already.*

"Amateurs, I'd say. A red Hongguang S1 picked us up outside the rental car agency, and it's been on our tail ever since. I pass, they pass. I drop below the speed limit, so do they."

"They?" *What the blazes is a Hongguang S1?*

"Yes, there are two of them. I'll wager that the third is following Joe and his FedPol pals." Horst glanced over at Rich and answered his unspoken question. "General Motors has hit China in a big way. The Hongguang S1 is kind of a sporty van, perfect for the non-growing Chinese family of two adults and one kid."

Rich began to relax, but only for a couple of seconds.

"Rich, keep your gun close by. These guys might do something stupid."

"Like?"

"Anyone dumb enough to tail someone in a red car is capable of anything."

"Do you think they are the guys you spotted at the airport?

"Probably. My guess is that they're Chinese military trying not to look like soldiers. Skinny lowlifes hoping for promotions that will never come, willing to do whatever they're asked."

Rich turned to look at the big German. He had grossly underestimated Horst Mueller. *He plays it—the male, 'roid-soaked version of an airhead—when he is anything but. His English is perfect and he probably speaks a couple of other languages as well. Joe knew just what he was doing when he assigned Horst to us.*

Just as Rich completed his musings about the German cop, all hell broke loose.

"Lindsey, Morgan, seatbelts on, heads down!" Horst shouted. "These idiots are ramming us!"

The air was filled with the sounds of tortured metal as the German fought to keep the small Honda on the ground and away from oncoming traffic. The car swerved wildly as he attempted to avoid the crazily aggressive thrusts of the big van behind, which seemed intent on rolling them into the lane of traffic heading to the airport. Then—as suddenly as it had appeared—the van was gone. The driver must have lost control and swerved directly into the path of an oncoming semitrailer. The lane heading into the airport came to a screeching standstill, and would be that way for the foreseeable future.

"Everyone okay back there?"

Horst's hands were at ten and two on the steering wheel as he jockeyed around stunned drivers who had gotten out of their cars to see what had happened. There were rattles and wheezes where before there had been only the sound of tires rolling along the asphalt, but they were still moving. Honda built durable cars.

Lindsey and Morgan were shocked speechless but looked okay.

Mueller said, "Rich, call Joe and let him know these guys are trying to kill us."

For just an instant, Rich and Mueller's gazes locked as each thought the same thing: *This isn't over. Next time they won't send amateurs.*

Watching the men silently in the rearview mirror, Lindsey caught the look that passed between them. She understood that the battle had begun and they were in the middle of it. Dragovik would do everything he could to prevent them from stopping his plan. She wondered if Morgan understood what was at stake and what they were risking.

As if on cue, the young girl spoke up, her eyes huge in the glare of the headlights. "There might be more men at his apartment, Lindsey. Waiting for us." Lindsey realized that Morgan had been living out this nightmare for months, in fragments that had slowly come together in the last two weeks. She'd seen the piles of dead and dying men, heard their screams for help. Of course, she knew precisely what was at stake. Perhaps it was even a relief to be living it with her eyes open this time. Lindsey stretched out her arm and extended her hand, allowing Morgan to decide if she wanted to touch. Instantly, Morgan grabbed her hand and squeezed it hard. They each managed a tight smile of solidarity.

At the sight in the rearview of the women clasping hands, Rich could feel himself relaxing for the first time since they had left Pismo Beach. Not because the danger was over—far from it. Like Lindsey, he had been reluctant to allow Morgan to come along on what could turn out to be a suicide mission. But, as he sat beside the silent Horst, now concentrating on pushing the damaged Honda past its limits, Rich considered the alternatives. Would Morgan be safer back at home with LJ?

His thoughts were interrupted by loud bangs and the grinding of the motor. He glanced over at Horst, but the driver's concentration was absolute, his hands white with the force he was using to keep the small car on the road. Although the accelerator pedal was on the floor, their speed had dropped to fifty. Rich turned sharply to his right just in time to see the car's muffler roll to the side of the road. Silhouetted in the distance was a most eerie sight—what looked like a large group of spire-shaped buildings. Were they pagodas?

"You're looking at the Kumbum Monastery," Morgan piped up. "That large shiny thing is called the Golden-Tiled Temple. Before the Chinese government instituted its crackdown on Tibetan Buddhism, there were close to 4,000 monks studying and teaching here. Now there's only like, 400."

Rich had no idea how Morgan knew such things, whether from reading or dreaming. At this point, he just hoped she knew enough to help keep them on track.

CHAPTER FORTY-ONE

Route G214, Xining

Cairns was making great time. It was just after midnight local time, and the tollways heading west from the airport and up into Gonghe were almost deserted. He was driving the Jeep Cherokee at eighty and had already eaten up over an hour of the four-hour trip. Just as he turned right onto the 315, the sat phone rang.

That would mean trouble from our other half.

Following the extensive wiretapping of Hank Reardon's offices and phones back in June, all of his employees, along with Rich and Lindsey, had switched to Cellcrypt mobile phones for their daily use. Although Interpol used a secret satellite shared only with other intelligence agencies, Evan had instructed the group to use the phones just for emergencies, and to keep their calls short and pepper them with words and phrases only native English speakers would understand.

Glancing over at Sebastian, then quickly back at the road—the last thing they needed was an accident—Cairns watched the spy's expression change as he listened to Rich Jansen's account of their near-death experience.

Shit, this is bad. If they're already having this kind of trouble, then so will we.

Cairns glanced at the rearview mirror to catch Dimitri's eye—but suddenly, the mirror was splintered glass. A dark sedan was coming up fast, heading west in the eastbound lane. The driver was leaning out his window with a massive gun and shooting erratically. Considering that the guy had to be going over ninety, Cairns had to concede that smashing the Jeep's mirror, which was less than a foot from his head, was not bad shooting. At the stomp of his foot on the accelerator, the Cherokee hurtled forward into the night. Cairns heard Dimitri lower his window, trying to get a bead on the shooter, but they were too far ahead of their pursuer. The range of Dimitri's Glock could not compete with the high-powered rifle behind them.

"In three seconds, guys, I'm going to turn around. Get ready to take out this guy when I do." Taking his foot off the accelerator, Cairns shouted, "three," and began to tap the brake harder and harder, "two," he practically stood up on the pedal, "one. Hold ON!"

Please don't flip, please don't flip...

Cairns had slowed the top-heavy SUV to just under forty. It careened, then swayed, the brakes screamed, and the passenger front wheels left the ground as it made a 180-degree turn. In under ten seconds, the car was now heading east in the westbound lane. The dark, nondescript car appeared over a rise, coming too fast to avoid the Jeep hurtling at him. Both Dimitri and Sebastian opened fire, one of them aiming at the driver, the other at the front tires.

The car shuddered, then veered into the west-going lane and onto an embankment where it rolled to a stop.

Cairns drove the jeep over to the embankment and parked behind the motionless car. The driver was slumped over the steering wheel.

All three men opened their doors and exited warily. There had been only one shooter, but each had learned the value of caution. Sebastian approached the driver, Cairns and Dimitri the passenger side.

"Nice shot, Dimitri," exclaimed Sebastian as he looked at the quarter-sized hole in the forehead of a thin Chinese man who appeared to be in his late twenties.

Searching through the car, Cairns plucked a neatly folded Chinese sergeant's uniform from the back seat. Holding it up so the other two could see it, he said, "Think our seventy-two hours have been cut in half?"

Both FedPol men exclaimed, "The Chinese Army? What the fuck?" Then Dimitri muttered, "You might be right Joe. Sam Wong warned us."

"Hand me the sat phone, Dimitri."

"You want to tell them our exact location?

Sebastian chuckled mirthlessly. "Like they don't know?"

Dimitri studied his colleague. "What are you thinking?"

"That we've got this all wrong. First, we should have known they had transmitters on the rental cars. Easy to do if you're the Army."

Now, Cairns was staring at him, too. *He's right, of course, They knew what vehicles we were renting, so why wouldn't they have placed transmitters in them?* But Sebastian's comment about getting it all wrong puzzled him. "What do you mean?"

"Three things. If there is any trace of the poison at the guy's apartment, we don't need to waste another eight or nine hours getting out to the prison to confirm what we'll already know. Second, if this dead guy is the third of the B team, then isn't it likely the A team will be waiting for us at the prison?"

Just then, Dimitri crawled out from under the Jeep holding a black box a little smaller than a package of cigarettes. "You called that one, doctor!" He looked admiringly at Sebastian, who merely nodded and continued.

"Joe," Sebastian continued, "I think we should be at Dragovik's lab in Frankfurt... back where we met. This is a wild goose chase intended to get us all killed. Viktor would not know how to aerolize the prion. It's got to be embedded inside a virus—preferably a simple, highly contagious one, like the rhinovirus."

"Rhinovirus. That's a common cold, right?" Dimitri's eyes widened at the implication.

"There's only one person at the lab who could accomplish such a thing: Farah Jabbour."

Tossing the small transponder up in the air, Dimitri quipped, "Dr. Cameron, your logic is, as always, impeccable." Catching it as it came down again, he stared first at his partner, then at Cairns. "So, this thing needs to be returned to the undercarriage of the Jeep. And then we need to split up. One of us should keep driving the Cherokee to Gonghe as bait for Dragovik's team. That lucky dude will get to face the A team, while the other two of us head back to Xining in a stolen car."

Dimitri eyed Cairns and Sebastian. "Want to flip a coin?"

Ignoring both of them, Cairns walked over to Dimitri, snatched the transponder from his hand, and slid under the Jeep. In a few seconds—before Sebastian and Dimitri had recovered enough to try and stop him—Cairns was opening the driver's door and climbing in.

"Joe," said Sebastian, grabbing hold of his arm. "No way are you doing this little jaunt. Dragovik's people nearly killed you a few weeks ago, along with me. They would have succeeded if it hadn't been for Mueller."

Cairns narrowed his eyes. "Look, I watched you and Lindsey working on the virus the whole trip over here. Only you and she can figure out how to stop this thing from happening. She can't do it without you. I'm no help with that." He turned his head to the right and regarded Dimitri evenly. "From what I hear, you were nearly killed last summer. Now it's my turn."

Neither Sebastian nor Dimitri spoke a word. There was nothing to say. They stared mutely at the man who had easily evaded their agent in Delphi and could have disappeared forever, but who chose instead to return to Lausanne and join them in this fight. What do you say to someone like that? Some guy you think is the enemy but who, for no good reason, risks his life to save yours?

Shaking off Sebastian's hold on him, Cairns slammed the door and drove off. He didn't look back.

CHAPTER FORTY-TWO

Pismo Beach, California

Yikes, Kate, how on earth am I going to get all of this organized?

LJ sat yoga style on the floor of Rich's home office. Twice she'd had to fill the fax machine with paper and yet the pages kept on coming.

Calling Kate Townsend, a reporter friend of Rich and Lindsey's, had been Julie's idea. Since the girls had returned to California, Julie had called just about every other night, concerned, to put it mildly. A woman of devout faith, Julie was also a realist. She had witnessed the power of evil in her own life and those of others. When LJ had explained the task given her by Jodi Tamarack, Julie had suggested asking Kate to help since she was an experienced investigative journalist. She also happened to be on maternity leave from her newspaper.

Kate couldn't have been kinder to LJ when she called. In under a day, she had called her back and warned her that she would need a mega box of fax paper to receive all of the documents she was about to send, some dating back seventy years.

Julie had warned LJ not to say too much to the reporter about the reason for the research, just to explain that Cal Poly was doing some background study on the mad cow epidemic that had decimated the cattle population in the UK back in the eighties. Luckily for LJ, Kate didn't ask many questions—probably because she was dealing with a newborn as they spoke. Once LJ had explained what she needed to Kate's satisfaction, she whispered a breathless, "Got it. Anything for Lindsey and Rich!" and rang off without so much as a goodbye.

By the time the fax machine stopped belching out pages, there were close to 300 of them, and Max and Gus were huddled in the far corner of the room whimpering. LJ smiled at the two dogs and said their favorite words, "Okay guys, let's go down to the beach for a run."

CHAPTER FORTY-THREE

Frankfurt, Germany

Viktor hung up on General Zheng again. The man was a fool, but he was not really angry at him; he was angry at himself for believing that Zheng's soldiers would be competent. According to the general, the two men tailing the doctor and her husband had been killed in their attempt to take out the couple. He'd attempted to excuse them for their failure, but Viktor cut him off. He had no patience for such sniveling.

It seems the general had assigned just one man to go after Sebastian and the two other men—Cairns and his anonymous German colleague. His only hope at this point was that the team that would be arriving at Gonghe Prison within the hour. He felt confident that those four men would not fail to take out the American spy and his meddling colleagues. *They'd damn well better.*

Viktor clasped his hands behind his back and paced the perimeter of his glass-walled office slowly, musing, questioning himself. Pondering his options. Thinking about the consequences of what he was unleashing.

It must be done.

"Gretchen, call Dr. Jabbour. Tell her to get here now."

"I need your help, Dr. Jabbour."

The woman sat motionless as she listened.

An unattractive face for a girl under thirty, thought Victor. *Her eyebrows are too thick, like a man's. Her forehead is too low, her eyes too widely set. Perhaps she could be pretty if she did something with that wild mane of frizzy hair. A smile once in a while wouldn't hurt either.*

He waited for her to ask how she could help, but the silence dragged on, just as it had in their previous conversation. The woman was exasperating. *If he did not have need of her…* Viktor cut off that line of thought and said, "You know what I need, don't you, Doctor?"

"Sir, I need the entire forty-eight hours to complete the task. It has been only sixteen." Dr. Jabbour's gaze met his.

She does not act like a Muslim woman. She should drop her eyes. She should behave like the servant she is!

Once again, Viktor forced himself to rein in his anger, but the smile on his face was frozen. He wished he had an alternative to this person, but there was none. "Yes, Doctor, I know, and you will get the time you need. What I need right now are men. Men who are able to get to northwestern China within hours; trained jihadists, eager to sacrifice their lives to stop infidels working against us."

For the first time, Dr. Jabbour's eyes lit up and she smiled. "On that front, I can help. I have some cousins in the Gojal region of Pakistan. They are young, fierce, and eager to engage in the Holy War. How many men are you looking for?"

"Ten, Farah. Five of them must get to Xining, China, tonight. I will give them the details once you put me in touch with the one you trust enough to lead the other four. The other five will have to come here to guard your animals and vaccine."

It was the first time Viktor had ever called the doctor by her first name, but he was not concerned that she'd misinterpret the gesture as anything other than respect. She seemed to have no interest in sex or romance—the common female weaknesses. Clearly, it was death that preoccupied her. Death and suffering. In that, they were somewhat alike.

"I need to get my phone," she said. "I'll return in under ten minutes."

As soon as she'd rushed from Viktor's office, Gretchen popped her head in and said, "General Zheng is on the phone. Are you in?"

The contrast between the striking blonde and the dark-skinned Arab was startling, Viktor thought. *Beauty and the Beast.* "Take a message," he barked. He suspected Zheng was calling to tell him that his third guy had been killed and to ask for more money to hire replacements.

Farah Jabbour walked rapidly down the hall. Although it was just under sixty-eight degrees in the climate-controlled corporate offices, she was perspiring heavily. When she got into her office, she closed the door, locked it, and leaned against it, breathing hard. She counted to forty-nine before making the call. She punched in a long series of numbers, then listened to the combination of hisses, clicks, and static that signified the call was secure.

"Yes?"

"Weiss."

"First Commando Unit."

"101."

"On whose orders?"

"Ben Gurion."

"When?"

"August 1953."

"Dr. Jabbour?"

She could hear the reproach in the voice of the man who

had transformed her from an Israeli surgeon and virologist named Naomi Weiss into Dr. Farah Jabbour. She had just used her name Weiss instead of Jabbour. It had taken close to two years of rigorous work to prepare her to blend into the world of radical Islam, and then several months more to help her infiltrate the highest ranks of Diedrich Gruppe Pharmaceuticals.

In hushed tones, she rapidly explained the situation—or the highlights, at least. She kept looking at her watch, and when her mentor began to question her, she said, "Listen, I have just thirty more seconds before I must return."

"Tell him the five men will be on the ground in Xining by midnight tonight, and five more will be in Frankfurt by eleven tomorrow morning. Tell him his contact, Uri, will call him at 11:01 tomorrow morning."

They both clicked off without pleasantries.

Breathing nearly normally now, the doctor took time to pour out a glass of water from the pitcher on her desk and drink it down. She then headed back to Dragovik's office.

CHAPTER FORTY-FOUR

Xining, China

"Take the Xining Stadium exit."

"What? I can't hear any bloody thing over this racket!" Horst had slowed the Honda to thirty, but the motor noise due to the missing muffler was still deafening.

"Morgan wants you to take the Xining Stadium exit," Rich repeated, this time nearly shouting.

Horst turned to stare at him, and Rich understood his dumbfounded reaction. How the hell could an American kid from Ohio be calling the shots here? He wondered the same thing periodically, but most of his heart and soul—if not his brain—believed that the mission the seven of them were on was in God's hands, and Morgan was His instrument. It helped that Rich had been a practicing Catholic his entire life, and that during those forty-six years, he had witnessed several events he could only attribute to divine intervention. Rich believed that God made use of people—sometimes unlikely ones. He'd sent King David to convert and recruit Joe Cairns, after all. Joe's conversion from a life of murder for hire to that of a warrior of God couldn't be explained any other way.

The Israeli King David was part of the line from which

Jesus Christ descended. To Rich, this was indisputable. If God could recruit Joe, it wasn't hard to believe that He might make use of this atypical girl.

Rich was unaware of the smile on his face until it prompted a flash of anger in Horst.

"You think this is funny? Could you explain the humor here, because I am not laughing."

Instantly, Rich felt compassion for the man. For over two hours, he had been operating under immense stress, and now he thought he was the butt of a joke.

Rich reached out and squeezed Horst's taut upper arm hard, then let go. *What the hell? When you don't have a clue what to say, try the truth.* "Horst, believe me. I'm not laughing at you. I'm actually laughing at God! But I agree—this is grave business, and for that reason, I suggest we listen to Morgan. Please take the exit. I believe she knows what she is doing."

Muttering something in German, Horst shook his head and changed lanes in preparation for exiting.

Although it was close to two a.m., the city of Xining was bustling. Apparently, nightclubs really *were* a favored pastime for Xining residents.

"Take a right here on Kunlun," Morgan said firmly. "The Lieutenant's apartment will be four blocks down on the right-hand side."

At this point, Horst knew better than to question Morgan's instructions. He slowed the car and eased it into a spot in front of the building she'd indicated.

"No! Wait for me!" the German shouted at Morgan and Lindsey as they sprang out of the rear doors of the Honda before he'd even turned off the engine.

Startled by his command, both froze until the two men caught up with them. The four stared up at the gray multistory apartment building. "They may have planned a reception for us," Horst said, in a hoarse whisper. "They must know where this guy's apartment is, too. Or he might have rigged it himself, before he left. Let me check it out first. Wait here."

The six-foot-five, 250-pound man moved surprisingly soundlessly up the wooden stairs.

Lindsey was impatient to get in there and look for any residue—a few crumbs, even—that might confirm her suspicions about the deadly pathogen. She was also curious about what else Morgan might know, including things she might not even *know* she knew until she got in there.

CHAPTER FORTY-FIVE

Xining, China

Rich jumped at the buzz of the satellite phone, then answered instantly. "Tell me you're not calling because someone's dead," he said urgently.

"What? Rich, is that you?" Sebastian was shouting to be heard over the sound of the traffic. Dimitri was at the wheel, pushing the Jeep over ninety.

Adjusting the phone so it was closer to his mouth, Rich replied, "Yes, Sebastian, it's me. We're here at the guy's apartment, waiting for Mueller to clear the place. He thinks they might have wired it or planted something. Are you three all okay?"

"Yeah, we're fine. That third guy Mueller spotted followed us and tried to take us out, but he is no longer with us. That was good thinking on Mueller's part. These guys seem desperate, and they're amateurs—which makes them dangerous as hell. Where is Lindsey? I need to talk to her."

Ignoring Sebastian's request to talk with Lindsey, Rich asked, "Sebastian, where are you at this point? Still heading to the prison, right?" Something had told Rich to ask the question.

Okay Rich, I'm just going to give you the O'Henry version, no details. "Joe is. We found a tracker on the Cherokee, and decided that throwing it away was a bad idea. So, Cairns kept going on his own—he should be there in a couple of hours. And listen. Your car had a tracker on it, too. We had to dump it. With luck, they will think we're dead—for a few hours, anyway. Dimitri purchased a Wuling Hong Guang from a shopkeeper on the outskirts of Xining. That guy must be a happy man; we paid him three times what the car is worth."

"Sebastian, tell Dimitri he needs to get off that road. Both lanes of the highway into Xining will be shut down for another couple of hours while they get that burning wreck extinguished."

"Got it. Thanks, Rich. We'll find another route into the city. Oh, and I need the address of that apart—wait a sec, Rich!"

Rich heard a screech of brakes. "Sebastian, you guys okay?"

"Yeah, sorry. Dimitri took the exit at sixty. He says *beaucoups,* thanks for the warning. Looks like traffic is backed up for miles on the main road. That address?"

Rich gave him the exact location of the apartment and they clicked off just as Horst reappeared, out of breath after jogging up and down three flights of stairs. He motioned for them all to follow.

"I'll take that, Lindsey," Rich said, grabbing her metal suitcase. "Man, this thing must weigh fifty pounds!"

"Fifty-five, I think. Basically, it's a mobile research laboratory. Sebastian's is far better-equipped than mine. His is what CDC investigators carry to outbreaks," Lindsey smiled grimly. "This qualifies as an outbreak, don't you think?"

By the time they reached the third floor, Rich was breathing hard, thanks to the extra weight. It had been a long time since he was in the Corps.

Chuckling, Horst reached for the suitcase. "Hey, need a hand with that?"

"Where were you about fifty steps ago?"

The apartment consisted of just one room, about 600 square feet, with plain sheetrocked walls. A small, grimy window overlooked the parking lot, and on the wall next to the door sat a tiny stove and small refrigerator. A twin bed and small metal nightstand with a lamp completed the furnishings. On top of the bed lay a carefully folded Chinese uniform with something protruding from the jacket pocket.

The four stood and stared at the grim little dwelling. Not a hint of color broke the unremitting gray that seemed to permeate even the air.

"Good Lord, even prison cells have a sink and a toilet," Rich said.

"Probably not in China," Horst replied. "The guy is clearly a soldier," he said, gazing at the folded uniform. "Or was."

Lindsey and Morgan said nothing as they each tried and failed to imagine living here.

Crouching down and opening the suitcase containing her mobile lab, Lindsey carefully removed the vacuum transistor and prepared to search for particles. She jumped at the sound of Morgan's voice.

"It was in that box."

"What box?" She stared at Morgan, who stood close to her. Standing as far away from the folded jacket as she could, the girl was riveted by the square box-like shape in the pocket. Morgan watched it as if the force of her concentration could keep its contents contained.

Both Rich and Horst stepped back from the bed. None of the three adults thought of questioning Morgan. It was evident to all of them at this point that the teen was getting reliable information from… somewhere. For several moments they stood, as if lost in a collective sense of wonder. Or was it fear?

The sat phone buzzed in Rich's pocket and the sound galvanized them all back to their senses. Rich ignored it. He wasn't sure why, but he had no wish to speak with anyone in this place. Both men stepped even further from the bed while Lindsey gingerly replaced the transistor back into its holder and plucked a pair of nitrile gloves—the latest in safety gear—from the suitcase, along with a bag from which she pulled out a complete Hazmat suit, including goggles and a hood.

The group watched as the methodical researcher grabbed a miniature microscope. Before donning a mask that would turn her into a giant insect, she said, "Rich, can you please get everybody out of here?"

"You got it," he replied, and grabbed Morgan by the elbow. He nodded to Horst and without a word, they walked out the front door, their concern for Lindsey's safety tempered by their own relief.

Just as the three began to trot down the stairs, the sat phone rang again.

"Sebastian, are you guys here already?"

"Dimitri found a shortcut. We're five minutes away. Did you make it into the guy's apartment? Find anything? Is Lindsey there?"

"Yes to all three. We'll meet you on the street. Lindsey is securing a sample now. See you in a few minutes."

Lindsey stood in the middle of the small room collecting her thoughts, the sound of her own breathing echoing within the airtight face mask. If only her med school infectious disease prof could see her now. Truth be told, she was more excited than she'd been in a long time. Soon, she'd find out how Dragovik had done it. She knew Rich was waiting and worrying, and it made her heart race and breath quicken.

Calm down, McCall. You're not accustomed to working in anything like this suit, never mind the gloves. Be very careful here. Take. Your. Time.

She thought about the villain she was dealing with. Were there hints in his dissertation as to how dangerous he would become? Could anyone have guessed that just five years after he finished it, the brilliant Dr. Dragovik would decide to annihilate the population of the world?

Mentally scanning the paper she'd so carefully read, Lindsey decided that none of his professors—even those who knew him and his work—could have predicted this. Ehrlich's book had been even more radical than *Malthus Revisited,* and he'd never launched an attack on humanity. She could only conclude that the seeds of Dragovik's evil had been planted during his horrific boyhood and were exacerbated by Braun's tutelage.

Recalling an in-patient she'd worked with during her psych rotation, Lindsey wondered if Dragovik could be categorized as a true narcissist. Those were exceedingly rare, and their pathology usually grew out of a massive insult to the ego—a trauma that imprisoned them in a psyche incapable of acknowledging the significance of anyone else. Knowing a bit about what the young Viktor had gone through, Lindsey could almost understand the hatred that drove him—and the doors to evil that it threw open.

Okay, get to it.

Despite her unwieldy gloves and full body covering, Lindsey's hands now flew. Carefully removing the small receptacle from the uniform pocket, she placed it on top of the hazmat trash bag in which she would safely store it. Lifting the lid from the box and setting it down gingerly, she used a micro vacuum to collect a few particles of the fine dust inside. Then, she delicately replaced the lid and sealed the box inside the hazmat bag.

Reaching back into her mobile lab, she located the packet of slides. While separating one of the slides from the stack, her heavy glove caught on the fragile piece of glass, breaking it into several sharp pieces, any one of which could pierce her glove.

Damn it, McCall!

Her entire body trembling, Lindsey found a metal probe with which to brush the sharp pieces away from the stack of slides and into a corner of the metal box.

Okay, breathe. One, two... and PRAY!

The eerie, distracting sound of her breathing began to recede into the background and the trembling abated.

You can do this. Returning to the small stack of remaining slides, she gingerly removed another and pivoted her body back to the waiting microscope.

Carefully placing the specimen under the microscope, she studied it intently. Puzzled at first, she rotated the glass just a millimeter clockwise and... there it was.

I KNEW IT!

CHAPTER FORTY-SIX

Xining, China

Mueller had insisted on remaining on the landing and Morgan wanted to wait with him, so Rich was standing alone on the sidewalk when Dimitri and Sebastian squealed to a stop. Sebastian exploded out of the passenger side of the car, slammed the door, and approached Rich at a sprint.

"Where is Lindsey?" Sebastian stood with his arms crossed, a study in pent-up anger. His pinched face was fraught with furrows and frowns.

Stepping forward so that he stood about six inches from the gangly Sebastian, Rich replied, "Upstairs. In the apartment."

Dimitri parked the car high on up on the pavement and walked nonchanantly over to where the two men stood, a knowing half-smile on his face. *Meet my partner Sebastian: on a good day, edgy; on a not so good day…God help you.*

"In the apartment? WHAT IS SHE DOING IN THE APARTMENT?" Sebastian's voice had increased in both pitch and volume.

Deliberately, Rich dropped his voice almost to a whisper. "Sebastian, what do you *think* she is doing?"

It's true what they say about other people criticizing your family, he thought. *Here I was, livid at Lindsey's insistence on playing Wonderwoman scientist while we stood out here cooling our jets. But when this guy comes along asking the same question, I'm ready to deck him.*

Rich glanced over at Dimitri, who stared at him with an amused expression. When he looked back at Sebastian, his gaze had shifted over Rich's shoulder and his expression had darkened furthur.

Rich didn't need to turn around to know what he was looking at. Lindsey must be coming.

When she, Morgan, and Horst hit the last step, Lindsey's smile was broad. She had clearly figured it out. *So why does Sebastian still look enraged?*

Without a word, Sebastian opened the hatch of the SUV and grabbed a metal suitcase half again as large as the one Horst had just carried down the stairs and set on the pavement.

"It's in the amyloid, Sebastian," Lindsey called out when she was still ten feet from him.

The other doctor didn't even look up to register her dazzling smile. He had opened his case and plucked out a Hazmat suit. "You've endangered yourself and everyone who went into that apartment, McCall," he growled. "Why didn't you wait for me as you promised?" His voice and hands were shaking.

"But... it's not infectious unless it's ingested, Sebastian. There's no evidence—"

"Do you *know* that, Dr. McCall?" he hissed. "No, you couldn't know it for sure. There is no way to confirm that it isn't transmissible by air. Until now, that is. Now we have you, your husband, Morgan, and Horst as guinea pigs, so I guess we'll soon know for certain."

Sebastian's expression may have looked like rage, but it was mainly fear. The anger was a defensive reaction he'd learned as a boy at school, as the sole black face in a sea of white ones.

Humilited and horrified—mostly horrified—Lindsey instantly understood the immensity of her blunder. Her eagness to learn just how Dragovik had transformed the prion could have catastrophic consequences, including her own death and those of three others she cared about.

Nauseated with fear, she crouched down beside Sebastian, who was continuing to extract equipment from his case. She knew what he intended to do. It was what she should have done. He would painstakingly use the microvacuum to seek out any particles that might remain on the furniture, floor, or rug, making certain he was protected head to foot while he did so.

"Please let me go back up there with you. Together we can clear the room in half the time."

Sebastian should have predicted this disaster and tried to prevent it. McCall had spent two weeks, night and day, looking for the key to weaponizing the prion and she was desperate for an answer. She was a seasoned researcher with an impressive track record, but she had never entered a potentially contagious biological zone and had no training in the protocols. Now his fury was directed at himself for not heading her off.

Sebastian nodded curtly at her in response to her plea, then said to the others, "You all stay here and wait for us. We'll try to get back down here in under an hour."

Rich's mind was reeling. Accustomed to viewing Lindsey as two degrees to the left of perfection, he considered Sebastian's reaction justified if a bit exaggerated. If he had known what Sebastian knew, he'd have colored the air with some choice language himself.

As he watched the two ungainly forms trudge up the three flights to the apartment, Rich ached for Lindsey. He could not imagine her feelings. And he was awestruck by her resilience, courage, and depth of character. She took it, without making excuses, or attempting to shift blame. She accepted the full weight of her own potentially fatal misjudgement and then set about helping to mitigate it. She'd always had a way of embracing the truth about herself—flaws and all—with quiet grace.

The four stood silently watching as the two cumbersome figures climbed slowly up the first, then second flight, and disappeared from view as they reached their destination. No one made a move to vacate the hallway, though there was little they could do from there.

Thoughts were colliding in Rich's jumbled brain as he tried to make sense of what was happening. First came his disdain for Sebastian. He had not admitted it to himself until now, but Rich blamed Sebastian for Cairns; for letting him take that one-way trip to Gonghe. For Rich, it was a rare instance of underestimating someone. His career—sometimes his very life—had always depended on making judgment calls about people, and he had learned to trust his instincts. They were usually spot on, but not this time.

C H A P T E R   F O R T Y - S E V E N

Route G109 to Gonghe, Xining, China

I'm close. I'll be there in fifteen minutes or so. Dimitri was right, Dragovik will have the A Team here, so this is probably my last hurrah. The last place I'd have expected to die was some godforsaken area in China. And I certainly never thought I'd head straight for it with my eyes wide open.

What was it like for you, David? All those battles, back in the day when the fighting was face to face... you must have thought you'd die in combat, and not in bed at seventy-something. The truth is, it feels weirdly passive, going out this way.

Cairns was sorry he was so close to the prison because he had finally found a decent radio station and was enjoying a little Creedence Clearwater. It was a great relief from the Chinese version of elevator music that seemed to dominate the English-speaking stations.

He had avoided thinking about anything of consequence during the trip, more than three hours now, such as a why he had insisted on being the scapegoat. He wasn't about to start thinking about it now, since he could already see the shadows of the multiple buildings comprising Gonghe Prison. Time was running out for him. Soon it would be done.

As the sun rose behind the snowcapped Himalayas, Cairns slowed and then stopped the car to gaze at the extraordinary sight. The light was transforming the mountain peaks to shimmering gold with just the faintest blush of rose, the colors deepening every second. He turned off the radio and pulled over. He got out, stretched, and stood… bathing himself in the celestial light.

If this is my last sunrise, at least it's a beauty.

The moment felt like a privilege, a gift for his eyes only. There were no other vehicles or people in sight. Emotions that he'd kept a lid on through all the years of killing for a living began to surface, and he realized his face was damp with tears of gratitude.

Weird. The last thing I should feel right now is peace and gratitude.

He chalked it up to the fact that he'd finally found in David a leader worthy of following into hell, and a mission worth dying for. Was that not the goal of every warrior?

He did not regret his rash decision to be the scapegoat. *That was what the priest called the goat who carried all the sins of the people, wasn't it, David? But they were supposed to be innocent, unblemished, right? In that case, I am no scapegoat.*

Just as his mind began to race down the path toward shame and self-loathing, his pejorative inner voice was silenced. Although he did not see the Israeli king, Cairns sensed David's presence in his mind and soul. And perhaps someone else as well.

Abruptly, he knew that Sebastian and Lindsey would succeed. They would stop Dragovik before he could poison the world. He even envisioned how they would do it. Utterly grateful for the insight, his sense of peace deepened to the point that when he turned his head, he fully expected to see David standing beside him. But there was no one.

Cairns' supernatural lucidity and serenity were suprising, considering he was working on a headache of monster proportions. Altitude had always caused him problems in the mountains of Afghanistan, and he was at over 10,000 feet here, but this pain was more ferocious than any he'd ever experienced.

Is it the result of the knowledge I'm receiving?

Cairns knew there was purpose to the pain. It would serve to orient him, to keep him focused on his surroundings as he watched for his own executioners. It would be a group of helicopters or small planes. The place was too remote for a ground team. They would come in low and fast, dropping cluster bombs to destroy everthing within 100 miles of Gonghe Prison. Dragovik and his Chinese associates could not afford to leave anything standing. The conflagration would be blamed on terrorists and the world would accept the explanation without too many questions.

As he waited, he was not really surprised at the words that appeared in his head.

How many are my foes, LORD!
How many rise against me!
How many say of me,
"There is no salvation for him in God."

But you, LORD, are a shield around me;
my glory, you keep my head high.
With my own voice I will call out to the LORD
and he will answer me from his holy mountain.

I lie down and I fall asleep,
I will wake up, for the LORD sustains me.
I do not fear, then, thousands of people
arrayed against me on every side.

Arise, LORD! Save me, my God!
For you strike the cheekbone of all my foes;
you break the teeth of the wicked.
Salvation is from the LORD!
May your blessing be upon your people!

CHAPTER FORTY-EIGHT

West Berlin, Germany

Viktor had decided to go home to his West Berlin penthouse on Pariser Strasse. He had begun to micromanage, as Diedrich had done when vital projects were in progress, and he hated himself for behaving like his dead mentor. Since there was nothing more he could do in his Frankfurt offices but hover, he decided to drive the 550 miles himself, happy for the solitude and numbing tedium of the drive. He drove most of the night, top down on his Mercedes convertible, enjoying the frigid January air as he roared down the wide, mostly empty lanes of the expressway. Driving never failed to clear his head.

He had been fighting the melancholia that always accompanied the completion of a significant accomplishment by concentrating on trivia—like the fact that he'd hounded Dr. Jabbour about her dress and adherence to Islam. Why would he do that? Viktor himself adhered neither to Islam, Christianity, nor any other religion. A memory of watching his mother and sister at prayer began to surface. Both women had worn their hijabs—like their faith—casually, letting their dark hair and joy spill out to those around them. The memory evoked feelings of love and gentleness, long suppressed and exquisitely painful. Viktor stomped on the feelings ferociously. *Don't. Go. There. They are dead, gone. Murdered. Religion and heaven are fakeries, witchcraft. The idea of Allah, of any God, is inane, a complete absurdity.*

The melancholia abruptly changed to something unfamiliar and frightening as a powerful sense of foreboding overtook him. A feeling of dread almost. The two years he'd spent at Porton Down, the military research institute in the UK, had amplified Viktor's profound distrust of governments and their motives. Although the British publicly asserted that the work of the scientists there was solely focused on defense, Viktor knew otherwise. He had seen the secret stash of bioweapons with his own eyes one day, when he unwittingly wandered into a forbidden area. He had been ushered out immediately, but not before he recognized the conditions required to maintain live, lethal organisms.

Stepping out of the elevator, Viktor continued to ponder this woman, Jabbour, and her curious effect on him. Absently, he wandered through the spacious, minimally decorated rooms of his penthouse as if looking for something lost.

The walls were white. A sectional couch, large chair, and ottoman were stark-white leather, accented by chrome-and-glass tables. The result, even on a cloudy wintry day, was jarring to the eyes. Like a vast expanse of snow.

The rugs and few paintings were a brown-black mélange, giving little relief to the sea of harsh brightness. Diedrich had visited just once, pronounced the furnishings hideous, and vowed never to return until Viktor added some color to counter the spartan, unlived-in feeling. He'd been right on that point, of course. It did look as if no one lived there.

Viktor's décor contrasted dramatically with Diedrich's own taste, which had run toward ornate furnishings, heavy woods, and ponderous drapes. Diedrich had liked it dark, even on the sunniest of days. Viktor had laughed at his mentor's appraisal and changed nothing. He liked the brightness and anonymity suggested by the neutral tones and absence of personal effects. It was merely a place to sleep, after all, and to occasionally relieve himself sexually.

Walking out to the patio, he stood watching the pallid January sun begin to light up the city. *The cleanup at Gonghe should be starting right about now. It's the end of history—literally—fifteen years in the making.*

Viktor smiled as he thought of that phrase, *the end of history.* The first time he'd heard it had been in an undergraduate philosophy class. The professor had been a crushing bore with no apparent awareness of the effect his insufferable droning had on his students. All of the classes at the Swiss school were taught in English, and this man had affected a British accent. *How inexcusably pretentious.*

Viktor had taken the class solely because a certain number of liberal arts courses were required. He saw no use for them, and even less for the pedantic egotists who taught them. Viktor's interests lay in the hard sciences: chemistry, biology, mathematics. Even physics was too unstructured for the damaged teen.

But no instructor had ever guessed what their handsome young student was thinking. By the time he was eighteen and a freshman in college, Viktor's manipulative skills were finely honed. With their help, he had achieved a close to perfect grade point average by graduation. Each of his professors had basked in the ingratiating comments he made in class, often cleverly disguised as questions.

Diedrich had taught him to always have a backup plan, and he did. Always.

Frowning, Viktor thought about Dr. Sebastian Cameron—the spy who had actually come close to stopping him. How could he have been so misled by the man?

If I was wrong about Sebastian, then surely I could be wrong about others. Even Jabbour?

Viktor cut off the thought and willed the disappearance of his unwelcome anxiety, insecurity, and self-doubt. Forcing himself to reframe the events of the last several days, he began to relax.

Sebastian was dead, finally, along with Joe Cairns and the imposter, that mysterious ally of Cairns who had appeared from nowhere to save them, posing as Stefan on the phone. They were ashes. Viktor's confidence returned, along with his conviction that his long journey from helpless victim to purveyor of the highest form of killing would soon be completed. The irony of converting a variant of mad cow disease into something so lethal was just too delicious. A pathogen that had introduced itself in the UK back in the late eighties, mad cow disease had killed hundreds before the government had taken action. Now, decades later, Viktor had only to wait. Once the pathogen was airborne, it would just be a matter of time.

Jabbour would get it done, he was sure of it. He had seen the earliest results of her laboratory work and she was better than Sebastian had been—and faster. She would create a viral vector for the prion, as well as its antidote. She would want to survive what was to come just as much as he did.

Still, troublesome thoughts about the doctor kept interjecting themselves. Viktor suspected her name was not really Farah Jabbour. Hell, she probably wasn't even a Muslim, but had affected the stance in a misguided attempt to please him. Once she delivered the virus, they would need to talk, this time without the lies. Meanwhile, he needed to sleep.

CHAPTER FORTY-NINE

About 10,000 miles over Kazakhstan

It had been over an hour, and still, no one spoke. The explosions had begun just as the six raced back up the stairs into Reardon's jet and Sebastian had shouted for the pilots to get the hell out of Xining and head for Frankfurt.

Glen Spencer and his crew had needed no inducement. None of the three had been able to sleep for longer than a few minutes during the thirty-six hours they had been waiting for the team to return. They'd had their guns at the ready the entire time.

The beaming smile of relief on Spencer's face when he spotted their cars had disappeared when only six boarded the plane. Before he could even assess who was missing, the first explosion had galvanized him into action. Within seconds, it seemed, the powerful jet was rolling down the airport runway without—he quickly realized—Joe Cairns.

Although the explosions at Gonghe Prison were hundreds of miles from Xining Airport, they brought back memories of Spencer's years in combat. He willed himself to stay focused on the present, as he'd learned to do during his years of treatment for PTSD.

A counselor at a Veterans Center had taught him the trick, soon after he'd returned from the war, when his hallucinations and flashbacks had threatened to incapacitate him. In danger of losing his job and family, he had been desperate, and willing to try anything to get his life back.

The brain was a clever trickster, the psychologist had explained. Memories were stored in specialized bundles of nerves in the limbic system. Traumatic ones, especially those involving life and death, can be triggered by such things as loud noises, bright lights, even certain scents.

"I get it, Doc. This is where I live. More and more. Don't tell me why it's happening, I really don't care. Just tell me what to do about it."

"Talk yourself out of it."

"I wish it were that easy—"

"Trust me. You can stop them. You can take back your life. The next time you hear or see something from the past, start talking, singing, recite a poem, a nursery rhyme, anything to get your mind back on track."

It had worked. Spencer had learned to maintain control over his traumatic memories. But this mission was unlike anything he'd been involved in since the military. This was a tough one.

You can do it, man.

The concussive effects of the blasts reducing Gonghe Prison to rubble would not send Glen Spencer back into the horrors of the past. Focusing on the familiar rituals of takeoff and rapid ascent into the ionosphere kept him grounded in the present, eclipsing the attempts of his brain to reverse time.

Sebastian had not stopped working since he and Lindsey had returned from the contaminated apartment, where he'd managed to find a few flecks of the powder embedded in the carpet.

Truth be told, he was grateful for the activity, as hazardous as it was. Anything to get his mind off the fact that he was the one who had sentenced hundreds of people to die a hideously painful death in that prison.

Sebastian had volunteered to work for Gruppe Pharmaceuticals. It had been the only way to learn what was going on. *Boots on the ground*, as they say. He knew there would be tests from Dragovik, there would have to be. He was clearly and homicidally mad, but he was the most brilliant man Sebastian had ever met. *Where should we test the prion, Sebastian?* As long as he lived, Sebastian would wonder if there was something he could have done differently. So far, he had always come to the same conclusion. He'd done what he had to do.

He had worked day and night on an antidote that could stop the madness as quickly as it had started—keeping himself from thinking about the fact that it would not save even one of the lives in Gonghe Prison. There was always another experiment to try, another model to look at... anything to keep from thinking about the consequences of the mission. He was engaging himself in busy work and he knew it—but the explosions reverberating in the air around him confirmed a prediction that had been nagging at Sebastian for months. He understood why the bombs were falling. He hadn't wanted to consider the possibility, but blowing up the place was the only way to deal with the thousands of potentially infectious corpses. And to cover Dragovik's tracks, of course.

Worried that some or all four of the team who'd gone to the soldier's apartment could have inhaled a microscopic particle of the poison, Sebastian drew blood samples the moment they hit the plane. It was Lindsey he was most concerned about, along with Morgan, who seemed never to leave her side.

Quickly and efficiently, the scientist set up his mobile

lab—a tricky undertaking as the jet gained altitude. But, by the time the steward informed his passengers they were at cruising altitude, Sebastian was studying the samples from Horst and Rich. When he was satisfied with what he saw under his microscope (performing the test several times to be certain), he moved on to the samples from Morgan and Lindsey.

Twenty minutes later, reluctantly, Sebastian got up and slowly walked through the plane toward Horst, Lindsey, Rich, and Morgan. He was surprised to see Morgan sleeping soundly on one of the plush leather seats that reclined into a comfortable bed. Horst lay breathing deeply on another one in front of her. Behind her, Lindsey and Rich sat upright, their heads downcast. He couldn't tell whether they were asleep or just lost in thought.

Sebastian collected himself as he approached the couple. He dreaded what he was going to have to tell them. He hadn't had any experience in patient care since he was a resident, and had always preferred organisms to people. By the time he stood beside them, he was trembling.

Sensing his presence, Lindsey looked up and smiled, letting the rosary she held in her hand drop back into her lap. Rich was out like a light, mouth open, sound asleep.

Lindsey is a Catholic?

For some reason, Sebastian expected all scientists to be atheists or agnostics, like he was—to have discarded their childhood faith along with their teddy bears.

Maybe her faith will come in handy right now, he thought.

"I owe you both an a-apology," he stammered. "Especially you, Lindsey. Forgive me for behaving like such a condescending ass." He took a deep breath and paused, his lips slightly parted.

"I'm positive. I inhaled the PrP," Lindsey said, calmly.

Dumbly, he just nodded.

"Consequences of my own stupidity and carelessness. Unforgiveable." Her self-deprecating grimace faded to dismay. "But—what about the others? Morgan, Rich, Horst?"

"All fine."

She smiled and exhaled, "Good." Then she closed her eyes. A few seconds later, she began convulsing uncontrollably. She was having a grand mal seizure.

"Holy shit—help me here!" Sebastian shouted, reaching out to try to pin her down by her shoulders.

Rich's eyes shot open. Although he had been almost comatose just seconds before, habits acquired long ago kicked in. Without even thinking, he grabbed the laminated copy of the crash instructions from his seat pocket, folded it in quarters, and jammed it between his wife's convulsing jaws. "*Do* something, Sebastian," he hissed, galvanizing the doctor into action.

Sebastian remembered the vial and syringe he'd tucked into his pocket and pulled them out. Shakily, he began to draw the serum into the syringe and somehow managed to aim it straight into the fleshy part of Lindsey's flailing upper arm. Still convulsing, she lost consciousness. The rhythmic contortions of her body slowly diminished.

Gently cradling his wife's head, Rich eyed the syringe and asked, "What in the hell was *that*?"

"It's an antidote, Rich, along with a powerful tranquilizer." Affecting a sense of confidence he did not feel, Sebastian added, "The antidote is going to make her violently ill for a while, but I'm hoping to God it neutralizes the pathogen she inhaled."

Rich was speechless, overwhelmed.

Lindsey's been infected. Holy God, she could die here. Right now, right on this plane.

He could feel himself shutting down.

Roused by the ruckus, Dimitri and the steward hovered

behind Sebastian. "Carry her back to the bedroom," said the steward. "I used to be a nurse. What can I do?"

"Once we get her moved, we'll need to start an IV for fluids," said Sebastian. "I have everything we'll need. I'll continue to administer the antidote intramuscularly." He dared not give Lindsey the antidote intravenously. Although he hadn't said as much to Rich, he knew the antidote—as yet untested on humans—might kill her. It was also the only thing that might save her.

CHAPTER FIFTY

San Luis Obispo, California

"LJ! This must have taken you the entire weekend! Thank you so much!"

Jodi was taken aback by the carefully assembled and labeled files the young girl handed to her. LJ had organized the more than 300 pages Kate Townsend had sent into three piles: amyloid aggregate, yeast-based research, and general prion study of the major diseases.

To look at her, no one would ever dream this girl was related to Lindsey, Jodi thought. At just eighteen, LJ was fully developed, buxom even, while Lindsey had always tended to be more willowy. But then there were those eyes… of the exact same shade of emerald green as her mother's. Jodi had assumed at first that Lindsey wore colored contact lenses. Then she got to know her and understood that for Lindsey McCall, looks were an afterthought at best. LJ's eyes were somehow more startling than her mother's—perhaps because of her hair, which was almost black. She realized she had done the girl a disservice by presuming her to be just another beautiful girl looking to land a guy or career in California. *This is an impressive kid. I should have figured there was a lot more to her than looks when she befriended Morgan Gardner.*

"LJ, honestly, I don't know how to thank you for this. You've saved Blaise and me tons of time."

The girl beamed at Jodi's praise, apparently unperturbed by her scrutiny.

Jodi's smile faded as she added, "The thing is… I'm afraid we're running out of time."

As if on cue, the priest waddled out of his office and raised his bushy eyebrows in surprise. "Hello, LJ, how nice to see you." He turned to Jodi then. "What's this about running out of time?" While waiting for an answer that wasn't forthcoming, he picked up and thumbed through the thick pile of files on Jodi's desk and plucked one out. "LJ, I presume we have you to thank for all this. I'm taking the amyloid stack, Jodi. Is that is okay with you?" Again without waiting for a reply, he sauntered back toward his office, turning before he went in to declare, "There are times when fear is good. It must keep its watchful place at the heart's controls."

"Hmm. That doesn't sound like something from the Bible," Jodi said. She knew zip about the Bible, but could usually tell when the priest offered up a verse or two.

"It shouldn't!" Blaise said, triumphantly. "It's Aeschylus!"

LJ laughed, thinking him rather irreverent for a priest. She knew she should leave and let them get to work—and anyway, the dogs needed to go out—but she couldn't resist asking, "Have you heard from them?"

Jodi stood to put an arm around the girl. "No honey, I haven't. But maybe it's time to try to reach them." She'd wanted to find out whether Lindsey had been able to get a sample of the poison and analyze it. Since China Standard Time was fifteen hours ahead of Pacific Time, it would be eight-thirty in the morning there—perhaps a good time to reach them.

"Won't the call cost Lindsey a bundle?"

"Oh, maybe two or three dollars a minute, but we won't talk all that long."

Jodi grinned when Rich answered. "Hey Rich, I'm here with LJ. We're so happy to hear your voice! Before you pass me to your wife to talk business, say high to a big hero in this story." She handed the phone to LJ.

"Rich? Are you and Mom okay?" She was stammering, and, to her extreme humiliation, starting to cry.

As he tried to chat calmly with LJ, Rich watched Paul and Sebastian taking turns at trying to bring down the body temperature of a now dangerously febrile Lindsey. He had stopped looking at the blinking digital readout when it passed one hundred and four. No longer convulsing but still unconscious, she looked half-dead.

"Don't you worry about us, honey. Your Mom and I are just fine—Morgan, too—but we all miss you. We'll see you real soon. Now, can you hand the phone back to Dr. Tamarack?"

Rich decided to keep Jodi in the dark about Lindsey's condition as well—not an easy thing to do. Giving in to superstition, he feared that speaking the truth aloud could somehow open death's door. "Sorry, Jodi, but Lindsey is tied up with the team at the moment—I'll have her call you back."

The minute he'd rung off, Morgan turned to him and said, "You lied to LJ and Dr. Tamarack." Her face was expressionless, as usual, and she loomed so close she was practically standing on his shoes. He just looked at her, waiting to hear what she would say next. He could not recall ever feeling so hopeless. The crushing despair flattening every cell of his body was something new. Even breathing was an effort.

Every fifteen minutes, Sebastian collected a fresh blood sample from each of them. When it was Rich's turn, he couldn't help wishing the doctor would slip and sever an artery. Sebastian claimed that the incubation period could be as long as twenty-four hours, so he wanted to be vigilant. Rich suspected he was just trying to keep himself busy. After all, Lindsey had succumbed in under two hours.

He thought about the conversations he and Lindsey had shared about the mission. They'd both known they were endangering their lives, but had agreed that fighting a madman intent on unleashing a lethal bioweapon was a no-brainer. But reason and logic pale in the face of mortality. He just couldn't fathom the idea that Lindsey might have to pay the price.

The truth is, Rich had assumed that *he* would be the one to die. Never once did he consider that it might be his wife. How had he been so selfish as to allow her to put herself on the line like this?

Some people would pray, I guess. The last refuge of the desperate. Rich Jansen felt so far away from God at that moment that the idea of praying was laughable.

At Morgan's touch, he jumped, jolted out of his poisonous morass of thoughts.

Her fingers grazed his cheek, then traced the edge of his mouth. Somberly, she declared, "She will not die, Rich. The antidote is working. Her body is destroying the poison. That is why she has the fever."

Sebastian looked up from Horst's arm as he untied the tourniquet. "Morgan is right, Rich." He smiled in shocked surprise as the realization sunk in. "By God, Morgan, that is exactly what's happening!"

CHAPTER FIFTY-ONE

Frankfurt, Germany

"Thank you very much, Mademoiselle. Indeed. This information is well worth the $750,000. I will wire the money to your Swiss bank account right now."

Viktor had returned from Berlin and was now feeling wholly refreshed after eight hours of uninterrupted sleep—a rarity for him.

Three messages from Dr. Jabbour were on his voice mail when he arrived in the office. At two forty-five that morning, she'd left one saying, "The new drug is ready." Four hours later, the second message, "The new drug has been tested and found to be ninety-six percent effective." And finally, just an hour before he'd gotten to work, "What population of patients do you want to be the first to benefit from the new drug? Please let me know the number of people and their locale."

This was proving to be a splendid day. Viktor's mole at FedPol was well worth her three-quarters-of-a-million dollar payout. She was keeping him one step ahead of the agents. Uri, Jabbour's man from Pakistan, had called at precisely one minute past the hour to inform him that he was in position and awaiting the arrival of Reardon's jet. In just under an hour, everyone on board would follow Cairns and become a pile of ashes. A knock on his closed office door prompted him to turn from the window.

"Yes, Gretchen, come in."

The young German woman looked flustered. "I thought you might like some coffee after your long drive from Berlin," she said. Her porcelain hands held a silver tray with an urn of French-press coffee and a plate of assorted biscotti.

"Wonderful. Join me for a few minutes, won't you?" Grandly, Viktor motioned for Gretchen to sit in one of the chairs arranged around the large square table in the center of his office.

Seating herself awkwardly, she smiled as her boss reached for one of the two chocolate almond biscotti on the plate. *I have worked here for almost four years and he has never before asked that I sit and eat with him!* Never wondering why the Pakistani scientist had offered to use her mother's special recipe and even bake the treats in the oven at her laboratory, or how the busy woman could spare the time to personally bring them over before they got cold, Gretchen had gladly accepted the unexpected gift.

"Gretchen, this may be the finest chocolate-almond confection I have ever tasted. Would you like the other one, or might I be a complete glutton and demolish it as well?"

"Oh, please do help yourself. I am so happy you like them!"

Gretchen had confided to Farah only a few days earlier that she had been taken with Viktor for years. She had dated other men, of course, but they paled in comparison to Viktor's charm, energy, and brilliance. Each relationship had fizzled out after just a few dates. But Viktor was so focused on his work he barely noticed her.

"He is a very handsome man, Gretchen. Surely, he has

many girlfriends, don't you think?"

"I actually don't think he does. He works pretty much all the time, you know. Not that he doesn't see women, but I believe they might be, uh-the business of—"

"You mean... prostitutes?"

Uncomfortable to find herself gossiping, about her boss, Gretchen lowered her voice to a whisper. "Yes, perhaps. I have seen rather large bills from what I assume are high-class escort services, as well as invoices for suites at the Ritz Carlton on occasion." At that point, Gretchen blushed and looked at the floor, knowing she had said too much.

Noting her discomfiture, Farah rose and said, "I need to return to my lab." Just as she was about to leave the coffee room, she turned back. "Gretchen, do you want to know the secret to the heart of a man? The one my mother taught me?"

Gretchen had stood to leave also, and had been making a mental list of all the things she needed to do before leaving the office. But Farah's question was irresistible.

"Yes, please tell me!"

"It's their stomachs!"

Gretchen began to giggle and placed a hand over her mouth. *Of course!* "What do you suppose would tickle his fancy?"

Gretchen was so pleased with Viktor's enjoyment of her baked goods that it took her a few minutes to notice the tremors in his hands and legs. It wasn't until he began to laugh that she started to think something must be wrong with him. There was no way she could know these were the classic symptoms of vCJD—the effects of a whopping dose of his own creation baked into the biscotti by her confidante.

He never laughs.

Within minutes, Viktor's body was no longer under his

control. So horrified she was rooted to her seat, Gretchen watched as a grand mal seizure racked his body, causing it to contort and lift out of the chair he had been sitting in. He went down hard, his skull hitting the corner of the table with a sickening thud before bouncing onto the carpet. His eyes were wide open, staring, as he shook and twisted.

Gretchen could not even hear herself screaming.

CHAPTER FIFTY-TWO

Wincing at the relentless clanging of the fire alarms she had tripped, Dr. Jabbour stood still in front of a floor-to-ceiling mirror. She had no idea why a research lab would be equipped with such a thing, but today she was happy to have it.

Gingerly, she massaged the lower portion of her neck with her right hand, then dropped it to her chest, just above her clavicles, and performed the same motions. Slowly the shift began. She could feel it loosen, the extra twenty-five pounds start to drop away. Looking into the full-length mirror, she shook herself hard. The cloak of "fat" she had worn for close to a year lay in a puddle at her feet.

Then Farah extended the fingers of both hands and dug them into her scalp. Methodically, she moved them side to side and up and down. This whole process had seemed impossible when they'd shown it to her nine months earlier. At her insistence that she'd never be able to pull it off—quite literally—Daniel had smiled. "You will be so eager to get out from under the thing, you'll be willing to do anything."

Then his smile had faded. "Listen to Uri," he'd told her—the same Uri that Viktor now believed awaited the jet at the airport. "He's done this before."

Returning to the present, setting her jaw, and reminding

herself she was a soldier, Farah inhaled once, twice, and once more. *On the count of three. This will hurt like—"*

The damnable mask took the first three layers of epithelium off with it. She blinked away the pain, then stared at a face she hadn't seen for more than nine months.

Well hello, Naomi!

Gone were the low forehead, the bushy eyebrows, and the mane of frizzy hair. In place of the odd-looking Dr. Jabbour was an arresting, almost exotic auburn-haired woman. Pinching her thumb and forefinger together, she reached into each of her eyes and removed the dark-brown contact lenses, revealing her natural blue-green orbs.

Naomi winced when she attempted a smile. Her skin was badly chafed from the removal of the mask and currently glowed a fiery red. *Second-degree burns,* she thought clinically, examining the inflamed and weeping skin. *It'll heal, along with everything else. There might be some scarring though..* There ws a time when the notion of a scarred face would have horrified her. But now, after all she had witnessed, such vanity seemed laughable.

Stripping off her shirt, carefully making sure that the fabric touched no part of her face, she breathed deeply in pleasure as she stepped away from the thick, rubbery undergarment that had added several inches to her torso. From the closet in her office, she grabbed and donned a black longsleeved sweater and a pair of skinny black jeans. Then piling her long hair on top of her head, she covered it with a black knit hat. She set a timer on her watch for fifteen minutes.

Please, everyone, get out. Now. Before all hell breaks loose. There was nothing she could do for the research animals, but at least their deaths would be quick and painless.

If anyone had been watching the security cameras, the lean black-clad woman striding down the hall would be unrecognizable.

Before the eighth of June two years before, Naomi Weiss had known exactly how her life would progress. She was about to become the wife of the youngest Israeli cabinet member, David Abraham—Minister of Science, Technology, and Space. Madly in love, Naomi was happier than she had ever dreamed possible. She'd even picked out names for the three girls and three boys she intended to have.

An act of fate had kept her from attending the pre-wedding party their friends and family had planned for the happy couple at one of the trendiest restaurants in Tel Aviv. At the last moment, Naomi had been called in to perform emergency thoracic surgery at the hospital where she worked. Just after dinner had been served to the fifty-five attendees, the sole female member of the waitstaff had pulled the detonator on her suicide vest. All but three people were killed, including David, his entire family, Naomi's parents, and her two sisters.

In the weeks that followed the horrific event, Naomi was sure she would die of grief. Unable to eat, work, or even move on most days, she dropped twenty pounds. But she lived, and gradually grew stronger in spite of herself. Eight months later, she accepted that the life she'd known was over. It was time to start a new one.

Years earlier, on the day she was discharged from the Israeli Army, a man with startling green eyes had come to see her. His name was Daniel.

"We are impressed with your competence as a soldier," he said. "So much so that I'm authorized to offer you a junior officer position in the Mossad. Today."

During her obligatory two-year stint, Naomi had come to the attention of officials in the Mossad, the intelligence agency of Israel. Unlike many of her contemporaries, she had genuinely enjoyed the punishing endurance runs, weapons training, and extreme discipline demanded by her superiors. She had delayed her service until after she'd completed medical school, figuring that the military training would help during her internship and residency in thoracic surgery and trauma—one of the more grueling specialties in medicine.

Naomi stared at the wiry man with strange eyes until he blinked. "You're joking." And then, "Sorry, the Mossad is not in my future plans. Not now, not ever." She didn't know whether to feel complimented or insulted by the offer. *A spy? Really?*

"There are many things I do, Dr. Weiss, but joking is not among them." His brief smile looked unpracticed as he handed her his card. "There may come a day when you wish... or need... to join us. Call me when that happens."

Naomi's mother had been Pakastani, and was proud of her heritage before the fundamentalists had hijacked her country and its citizens. One of the many reasons Daniel and his associates had been interested in Naomi was her fluency in Urdu.

Staring at the card she'd received nearly ten years before, she'd called the number, almost hoping it would no longer be valid. He picked up on the second ring.

"Captain Levin?—Daniel. My name is Naomi Weiss. I don't know if you remember the conversation we had some years ago—"

"I remember you well, Dr. Weiss."

"Well, events have occurred in my life that make it—well, if your offer is still on the table, I'd like to work with you. In fact, I believe it to be urgent that I do so."

"Pack a bag, doctor, but only with things you cannot do without. Plan to be away for close to a year. Tell your associates at the hospital that you need to get away, nothing more. I'll pick you up outside your condo in thirty minutes."

But he didn't hang up. She could hear him breathing across the open line. Then, in a different voice, one that was soft and sad, he said, "Naomi, I cannot tell you how very sorry I am that this day has come for you, too."

CHAPTER FIFTY-THREE

Entering Polish Air Space

Lindsey opened her eyes and found herself looking into another pair of eyes featuring unusual coppery dots. She moved her lips to speak, but nothing came out. Her mouth and lips felt sticky, her throat like a very coarse sandpaper.

"Get her some water, Morgan. Just half a glass with a few pieces of ice."

A minute movement of her head to the left so she could see Sebastian caused such intense pain that Lindsey sucked in an involuntary breath and gritted her teeth. "God." It sounded like a plea or a prayer more than a complaint.

The water appeared, complete with a straw. Lindsey looked at it longingly, but knew better than to move. Even her eyelids hurt.

Suddenly Rich was there. Not bothering to hide the tears streaming down his face, he lifted her gently, just high enough for Morgan to hold the glass in front of her and place the straw between her lips.

"Welcome back to the world, Dr. McCall." Then his voice cracked and there were no words. He just held her very carefully, as if he were afraid she would break into pieces or disappear if his grasp was too tight.

"Don't let her drink too much, Rich," Sebastian barked. "Just a few sips every few minutes, She doesn't need the torture of vomiting on top of the overall agony she is experiencing right now."

Sebastian was stunned. Overwhelmed. Still reeling from the now receding tsunami of natural corticosteroids that had been assaulting his system ever since he'd learned about the contagion. As exhausted as he was, he had never been more excited or grateful.

It worked! By God, it worked! I had exactly enough, and she'll be fine.

Gently, Rich laid Lindsey back down on the bed. *She looks like death warmed over.* He'd always thought that an inane phrase until now, seeing what seizures and life-threatening fever can do to a healthy woman. Her skin was waxy, her hair dark with sweat, and she looked like she had lost ten pounds in twelve hours. Her eyes were closed but it was clear somehow that she was sleeping now, no longer in a coma.

"You saved her life, Sebastian. How—"

"Payback, Rich. She saved mine, remember? That tension pneumo she spotted back in Germany?" He paused, thinking about his own close call with death. "I've known Franz for a couple of years now, and I don't think I've ever seen him so shaken." Looking down at Lindsey, Sebastian closed his eyes. *It seems impossible, but she's going to be okay.* Abruptly, a vision of the rosary Lindsey had been holding came to mind. The silent motion of her lips as she prayed. *Could her prayers be the reason?*

For the first time, the person behind the mask appeared. Sebastian's face suddenly seemed transformed by the smile that lit up his face as he lifted his gaze to Rich. "The truth is, I didn't have a clue if it would work. Prion disease is resistant to radiation and almost all of the usual ways of eradicating infectious organisms. So, back when I was still working for Dragovik, I began experimenting with autophagy. I knew the effects would be horrific, but if the patient survived the antibody, they had a chance to live through Dragovik's vile creation."

"Auto—what?"

"Oh, sorry. The word literally means *self-eating*. I reasoned that for all mammalian organisms—including us humans—the natural process by which cells detoxify and repair themselves could be used to destroy prion disease. It's the concept behind our current work on cures for cancer, inflammation, and some other diseases. In my experiments, I managed to stop the binding of the distorted filament in mice—the amyloid aggregation that spreads by a mechanism we don't understand. But I lost half of them to seizures from the fever induced by the antidote. I wouldn't have tried it on Lindsey if—if we'd had anything to lose."

Just then, Dimitri appeared in the doorway of the now crowded bedroom of the jet. He looked like a little boy on Christmas morning, eyes bright. Grinning as he glanced from Rich to his partner, he said, "Evan just called. There's no need to land in Frankfurt after all. An unexplained explosion has demolished the entire lab. The strange thing is that almost no one was hurt because somebody tripped the fire alarm about ten minutes before the building blew. The authorities believe the causalities were limited to Dr. Viktor Dragovik. I've just asked our captain to return to Lausanne."

CHAPTER FIFTY-FOUR

"It *was* the amyloid, wasn't it?" asked Lindsey. "The prion molecule was conformationally altered, and then Dragovik accelerated the sequencing of the disordered sequences. That's how he shortened the incubation period of Creutzfeldt-Jacob from years to hours, right?"

Just as Sebastian was about to answer, she cut him off, "No, wait. He had to be using vCJD, the variant, because it can hit in a far shorter period of time." Lindsey leaned back against the stack of pillows that a thoughtful nurse had supplied when the number of visitors expanded to eight. She could tell by looking at Sebastian's face that she'd nailed it. Not that being right compensated for her rash stupidity. She'd endangered them all when she barged into that apartment, and she'd regret it for the rest of her life. A life she now owed to Sebastian. But there was some satisfaction in answering the riddle.

Her eyelids flagging, Lindsey soon dropped back into a deep sleep.

Rich smiled and slowly shook his head in reply to Sebastian's incredulous look—*Can you believe her?*—but he said nothing. Indeed, he *could* believe that ferocious, almost ravenous intellect of hers. But he was overwhelmed by all that had transpired, his mind and body still processing the emotional roller coaster of the last few days.

For a rat doc, Sebastian Cameron, you're not half bad. After all that, look at her—she looks... healthy. Awed by the precariousness of life, by how everything can change in an instant and then change back again, Rich sat quietly, feeling no further need to understand the complex science that had brought his wife back to the land of the living.

Something had changed, something unutterable but vital that commanded attention. Rich's mind flashed back to those dreadful hours of bottomless despair. It brought to mind a comment made by his friend and spiritual advisor, Father John Tobin, years before. *The original sin of man was not disobedience, but distrust.* He had been puzzled by the priest's remark, replying that he didn't see the difference between the two. Now, he understood what Father John had been getting at.

Rich had always been a man of faith. Catholicism had been a constant for him, even during college and law school. Unlike Lindsey and many of his friends, he had never walked away. But much of his practice of religion was rote and routine—as comfortable as a pair of well-worn slippers. Perhaps for the first time, he was now aware of what he could only describe as *a presence.* Yes, that was the best, maybe the only word for it. His anger, fear, and hopelessness were gone and in their place, something joyous inhabited his soul. Lindsey would recover. Inexplicably, they had their lives back. It was as if he had opened a door and crossed to a new place.

Rich turned his thought to Joe Cairns and the sacrifice he had made, and he was filled with sorrow. He knew that Cairns had freely offered himself up in exchange for their lives and those of countless others, but his sadness would take time to resolve and dissipate. Intentionally, Rich pushed those thoughts into a compartment in his mind, to be dealt with later. It was all too much to grapple with now.

They'd been through three weeks of hell, but in two days, they'd be home, back in peaceful Pismo Beach, gazing out at the ocean. *Would this all just seem like a bad dream?* Closing his eyes and leaning back into the chair he had been rooted to for three days, Rich could hear several muted conversations in the air around him. Horst, Dimitri, Sebastian, and Pierre were discussing the events in Frankfurt. Too drowsy even to turn his head, Rich took in only snippets, "...Mossad picked him up during the two years he worked at Porton Down..."

Hank and Liisa Reardon stood quietly talking with Morgan. When Lindsey had explained precisely how Dragovik had modified the prion, the two had looked at each other with genuine understanding and the relief that comes with it. They stood at the back of the spacious suite where Lindsey had immediately been moved so that she could receive parenteral nutrition. *She still looks pretty ragged,* thought Liisa, *but I can see the old Lindsey coming back.*

"You used CMA autophagy to kill the prion didn't you?"

Sebastian hadn't noticed Liisa moving across the room to stand next to him, and was surprised by her whispered question—until he remembered what she did for a living. He nodded and murmured, "Yes, but the antidote and the encephalopathy nearly killed Lindsey anyway. She's a tough lady—and a fortunate one."

Liisa's direct gaze conveyed both sympathy and admiration. "Hell of a risk, Dr. Cameron but," she scanned the faces of the men standing around Sebastian, "we're all thankful you took it."

Extending her hand to the director of the Tigris team, Liisa introduced herself. Graciously, Evan took her hand, shook it and replied, "I know of your work, Dr. Reardon. It's a pleasure to meet you."

"I fully understand that you may need to kill me if you answer my questions," Liisa said with a sardonic smile, "but, can you explain a couple of phrases I heard just a moment ago? *Porton Down* and *Mossad*? Is Porton Down still functioning as a British biochemical industry? Was Israeli Intelligence involved in this thing?" Eyes wide, she glanced at Dimitri, Horst, and Sebastian, who had approached to listen in on Evan's response. Clearly, they were curious as to how their boss would handle this most inquisitive scientist. When he didn't immediately say anything, Liisa pressed on. "I understood that the UK, like most of the western world, had stopped all research into biochemical weapons decades ago. Is that not so?"

Pierre opened his mouth to reply, but Liisa's line of inquiry was gaining steam. "Sorry, but more importantly than all that, did Viktor Dragovik work at Porton Down? And was it a Mossad agent who took him out? And blew up Diedrich Gruppe Pharmaceuticals?"

Dimitri and Sebastian exchanged glances and began to study the suddenly mesmerizing floor of the hospital suite. *How the bloody hell did she figure that out?*

Evan Pierre studied the red-headed researcher. After almost thirty years in intelligence, little surprised him, but Liisa Reardon just had.

Withstanding the intense scrutiny of the head of covert intelligence for FedPol, Liisa merely eyed him back, her expression now grave. *These people nearly killed Ariana and me a few months ago. That gives me the right to a few answers, don't you think?*

Feeling the suddenly charged nature of the energy in the room, Hank Reardon wandered over to stand beside his daughter, followed by Morgan. He had heard enough of the whispered exchange to whet his own curiosity, but he remained silent.

Evan's chin jutted out. He stepped back and adopted what looked like an at-ease military posture. Watching him, Hank expected a rant beginning with, "In the interest of national security..." He was pleasantly surprised when Pierre proved him wrong.

"All right, Dr. Reardon, you've raised some rather large questions here—questions I feel it would be unfair to dismiss. You've all risked your lives by being here, after all. Therefore, I'll try to respond to you candidly—though unofficially—provided you never speak of it again." Evan looked over at the now sleeping Rich and Lindsey, then at his two agents Dimitri and Sebastian, then stopped at Horst. "Before I continue, I'd like to offer my thanks to all of you; and Mr. Mueller, if you'd like a job with us at Tigris, now or at any time in the future, I'd be honored to have you."

Recognizing the comment as rhetorical, Horst acknowledged the statement with a slight nod, and they all waited for him to continue. His gaze returned to Liisa and her father.

"Viktor Dragovik worked at Porton Down for two years. We believe that was where he got the idea for the infectious prion disease. He worked in defense, where they developed agents to defend against poisons, such as sarin and anthrax, as well as the safe disposal of old chemical weapons. He would also have come to see just how complicated the creation of a bioweapon could be, and how impractical. But for a man like Dragovik, this must have seemed like a challenge." Evan deftly sidestepped Liisa's question about ongoing bioweapon research.

Nodding to Liisa, he continued. "He'd come to the attention of Israel while Hezbollah was courting him in college. When he worked at Porton Down, he attracted the overtures of ISIS. Although Dragovik spent several weekends in Aleppo in those days, we doubt that he had any real connection with any of the extreme fundamentalist groups. He had no need of their money and seemed to have only contempt for their religion. To answer your question, yes, it was a Mossad agent who ultimately rid the world of Viktor Dragovik."

Evan eyed Sebastian as if inviting him to speak, catching him by surprise.

After a confirming nod from his boss, Sebastian took up the story. "I knew her as Farah Jabbour. A brilliant virologist, she was the only person we believed Viktor might entrust with the process of aerolizing the prion." Sebastian frowned and seemed to be deliberating about whether to say more about the woman. "I wish I could tell you that I knew all along she was one of the good guys, but I didn't have a clue. Farah was convincing. Her story was that she'd lost all of her family in Pakistan while she was in med school in the UK. But, as it turns out, Farah wasn't Farah." Again, he checked with Evan and received a slight nod. "We have come to determine that she was actually an Israeli surgeon—Dr. Naomi Weiss—recruited by a man so protected by the Mossad that he is known only as The Ghost.

"Dr. Weiss was operating on a trauma victim in Tel Aviv when her fiancé and fifty-odd other people died in a terrorist attack. Shortly after that, she offered her services to Mossad and disappeared, only to later re-emerge as Dr. Farah Jabbour."

The group was quiet as everyone absorbed what he was saying.

CHAPTER FIFTY-FIVE

Pismo Beach, California

Reardon had instructed his crew to fly Lindsey, Rich, and Morgan home in his Lear jet, but before that was to happen, the six reconvened and agreed to commemorate Cairns in some way. The details would have to be worked out later, when they were all feeling a bit stronger and saner. Meanwhile, Evan, Dimitri, and Sebastian had extensive debriefing to do, not only with Tigris but with their partners in Jerusalem.

For the first several days after Rich, Lindsey and Morgan got back, LJ had gladly kept both dogs with her. More than anything, she wanted them to sleep, rest, and recover.

"What day is it?" Lindsey asked LJ as her daughter filled her coffee cup.

"Thursday, the 29th of January." Ignoring Lindsey's stunned expression, LJ placed a plate in front of her with eggs, toast, and bacon burned just the way she liked it. Setting a fork into Lindsey's left hand, LJ said, "Eat... please. You've lost, like, fifteen pounds."

Squinting up through the bright sunny morning, Lindsey could see only the blur of a face and riotous dark hair. The fragrance of the food wafted up through the ocean breeze.

Suddenly ravenous, she obliged.

"This tastes really good, LJ. Thank you for cooking my favorite breakfast."

The doors from the living room to the patio opened and out spilled the dogs, followed by Morgan and Rich. "Sleep, glorious sleep!" proclaimed Rich. "As much as we want! Can it get any better than this? And bacon and eggs, too!"

Rich studied his wife. LJ was right. She was thin. Too thin. But to him, she looked more beautiful than any woman in the world. "What would you think of asking everyone to come this weekend?"

"Everyone?" Lindsey stared at Rich, uncomprehending.

"Dimitri, Evan, Horst, Sebastian—I'll bet the Reardon's would come, too."

"A party?" Morgan asked.

"Not exactly," Lindsey said. She and Rich looked first at Morgan, then at each other. Both were thinking the same thing. *It will be that "something" we all need to do for Joe, and for ourselves.*

As it turned out, the six were joined by everyone who had helped make the impossible happen. The three-man crew of Reardon's jet, Ariana Dumas, Sam Wong, and Evan Pierre. Father Blaise and Jodi came, plus Julie and Ted Grayson flew out from Texas. It was to be a quiet celebration of a complex and meaningful life, much of it lived in secret. For those present, it would allow the expression of a gratitude too vast for words.

Morgan, Jodi, and LJ had declared themselves the hostesses, and were doing a bang-up job of serving and making everyone feel welcome. This freed up Lindsey and Rich to speak to everyone in turn, and they circulated through the group at a relaxed pace.

Lindsey smiled as she eyed Jodi and Dimitri. The Swiss cop

was laughing at something the scientist had said. *I've never seen him laugh! He's quite attractive when he drops that Tigris persona.* Her gaze diverted to Jodi. *Yesterday worked magic on her.*

Julie approached with two glasses of something white and bubbly. "You have two empty hands, Dr. McCall. Join me in a toast to friendship, family, love, and life!" As the two clinked glasses, Julie's eyes wandered to Morgan, who was offering appetizers to Hank and Liisa Reardon, and Sam Wong. With her new haircut and glasses, she looked quite pretty. Turning back to Lindsey, Julie made a fresh toast, "To the miracles wrought by a good haircut!"

Chuckling, Lindsey replied, "And to my wise best friend. How can I thank you for your advice about taking Morgan?"

"You're thanking the wrong person, Linds." Julie's almond-shaped eyes were vibrant and crinkled at the corners when she smiled. "We have so much to be grateful for... so many gifts… from Him." Her words were whispered, but Lindsey could hear them.

In the far corner of the room, Evan stood talking with Sam Wong and Hank Reardon. Rich approached them and said, "Thank you for coming, Mr. Wong. And for all the help you gave us."

Sam's wide mouth broadened into a smile. "Call me Sam, please. May I call you Rich?" Without waiting for the yes, Sam deflected the praise. "I am the one who should say thank you. My country—the whole world in fact—is in your debt. All of you. We live in a world that will never know what you accomplished." He took a sip of amber liquid over ice. "But it's better that way, isn't it?"

When no one replied, Rich grabbed his chance. "Thank you, Mr. W—Sam. But I still have a few questions." He moved his gaze and said, "Evan, there are a few things that don't make sense. I know how top secret all of this is, but—"

"Go ahead, Rich, ask away. Sam's right, you've earned it. Whatever you would like to know. If I can answer, I will."

"How was Dragovik so far ahead of us at each step?" He glanced at Sam. "We figured out that they had tracked us through the rental cars, but Joe was sure there was a leak in your office. Was there?"

"Yes. Our receptionist. She agreed to pass on false information if Viktor took the bait. It took a few weeks, but she hooked him. Most of her intel to him was fake, but she told him precisely when you were arriving at Frankfurt airport."

"And had people waiting to kill us or blow up the plane?"

"He thought he did. Naomi Weiss, the Mossad agent Sebastian knew as Farrah Jabbour, had assured Viktor that she would bring in her ISIS friends from northern Pakistan."

Rich shook his head at the complexity, the sheer audacity of the thing. He glanced at Morgan, who was approaching them with a tray of fresh canapes. Quickly, he asked, "Did Weiss make it out before the explosion? And was Dragovik really the only casualty of that explosion in Frankfurt?"

Once again, Rich found himself shaking his head in amazement as Evan explained about the infatuated assistant and the poisoned biscotti. The plan could have failed so easily—*A house of cards— What if he wasn't hungry? Or wouldn't eat the poisoned biscuits?* To his relief, Evan assured him that Dr. Weiss was back in Jerusalem trying to decide whether to return to her former job at the hospital or stay on with Mossad.

"What's your guess, Evan?"

"I think she'll stay in Mossad. She's a natural, and once it's in your blood—"

San Luis Obispo, California

The Memorial mass had been Father Blaise's idea. Once the priest understood just how close this flawed, sinful, and utterly precious population of seven billion souls had come to virtual extinction, he had scheduled the service for Sunday, the first of February. He noted that it was the Feast Day of Blessed Andrew of Segni, one of the thousands of obscure saints that only hagiographers such as himself knew as friends.

In the priest's eyes, the confluence of dates was more than fitting, as Saint Andrew of Segni, born as nobleman in the thirteenth century, had eschewed his material wealth and emerged victorious over a life-long battle with the devil. The mass would be celebrated for a man who had done the same, not only for himself but for the world.

Lindsey looked around the chapel at the attentive faces. *Just five of us are Catholic—Rich, LJ, Julie, Ted, and me. But nobody seemed ill-at-ease, even during the Consecration and Communion. Even Sam Wong took the blessing!*

Her prayer was a simple one, a litany of *thank you, thank you,* over and over. She was awed by just how close Viktor Dragovik had come to achieving his monstrous goals—including her own death—and that made re-entering normal life disorienting, to say the least. Above all, her ability to find joy in the most basic things was amplified beyond description. Her husband, LJ, Morgan, Julie… these people and the rest of them filled her with wonder. *I'm surrounded by miracles,* she thought. *Miracles unseen and therefore unnoticed.* Her chest hurt, it was so full.

The Newman Center Chapel was a large, plain room equipped with folding chairs. Windows high on the walls let in a flood of California sunshine. Without the altar and crucifix, it could have been a classroom. At pauses in the service, the silence was profound. There was no shifting around, coughing, or clearing of throats; no chatter of students passing by. This was one benefit of the fact that it had been scheduled at three on a Sunday afternoon.

Father Blaise had slightly adjusted the mass so that the Eucharistic Celebration preceded his prayers for the soul of Joe Cairns. His opening statement riveted the small group of mourners.

"Had anyone told me a mere three weeks ago that I would celebrate a funeral mass for a man once engaged in murder for hire—an assassin, who had come within an eyelash of killing four of the people in attendance today—I would have laughed."

Blaise paused for dramatic effect, his expression grave, his gaze focused on Ariana. This was understandable. She had spoken to him the night before, about her own near death at the hand of Joe Cairns hands. Dimitri and the Reardon's had added their accounts of those four eventful days in June, and the entire improbable story had come into focus in the priest's mind.

Ariana's beautifully gamine face glowed back at Father Blaise as he spoke.

"But here we sit in praise of a God whose thoughts are not ours; a God who desires mercy, not sacrifice; a God who listened to the heart-felt prayer of one about to be killed. She did not pray for her life to be saved. NO!" Father Blaise brought all the power of his massive bulk into the flat of his hand as he smacked the lectern in front of him. The echo of the THWACK reverberated through the chapel. Then he whispered so softly that everyone had to lean forward in their chairs to hear. "No, she did not. She prayed for the good Lord to forgive her murderer, Joe Cairns, for what he was about to do." Pausing, the priest scanned the faces of his listeners.

"Imagine yourself badly bleeding from a knife wound. A man is kneeling beside you with the barrel of his gun pressed against your temple." The priest took the second and third fingers of his right hand, curled the others and pressed the two fingers against his own temple. He waited.

Sam Wong was the first to mimic the motion. Hank Reardon followed. Then almost everyone else mimicked the motion.

"We can't really imagine it, can we? Sitting here, pretending. It doesn't come close to the feeling she must have experienced." Lowering his voice to a whisper yet again, he brought his point home. "Lest you ever doubt the power or the possibility of God's mercy, remember this story. Remember Joe Cairns—a killer who was converted by the prayer of his intended victim."

The priest looked around the room and smiled. "I believe as I stand here that Joe is in heaven with Our Good Lord." He grinned, "But. just in case I'm wrong about that, we are here today to pray for his soul." He then nodded at Rich so slightly that the move was almost imperceptible.

Rich knew it was an invitation. He rose slowly and walked to the altar. Then he turned to face the small group.

Now standing behind the ambo, where the priest had delivered his quasi eulogy for Cairns, Rich declared, "Joe Cairns didn't get out of bed one day and decide to become an assassin. To work for a man for whom the extermination of corporate bosses, employees, and a number of us was merely business. Joe was a soldier. And soldiers follow orders."

He paused, gaining steam, his eyes directed over the heads of his listeners out at the California sunshine, and blinked, twice. "But Joe wasn't *just* a soldier. He was a Marine. The last several years of his service, he was a Marine Raider." His smile was sad as he said, "Combat marines are trained killers. The Raiders are the elite of Force Recon. These guys have seen and done things few of us can imagine—or want to. And they get medals for it. I doubt that after close to twenty years, there was much difference in Joe's mind between working for Braun or working for the US government. Most likely, it felt like more of the same. Except for the money, of course." Once again, Rich paused, this time to regard Ariana, who sat with her head tipped to the side, listening. "Until it wasn't."

"We know that Joe didn't make the switch from the "dark side" because of some momentous moral transformation." Glancing at the crucifix, then back to Ariana, Rich said, "Like the 'good' thief, Dismas. No. Instead, Heaven reached down and stopped him cold. Ariana, Joe told me that King David's hand was like an iron band around the wrist that held the gun to your head." He shot a quick look at the priest. "Like you, Father Blaise, I believe it was Ariana's prayer that summoned David. But mustn't there have been more to it than that?

"I've always believed that our Lord places each of us here for a specific reason. To complete a task that only we can accomplish. Many of us may never know the reason we are here. We may find out only after it's over. But a few of us are blessed to become aware of our mission in a most spectacular fashion." Without taking his eyes off Ariana, he continued, "Joe told me that he was a little kid when he first met King David. Throughout his life, David appeared to him during times when Joe urgently needed help or counsel. One day, abruptly, he disappeared. Joe didn't hear or see his old friend for many years—until the day he placed a gun to Ariana's temple." Rich paused for a moment and listened to the awed silence around him. "Was it just coincidence, Ariana, that you were sending up a prayer for his soul? A prayer for him instead of yourself?"

Her eyes glued to his, Ariana smiled. She mouthed a silent, "No."

"For years, I've believed that our Lord has a certain…" Rich paused as he searched for the right word. "A certain *sympathy* for soldiers. Perhaps respect, even admiration. Why else would David have been His anointed one? A man whose genealogy descends directly to Christ?" These last words were uttered so softly that only those in the front seats could hear them.

"Christ, the True Warrior, we fight for You. Semper Fi, Joe."

Just like all of my novels, *Malthus Revisited: The Cup of Wrath* is entirely a work of fiction. The background, however, is based on real world events. The horrors of the Balkan War are all too real and impossible to overstate. The events at Srebenica are a matter of record, as is the account of the Dutch United Nations Battalion and the Serbian Army. Interested readers can find riveting information about these tragic missteps in Laura Silber's *Yugoslavia: Death of a Nation*, and Peter Maas's *Love Thy Neighbor: A Story of War*.

Not infrequently, characters simply appear in my head. Morgan Gardner did so about a year before I started to write *Malthus.* She was "different"—a teen who was smart, but weird. It was at the suggestion of Susan Toscani, a most helpful reader of all of my books, that Morgan be autistic. Autism and autistic spectrum disorder are fascinating conditions that are just beginning to be fully understood. Since diagnoses of autism are increasing each year, there are scores of books on the subject. Morgan Gardner's qualities are a composite, based on the many that I read. Dr. Temple Grandin's books stand out among them as clear and practical, with an understanding of the condition that only an autistic individual could possess.

Thomas Malthus wrote *An Essay on the Principle of Population* in 1798. Since then, periodically, "experts" such as Peter Ehrlich have emerged to forecast the dire effects of overpopulation. The Vatican did hold a conference on biologic extinction in 2016. To the dismay of many Catholics, Ehrlich was a featured speaker.

The idea of chemical warfare as a "higher form of killing" is taken from the life and works of the man known as the father of chemical warfare, Fritz Haber. Robert Harris's *A Higher Form of Killing: The Secret History of Chemical and Biologic Warfare,* provides an excellent and eminently readable source for more information.

Creutzfeld-Jacob disease—otherwise known as mad cow disease—and its variants are real. Thankfully, the incubation period is many years and its incidence remains extremely low. The variant of the disease was first seen in the UK during the late eighties and caused 200 deaths. Several hundred thousand cattle were killed because of infection.

Dragovik's modification of the molecule to shorten the incubation period is the work of my over-active imagination. Autophagy, however, is a real and fascinating process of these remarkable bodies of ours. It's possible use in cures for much of the chronic disease affecting us is being studied actively by scientists.

FedPol and Tigris are actual agencies in Switzerland, though the characters in the book who work for them exist only in my mind—and now, hopefully, in yours! To my knowledge, there is no high official known as The Ghost in the Mossad nor a Captain named Daniel Levy.

I'd like to offer a huge thanks to my early readers: Susan Toscani, Margaret Caddy, Lori Ann Finn, and my husband, John.

After four books, I have found partners in this intricate work of getting a story into you're your hands. One that is plausible. One that will stimulate. One that will challenge while providing a darn good read. Laura Ross, for the very first time, you have made the process of revisions... enjoyable—

well maybe not always. I thank you for calling me out when I get lazy and attempt shortcuts. Lori Hawkins, I thank and admire you for your attention to the details of proofreading.

Ardis Braunn, thank you, both for the work you do for our beloved abandoned Dobermans and for permission to cite Dobies and Little Paw Rescue in the book. Last but certainly not least, thanks to Nancy Cleary at Wyatt-MacKenzie for your consistently high-quality cover designs and careful formatting, as well as your consistent support.

It's a wrap. I hope you have enjoyed the book.

I, Claudia

I had no intention of switching from medical mystery to historical fiction. In fact, in the fifth of the Dr. Lindsey McCall medical mystery series, I planned to bring back Zach and Harvey Cunningham—and a few other characters from *Do You Solemnly Swear?*—to solve a weird homicide. But, writing fiction is akin to a canoe trip along a river known, but not well. Hours of smooth, calm waters can turn abruptly into a rollicking white water adventure!

The story of Claudia Procula, the wife of Pontius Pilate, appeared in my mind over several months while finishing *Malthus,* and proclaimed itself ready to be grappled with. It will be told in her voice.

I hope you are tantalized by the prologue to *I, Claudia.*

—Lin Wilder
December 6, 2017

PROLOGUE

I, Claudia

I am nearing the end of my life. Seventy-nine years lived as a shadow, a face behind a curtain, whispering the residues of a dream. Insubstantial, unheard. But my time of silence is done. It is time to write the truth for those with ears to hear it.

My name is Claudia, wife of Pontius Pilate. My husband has been dead for over a decade now, and is the subject of vast ignorance and injustice. The very name of Pontius Pilate has become synonymous with cowardice and betrayal. Those who claim to know the substance of my dream believe it emanates from evil. Others insist that the words recited by Christians for the last ten years, "suffered under Pontius Pilate, was crucified and died," terrorized me in my dream, echoing as they will, as I have seen in my visions, through the centuries. To be memorialized in something that will be called the 'Apostles Creed.'

These silly claims, and all the others like them, no longer sadden; but merely annoy. I often think of the writing of Socrates, a man I consider a good friend though he died before I was born. His wisdom and humility await those rare searchers of truth. "I know I am intelligent because I know I know nothing."

My husband asked that I tell our story, but he cautioned me to wait until the last possible moment, for even in death, he fears for me. Writing the truth always comes with consequences, often persecution and even death. So, I waited… but now, the proper moment has come. In just two months I will be dead, so there is little anyone can do to me. There is much to tell you. About my husband. About the Christ. About me.

I was born in Delphi, the last of the Oracles of Pythia. It was a time of disorder, chaos, great fear, and the death of nations. My mother broke her vow of virginity in lying with my father. She feared for both our lives, because what she had done was punishable by death. The time of the Oracles was coming to an end. Men no longer listened to the whispers of the prophets, certainly not the women. Not even when we had the words of the gods on our lips.

I survived, but my mother did not. I was taken to Athens, where I was raised by Demetrius and Sabina. Only they knew that I was the last Oracle. My true identity remained a secret to all others—even my husband.

Now, the world will know my story.